A MOST PARISIAN MURDER

A MOST PARISIAN MURDER

Millicent Binks

Bookouture

Published by Bookouture in 2025

An imprint of Storyfire Ltd.
Carmelite House
50 Victoria Embankment
London EC4Y 0DZ

www.bookouture.com

The authorised representative in the EEA is Hachette Ireland
8 Castlecourt Centre
Dublin 15 D15 XTP3
Ireland
(email: info@hbgi.ie)

ISBN: 978-1-83618-314-3
eBook ISBN: 978-1-83618-313-6

For my beloved mother, Mary, who loves everything French, and with whom I enjoyed research trips to Paris and whose encouragement was unwavering. Also, for my beloved father, John, whose support made this novel possible. I've enjoyed many a Hammer Horror film with you and I hope this novel is just as gripping to read!

Secrets travel fast in Paris.

Napoleon Bonaparte

ONE

THE IMPOSSIBLE INCIDENT IN THE
LAURAGUAIS SUITE

Paris, April 1934...

The Reinette Hotel stood out from the other sandstone edifices on the Rue de Rivoli as its façade was painted an obsidian black. It was one of Paris's chicest hotels and had been given the name 'Reinette', meaning *Little Queen*, because its suites were named after the many mistresses of Louis XV. It was a hotspot for couples' rendezvous.

The owner, Sylvain Leclerc, was used to a symphony of kisses, laughter and quarrels reverberating around his hotel. Of course, wherever there are lovers residing there will be bust-ups, but there had never been a dispute that ended as horrifically as it did on this particular April night.

On the evening it happened, there was only one room lit in the entire hotel, on the top floor to the far right. In that room, a woman was dancing, repeating the same eight-beat ensemble over and over in a kind of perfectionist frenzy. The cabaret dancer – Valentine Beaumanoir – was practising her dance routine in a steel-boned corset, getting used to the restrictions it made on her body while moving. The shrill sound of saxophones and bass blasted out of the wind-up gramophone that was perched on the dressing table.

A moment later a second light flicked on in the hotel in the room below. It was the bedside lamp of Zsa Zsa Desmarais, another showgirl.

Unable to sleep due to the noise, Zsa Zsa huffed and swivelled out of bed. Flinging her black kimono around her shoulders, hissing to herself, she prepared an indignant speech. *This was too much!*

Zsa Zsa was about to march upstairs to tell Valentine to *cease the racket* when the music and stomping stopped abruptly. Silence.

And suddenly, Valentine started to shout.

'Christophe Tasse! Get off, get off me! Someone, please, help me! Bastard! Christophe!'

Zsa Zsa frowned. It didn't sound like anyone was coming to her rescue. Christophe was Valentine's beau and the cabaret's costume designer. What was this brouhaha about? Zsa Zsa left her room and hurried out into the corridor, up the wooden spiral staircase to the floor above.

Arriving at Valentine's room, Zsa Zsa could see the light shining through the gaps of the doorframe. The shouting had stopped now, which made Zsa Zsa a little anxious. She felt for the door handle and rattled it hard.

'Valentine? Christophe? Are you alright? Please open the door!'

There was no answer, and an alarming lack of movement in the room.

Zsa Zsa pushed her ear to the door and squinted her eyes in concentration. After knocking again, there was still no noise at all, only the sound of her own breathing. A couple of minutes later, the hotel's owner, Sylvain Leclerc, came bumbling down the corridor, a small, greasy-looking man with a round face like a perspiring peach. His eyes were bloodshot from being woken abruptly from a light sleep in his office armchair, presumably from the racket. A bunch of mortice keys jingled in his hand.

M. Leclerc brushed Zsa Zsa aside and knocked solidly on Valentine's door. 'Open the door please.'

'I've tried that,' Zsa Zsa said impatiently.

Sylvain cursed under his breath and fumbled with the key in his fat fingers, inserting it into the lock.

'*Zut!*' he said, stabbing the key in the keyhole. 'The key is in the lock on the other side of the door.'

'Well, we'll just have to kick it down,' said Zsa Zsa. 'She sounded desperate for help, as if she was being attacked!'

Sylvain shut his eyes and breathed in very loudly through his nostrils, likely thinking about his damaged door and how much the handyman would fleece him for 'materials and labour'.

Three rams of the man's shoulder broke the lock. The door swung open and Zsa Zsa peered inside. A cool breeze pricked the tip of her nose.

The bed was made and untouched. On it was a handbag, the contents of which were strewn across it. On the floor was a pair of snakeskin heels, and oddly, a broken pencil. The curtains at the French windows were billowing and flicking upwards in the breeze.

'Valentine?' Zsa Zsa called.

No reply.

Sylvain brushed past Zsa Zsa and entered the room. His eyes darted around the suite. There was nobody here.

At that moment they heard animated tittle-tattle coming from the street below and Zsa Zsa went to the French windows to investigate. As her eyeline hit the ground she breathed in so sharply the cold air sliced her throat.

Valentine was sprawled on the pavement, lifeless. She was on her back, one hand slumped above her head, the other stuck inside the front of her corset. One of her legs was bent upwards underneath her. It looked twisted and unnatural. Kneeling over her body were three people all of whom were talking loudly. Zsa Zsa heard one of them shout, 'She has no pulse!'

Zsa Zsa's stomach lurched.

'We're too late. He must have pushed her. She's dead.' Zsa Zsa's voice was toneless with shock.

'But how would he have got out of the locked room?'

Zsa Zsa didn't reply. She then shrugged and hung her head.

'I will alert the police.' Sylvain put a gentle hand on Zsa Zsa's back and led her out of the room.

Zsa Zsa muttered to herself all the way along the corridor in a daze. Something wasn't adding up. Valentine was pushed off the balcony. But wouldn't you scream if you were pushed from a great height? There had been no scream. No scream at all.

TWO

THE LAPLUME MILLINERY SHOP

Marylebone, London, five days later

It had been yet another unremunerative day for the hat shop, but the lack of revenue wasn't the problem for the Honourable Opal Laplume. It was the beastly loneliness. Young Opal eyed the pavement through the glass shop door and wished a shiny pair of feet would stop and swivel and step inside. They didn't. They kept scurrying along on their London business as if the shop didn't exist. Even if someone were to walk in and complain about a tulle tulip pinging off their cloche, she would be happy.

'I should be thoroughly accustomed to the solitude really,' Opal said to her miniature black poodle, Napoleon, just to break the silence. 'Though I know I've got *you*. But fancy being twenty-two and never having a solid friend. Did you know my name was "Carnival Float" at school?'

Napoleon, ensconced in his basket, made a kind of perplexed squeak with his head on its side.

'No, the nickname wasn't out of any fondness. I had a flair for sticking ostentatious decorations in my hair. A veritable garden of berries and wildflowers and rather too much paper origami. They thought I was a trifle barmy.'

She crouched down and caressed his pom-pom tail. 'That wasn't the only thing that ostracised me. After losing our estate, the society lot think me too *declassé* to invite to parties and the ordinary girls think I'm to plummy to relate to. An awkward position to be in, wouldn't you say?'

Napoleon rested his chin between his paws and groaned in despondency.

'Daddy is perpetually off somewhere. Mother is absorbed with herself, as usual, and there are, regrettably, no siblings to share this predicament.'

She picked him up and looked into his onyx eyes. 'So here we are, Napoleon. You and I, destined to spend our days in this frightfully dull hattery, with nothing for company but straw, felt, and the occasional feather. I daresay I shall meet my end here, an old maid, sporting some ghastly aluminium fez or whatever the style will be in 1990.'

She flopped onto her stool behind the counter, popped the dog on the floor and flipped the pages of the *London Evening Standard* with a lazy, red-lacquered finger. The birds of paradise feathers that were stabbed into her tilted fedora billowed upwards as she sighed.

Suddenly, she noticed a familiar name in the left column and her eye pulsed. Her iris became as blue and alive as the flames of a gas ring. Her pyramidal nose moved closer to the paper as she scanned the column. She cupped her chin in her hands and weaved her fingers into her fashionably cropped dark curls.

REPLACEMENT WANTED FOR KILLED DANCER, PARIS

Cabaret dancer Valentine Beaumanoir was killed last week in mysterious circumstances at the Reinette Hotel. The Paris authorities remain diligently at work on the case, which is not yet solved. She was set to appear in the much-anticipated Clementina Lalonde revue at the Casino de Paris in the French capital. In light of this grievous incident, an audition to find a replacement will take place tomorrow at the Casino de Paris, Rue de Clichy, Paris, commencing at 10 o'clock. The management seeks a competent dancer with balletic training and an approximate height of 170 centimetres.

Clementina Lalonde, the star of the cabaret show mentioned, was Opal's cousin. She'd never met or spoken to her, but she very much wished she could, seeing as Opal didn't have any siblings. The fact she was a glamorous Parisian celebrity always fascinated her too. But Opal's mother didn't want her to associate with *that* side of the family.

Opal made a mental note to mention this article to her mother later. She kept the page open and swished it aside on the mahogany shop counter. She sipped some Earl Grey, drumming her nails excitedly on the china.

'A delectable titbit of family gossip to enliven the day. Eh, Napoleon!' She gave her beloved poodle an ear scratch. 'At least I've got you to converse with. Not long before our Regent's Park walkies. What shall I do in the meantime? I'm not inspired to do any more hat sketches right now.'

Napoleon nibbled and dragged a copy of *Tatler* out of the magazine basket. The pages fell open on an advertisement for the current season of Chanel headwear, Opal's favourite Parisian designer. Her eye fluttered delightedly over the models in the à la mode cloche hats. They demonstrated the new vogue for wide, swooping brims. There were also cartwheel hats in Baku straw with metallic brocade and luxurious silk lining. She admired how Chanel was brave enough to introduce masculine headwear to the female wardrobe, she thought it *simply ripping*. There was nothing more chic than a woman in a man's boater. But her mama did not agree with this ideation.

Opal compared the styles to her mother's designs in the shop window ahead of her. Lady Phyllis Laplume's taste seemed to always be at least five years behind. Opal wished she had a magic wand to widen the brims, heighten the crowns and morph them into all kind of inventive shapes. She wanted to stock more silhouettes, like turbans, calots and capulets, and spray jewel colours over the current anaemic tones.

Her father, Lord Edmund Laplume, who Opal missed terribly, had said that millinery was a rather shallow thing to occupy oneself with. But Opal had debated the contrary. Her fascination with hats was akin to his ornithologist fascination with birds. A bird's pretty plumage would evolve depending on changes in their environment; and hat fashions would evolve depending on social environments. Like a male bird of paradise's feathers, a woman would use a hat to express herself.

Wearing a hat confers undeniable authority over those without one. Seeing as men have to remove their hats upon entering a room as a mark of respect, while women are not required to do so, this gives women a certain power over men. Or so Opal would like to think.

Even Napoleon donned a hat. The day she had rescued him, Opal had just hand-delivered a bridal headpiece to a client staying at the Café Royal and noticed a sad scene out the back of the kitchens. There was a heap of coal sacks and a poor stray pup, no bigger than Opal's hand, had his paw wound up in a piece of ripped burlap. The burlap fabric had also created a mini bicorn hat on his head. A tiny Napoleon! Opal could not resist. She had untangled the whimpering lump of coal and made her driver Thompson keep shtum about it to Mother.

'What a wasteful endeavour that thing is. With an absurd

moniker... Napoleon!' Lady Laplume had said when she had found out what Opal had been hiding in the apartment.

'Seeing as your most noble friends in society are named Stimpy and Turkey, I don't see how Napoleon is any more absurd,' Opal had retorted.

Her mother had warmed to the creature once she realised how much attention they got in Regent's Park and what a brilliant advert Napoleon was for their business. Someone would stop them and compliment the charming pet and Phyllis Laplume would give them a Laplume Millinery business card. Opal had started to make Napoleon miniature bicorn hats as an extra conversation piece – much like the one he was wearing now, pricked with a macaw feather.

Suddenly, a whimpering sound came through the plaster ceiling, then a wail, then more whimpers. Napoleon looked up and whimpered back. It sounded to Opal like Effie, their maid, was crying. Then footsteps hurried down the wooden staircase, and Lady Laplume burst through the door to their upstairs apartment. She had sapphire eyes like Opal, but they were drained of colour and seemed to have a freight train of thoughts rushing behind them. Opal had noticed her mother's eyes had been like this for several days.

With an impatient fumble in her pocket, Lady Laplume pulled the shop keys out of her skirts, shook them out like a metal spider and shoved the correct key into the entrance door. She locked it, flipped the Open sign to Closed and whipped around to face Opal.

'Mother? Are you alright? Your face is red.'

'Yes,' she replied, out of breath.

'Why are you closing so early?'

'Pray. Wait until I explain.'

'Is Effie crying?'

'She'll be alright. Firstly, my daughter, I have a request. I implore you not to oppose me in what I am about to say.'

Lady Laplume took Opal's shoulders and pushed her down gently onto a customer's armchair next to the full-length mirror. She herself sat in the one next to it and laced her hands around her knee.

'What request? I do wish you'd spit it out,' Opal said.

'Your cousin, Clementina,' Lady Laplume began.

'Clementina? That's funny I was just reading about her Casino de Paris show in *The Standard*. It seems one of the dancers was killed in mysterious circumstances...'

'Yes, well, it relates to that incident. I've been speaking with her on the blower and she needs you to help her at the theatre with feather headdresses for the dancers. They've been manic since it happened and desperately need your help.'

'Steady on, Mother. You spoke to Clementina? The last I knew you were never going to speak to your sister-in-law, Florence, or her daughter, Clementina, ever again. You said they were degenerates, and you were never going to let me meet them.'

'Well, I've changed my mind. You are twenty-two now. Paris could provide a stimulating environment, especially with the current jewellery exposition that is on. And while you're working at the historic Casino de Paris, you'll be learning a lot about the *plummasserie* trade. You can tell the bourgeoisie about our Laplume Millinery business and be a beautiful ambassador for us. You've got a new stash of business cards printed, haven't you?'

'I'm utterly dumfounded, Mother. Why are you so keen on my going?' Opal hugged her own shoulders as she continued in a bitter voice. 'I'm going to be even more lonely there than I am here. I won't know a soul there!'

'You will get to know your cousin. And it'll only be for a few months.'

Opal sighed.

'You'll be in a splendid hotel on the Rue de Rivoli and your father has sent two thousand francs to start with and we shall see how fast that swirls down the plug. Now, your Golden Arrow train leaves from Victoria first thing.'

'First thing? But I've got an appointment at the haberdashery tomorrow to look at the new lace trimmings they've got in. And my poodle needs a trim the day after. We can't let him get ratty.'

'Opal. I need you to comply with my wishes. Clementina needs you to be in attendance *tomorrow*.' Lady Laplume looked fervently at Opal without blinking. Only the clock could be heard strumming low and slow tocks.

'You're abandoning me like Father has us both.'

'Opal Marion Laplume you are a grown woman. It's time to spread your wings. Then you *might* make a friend.'

'I guess you will have to go to the lace appointment at the haberdashery for me then, Mother.'

'I can't.'

'Why ever not?'

'I'm also going away tomorrow. I'm going to Papua to visit your father for awhile.'

Opal gasped and clasped her cheeks. There was most certainly something going on... Her mother looked down at her knees and pursed her lips into a tight prune. Opal could discern that she was exerting her utmost effort to appear blasé and that nothing was untoward. *Why was she trying to get them both out of the apartment?*

'Mother, are you ill? Is Father ill? You told me you would never go on one of Father's ornithology expeditions ever again! You don't like birds or the outdoors. You come back insect-bitten and furious every time.'

'I need to get away from this tiresome town for a time. I do feel I need to make more effort supporting your father.'

'But I won't be able to contact you out there. Father won't pay for the telephone at Port Moresby unless it's an emergency and he only sends a telegram when he's in the village. We've given up on letters arriving in under three months.'

'I will do my best. Now, desist from this impudence and go and instruct Effie on the contents to pack in your trunk.'

'Well, you must tell me why she is whimpering if I am to speak with her.'

'We are taking a flight with Imperial Airways to Rome, then Cairo, then Singapore. She is terrified, the poor thing. She's never even been at sea, let alone in the air.'

'Effie is going with you? Mother, why would one need a lady's maid in an isolated forest outpost? What occasions will you need to be dressed for? A state banquet with stick insects? Nobody is going to see you and it doesn't matter what you look like.'

'Lord Laplume will see me. There are the missionaries and your father has Dutch friends at Port Moresby. But you're right. If my maid can't pull herself together, I may have to... fly solo.' She swallowed a large marble-sized gulp. 'But, Opal, you must simply grant me one favour. Please do not tell anyone on the Paris circuit that Clementina is your cousin. She is merely your employer. I will not have London society knowing we are related to a *danseuse de cabaret*.'

'But what if they enquire as to how I obtained the millinery position?'

'Tell them she is an acquaintance from the millinery business. Use your imagination, my dear girl... you seem to have quite enough of it when talking back to me.'

By midnight, Opal had a packed trunk of essentials, a hatbox stacked with her favourite headwear, a wad of francs, a Golden Arrow ticket and her sketchbook nestled in her handbag. Napoleon was curled up on the hatbox in blissful ignorance of the journey he was to make in the morning. But he had one eye on his mistress. He was perplexed by her tossing and turning under her sheets, scrabbling her fingers inside her French dictionary at intervals in the night.

Opal's mind could not stop circulating. *Why does Mother want us both out of London so suddenly? She to Papua, I to Paris...? What on earth is going on?*

THREE

THE AUDITION

Pasted above the glass doors of the Casino de Paris theatre was a huge colourful billboard. It was a painted depiction of three cabaret dancers. The artist had peppered their bodies in jewels that crept up into their coiffures. They were wrapped in a whirl of plumes that flicked and blurred around their dancing limbs.

Their stage names were printed above their heads in scarlet. The brunette on the right was 'Zsa Zsa Desmarias'. The ash-blonde on the left was 'Valentine Beaumanoir'. The redhead in the centre was the evident star of the show, her name printed in the largest letters, surrounded by a corona of colours, 'Clementina Lalonde'.

On the street, below the murdered Valentine's picture, was a little shrine of mourning. Half a dozen posies and some minia-ture crucifixes were tied with ribbons and string to the railings. Beyond the railings to the left were the stage doors. They were hung with a sign saying, 'Audition' and an arrow indicating to enter.

Many ambitious girls from Western Europe had turned up to the audition to replace Valentine Beaumanoir. It had been an open call printed in all the major newspapers and gazettes, creating a frenzy of publicity for the show.

Opal Laplume waited by the gate. The winged lapels of her trench coat jutted up to meet her fedora. A firework of feather fronds hovered above it. One blue-gloved hand pinched a cylindrical hat box. The other held onto a black-leather dog lead, with Napoleon at the end, sitting to attention with a puffed chest.

She stood for a long time alone outside, every now and then checking her watch and glancing up at Clementina Lalonde on the billboard. *My marvellous long-lost cousin should be coming out to meet me any moment*, Opal thought. *I do hope she likes me. If not, I will feel completely alone in this city. And I must ensure my hat's sitting in the correct position. A true milliner's hallmark is a perfectly poised chapeau.* With the practised precision of an artist at her easel, she deftly plucked out the pin holding the hat in place and gave it a judicious tweak.

In that moment a wave of wind blew her aside. She tottered and twisted around to witness a whole team of cyclists hurtle past, piles of newspapers strapped to the front of their cycles. Scores of berets and baker boy caps, with the occasional top hat wrapped in newspaper, flashed before her, accompanied by the echoing clamour of their bells. *Must have been some sort of newspaper boy criterium or race.* Opal smiled. *Nice to know Paris was just as crackers as London could be.*

Her countenance dropped when she noticed her favourite hat on the dirty pavement. Before she could salvage it, her poodle happily added drool and teeth marks as it picked it up for her. The canine wagged his pom-pom tail like a speedy metronome, convinced he was helping.

'Napoleon, this isn't Regent's Park and this isn't a flying toy. It's my velour felt and paradise-bird masterpiece. Although I know you were only trying to help. Thank you!' Opal said firmly.

Napoleon yapped and his front paws lifted off the floor. This was because the stage door had flung open with the sound of metal colliding with brick. A gaggle of five girls fell out with stormy facial expressions. One of the girls was muttering obscenities in English about what she thought of the audition judges. Opal clasped the railings, stuck her pointed nose through and addressed the girl who spoke English.

'Excuse me... have the auditions ended?' Opal's voice was a small, woodwind tone.

'No... they're running behind. We've just been cut. You can probably go in and try. I don't think you'd be too late.'

'Oh no, I'm not auditioning,' replied Opal.

'What you 'ere for then?'

'Oh... I'm here to see Clementina Lalonde.'

Opal desperately wanted to show off and say that the famous dancer Clementina was her long-lost cousin. But she'd promised her mother to keep that a secret and that Clementina was simply an acquaintance.

'What do you want to see Clementina for? She's awful!' the rejected auditionee said, and scrunched all her features into the middle of her face.

'I'm going to be helping in the atelier with the headdresses. I'm a milliner from London, you see.'

'Oh, well I'm on my way back to London now, I suppose.' The girl rolled her eyes and put her hands on her hips.

Opal eyed the girl's pretty but outdated cloche hat. 'Here, take my business card. If you ever pass by Marylebone do pop in.'

The girl took the card and said flatly, 'Oh, I can use this as a bookmark.' And passed through the gate.

Opal's smile withered a smidge. She didn't know whether that was a backhanded comment or compliment to how pretty the illustrated card was. She decided to take the latter.

She sighed and looked at her watch. Four thirty. Clementina had said she'd meet Opal at four o'clock when the auditions finished. But they had overrun. *Would it be impertinent to just go inside?* she thought to herself. *It is getting slightly chilly...*

Opal was about to put her fedora back on when she remembered the pavement dust and canine teeth impressions on the felt. She couldn't possibly let Clementina meet her for the first time like this. She needed a hanky to brush off the dust. The indents could be covered by the feathers.

The stage door had been left ajar when that girl had come out. Perhaps she could slip inside and find something to brush it with?

Without giving herself a second to change her mind, she slipped inside the gate in the railings, led Napoleon through, then entered the crack of the stage door.

There was a faint swell of piano music coming from behind a door at the end of the corridor. She floated towards it, past various retired props and dusty pieces of old stage set. She very slowly opened the door just wide enough for her right eye to peer through.

She squinted as the red auditorium came into focus. There must have been at least two thousand seats, like seeds of a ripe pomegranate. They were all empty apart from three silhouetted heads in the front row. The adjudicators, Opal assumed. One of them must be Clementina.

The stage was infinite, bigger than any stage she'd ever seen. Stretching its width was a staircase that grew up a vast thirty steps. It was lit up brightly by bulbs inside the Bakelite. It illuminated dozens of legs, daintily descending it like willow branches. The owners of the legs were smiling desperately and pulling their torsos up as if to make the numbers pinned to them magnify.

'What are you doing?' A female voice stabbed Opal's earlobe, it had a hint of an East End of London accent to it. Opal turned round and parted her lips to apologise but was shocked when she was grabbed by the wrist and pulled to the very end of the corridor, shutting them inside a pitch-black doorway.

FOUR

THE CUT

Opal's eyes quickly got used to the blackness and she realised she'd been pulled backstage. She was in a dark forest of ropes, wires, ladders and metal poles. A line of about two dozen dancers stood in a queue, their bodies bisected by the shadows of the wings.

The person who'd grabbed her wrist was shrouded in black mink. She looked like the raven-haired woman depicted on the billboard outside. The woman let go of Opal's cuff and turned around, her Cupid's-bow mouth pursed tightly, her arms folded.

'Pardon, madame,' Opal apologised, her English accent peeking through. She was certain she was going to be reprimanded for entering the theatre uninvited.

The woman's eyes flashed brightly, and her lips stretched into a pleasant smile. 'Oh, you're Rosbif!' she said. 'I'm Zsa Zsa... I'm English too. Don't let my name fool you. It's Hungarian but I got given it by my dance peers because I move with real pizzazz! "Zsa", "Zsa".' She demonstrated with a fusillade of vampish hand movements.

Napoleon yapped at each of Zsa Zsa's gestures as if they were somehow a threat. Opal gently tugged the lead to quieten him. *I say,* she thought, *she seems a jolly good sport. Off her rocker slightly but entertaining none the less. I wonder if she could be a potential friend?*

'Yes, I am English... I'm Opal. From London,' she replied politely.

'What part a' town? I'm from Stepney Green. But I used to perform at Grosvenor House before they chose me to be in this.' Zsa Zsa's cockney slipping out a tad.

'I was born in Suffolk, then travelled a bit with my father but have lived in Marylebone for a long time.'

'*Marylebone?* That's a fancy part of London. And you sound spiffy.'

'Well, it's not that fancy really,' Opal said modestly. 'I live in an apartment above my mother's millinery shop.'

'Oh? Which one? I love window shopping around there. Not that I have two nickels to rub together. But I think after this job I'll be able to go inside those kinds of shops.'

'It's the Laplume Millinery shop on Ivor Road.'

'Not fancy? You gotta be jokin'. I know that shop, it's got a four-floor apartment above and the hats. My gosh, the beading and ribbon work on those treasures.'

'It is rather a nice hat shop, yes.' Opal felt herself blushing. 'So, Zsa Zsa, you're one of the three stars of the show, aren't you?'

'Yes. I've not been able to rehearse today because this audition has been on. I've just been watching from the wings... It's pretty boring. I was on my way out to the tobacconist when I saw you in the corridor and thought I better bring you to where you're supposed to be. You know you're very late, but I think you might be able to go on with this last bunch of girls.'

'Oh... golly... I'm not auditioning...'

'Why are you 'ere then?'

'I... I've been waiting to speak with Clementina. She's

kindly offered me a position in the costume atelier to help with the headdresses.'

'Oh... I guess you'll be working with Christophe Tasse.' Zsa Zsa looked down at the floor.

'Oh... who is he?' Opal replied, detecting awkwardness in Zsa Zsa's demeanour.

'He's the costume designer. I thought... he might have something to do with Valentine's death and that's what I told the police, but there wasn't anyone in the locked room when we opened it. He's got it in for me now.'

'Oh goodness gracious.' Opal fluttered her lashes and looked Zsa Zsa up and down concerned. *Would I be working with a murderer?*

'This is what the audition is for... to cover for Valentine. Showbusiness is cut-throat, eh? A girl is killed and they just carry on with someone else.'

Napoleon yapped playfully. He was trying to catch the feather fronds hanging from Opal's hat that was still in her hand.

'Shhhh, Napoleon!' Opal whispered, and remembered she had to clean off the dirty marks. 'Zsa Zsa, I dropped my hat in the street. Is there anything I can dust it with?'

'How did I not notice this cutie-pie before? The little pom-pom tail!' Zsa Zsa beamed down at the mutt. 'And eeeer, yes, just use this wing curtain to wipe it.'

Zsa Zsa plucked the bottom of the black avalanche of fabric and held it up into a patch of light, beaming in from the stage.

Opal scrubbed away the blemish and placed her favourite adornment back onto her head, affixing it again with its pin, tilted half over her right eye. She was the Honourable Opal Marion Laplume once more.

She now had a good view of the judging panel. Opal gasped when she laid eyes on her cousin sitting in the middle. Clementina's famous fire-opal curls were combed back and

clasped on top of her head with what Opal could decipher as a
Schiaparelli diamond clip. Her calligraphic eyebrows arched
harshly as she observed the auditionees. But despite her harsh
expression, Opal thought her beauty remained set in her heart-
shaped face. *Papa's got the same face shape. The Laplume
visage,* Opal thought.

Every now and again, the voluminous puff-sleeve of
Clementina's gown was deflated by a poke of the finger of the
man to her left. He whispered to her and she nodded vacantly.
This man's receding black hairline was that of a man in his mid-
fifties, though his physique was youthful and filled out his Kent-
cut suit well.

'Who is that judge, the one on Clementina's left?' Opal
hissed over her shoulder to Zsa Zsa.

'That's the American impresario, Leon Dumoulin. We've
been seeing each other... sort of. He's a *diamantaire* who was
persuaded by Clementina to whip out his chequebook and fund
the show and acquire a "producer" credit. He gets to advertise
his jewellery by putting it on the dancers. He seems to think he
has influence over which girl they choose and Clementina
humours him, but he's not really a judge. He doesn't have a clue
about picking the right girl, he's just sweet on them all. He's not
particularly good-looking but he thinks he is. He's one of the
few men who isn't a Hollywood actor to get porcelain veneers
fitted on his teeth, ensuing to his extreme vanity.'

'I see. Who's the man on the other side of Clementina?'

'Oh... that's the choreographer, Monsieur Blanchett. He's
very cruel with the dancers but whips us into shape like the
navy.'

M. Blanchett sat very straight in a black turtleneck, giving
the illusion that his pale head was floating in mid-air, a cobalt
blue beret atop. Instructions for the dancers came screeching
out of nasal orifices, disturbing the clement chords of the pianist

in the pit. Something about M. Blanchett made Opal feel very nervous indeed.

She flinched when two elongated paws flopped onto Clementina's lap. The rest of the beast's body was like a sleek, grey-blue moonbeam. Was it? It was. Clementina's famous pet greyhound, 'Yvette'.

Now, a very young waitress in a white escalloped pinny rattled a trolley along the carpet and halted in front of the three judges. She then proceeded to pour out three cafés noisettes in china cups. Opal watched as Clementina adeptly removed the fingers of her tight gloves and placed them on the trolley to receive her cup and saucer. She was just so elegant in the way she moved her hands. The waitress then handed the gloves back by the tips and wheeled the cart to the back of the auditorium. She pushed the trolley through the swing doors. Before they swung shut behind her, an illuminated sign 'RESTAURANT' could be seen.

M. Blanchett casually gesticulated a guillotine slice at his neck with one hand while his other held his china cup with pinky extended. The girl onstage to whom he was gesturing, dropped her shoulders as if her marionette strings had been flung onto the ground and scurried off stage-right.

Roughly three piano tunes later and a dozen or so more girls cut, a scream shot above the piano music. It was coming from the judging panel. Clementina jumped up out of her seat and continued to caterwaul like a broken saxophone. She was clasping her left wrist and gawking at her ring finger.

'*Ma bague de fiançailles!* My engagement ring! It's gone!' she yelled.

Opal stuck her nose forward for a better look at what was going on. The pianist tinkered inharmoniously to silence, and his furrowed brow appeared up over the pit. The other judges got to their feet.

'Are you sure you had it on this morning?' Leon Dumoulin asked.

'*Oui, oui.* I always wear it.' Clementina's voice echoed in the great hall.

M. Blanchett and Leon Dumoulin scrabbled below the seats, while Clementina just stood muttering madly at her finger.

Opal's eyelids flickered briefly, as if trying to adjust to a sudden realisation. Before she could stop herself, she handed Napoleon's leash to Zsa Zsa and stepped out of the wings into the warmth of the stage lights. She piped up as loud as she could.

'I... I think I know where the ring is.'

FIVE

THE RING

Opal felt all the eyes in the theatre settle on her like a hundred spotlights. She didn't know whether it was the heat of the Fresnel lights above her or whether she was hyperventilating, but she could feel sweat gather on her forehead.

Clementina was looking at her with almost viscous incredulity. But then her calligraphic eyebrows softened. 'Opal? Opal Laplume? It must be! Look at those glorious paradise feathers on your head.'

'Yes, yes, it is me. I'm sorry, it got rather chilly outside, so I thought I'd watch the auditions until you'd finished. I was watching you all very carefully and I think I know where your ring is, Clementina.'

'Pardon, I lost track of the time. Welcome, *ma chérie*. But how could you see what happened to the ring from all the way over there?' she said in her thick accent with lots of Zs and missing Hs.

'Thank you. Well, I'm not entirely sure but I have an idea where it might be,' her voice quivered. 'Let me just go and see.'

With hot cheeks Opal tiptoed down the front steps of the stage. She assumed Clementina must think she was crazy, or colluding in the theft of her ring by the mildly suspicious way she was looking at her.

Oh fig, please let me be right! Opal floated up the carpeted aisle as fast as she could. She went through the swing doors that the waitress had exited through earlier and careered around the grand pillars of the foyer, under the illuminated 'RESTAU-RANT' sign. She spotted the waitress serving coffee to a couple of old women wearing acorn-cup shaped hats, squirrel furs and strings of beads.

She approached the trolley and inspected its surface and the inside of coffee cups and saucers. Nothing. Opal blinked rapidly at all the customers who had coffee. Her chest began to tighten against her heartbeat again. *Perhaps I was wrong. Maybe I won't be able to find the ring and I will look like a complete berk. I need to win my cousin's trust.*

Suddenly a splutter sound came from the table over by the bar. A young couple were sitting shrouded in a grey mushroom of cigarette smoke. The girl had a café noisette cup on the table in front of her and was coughing the brown liquid up into her cupped palm. She then plucked an object out of the dribble and held it aloft in front of her nose.

'Joseph! Oh my God! Trust you to come up with something as spontaneous as this! Putting a ring in my coffee!' She planted a large kiss on his bewildered face and coffee from her chin splurged onto his cheek. 'Yes, yes, *I will* marry you!'

The old ladies in the acorn hats started to clap faintly in the background, their beads jangling in their own congratulatory way. *Oh, what a ghastly debacle,* Opal thought. *How do I let her down?*

'What are you talking about?' the boy replied, glaring at the object in his girlfriend's hand in horror.

'Excuse me for interrupting.' Opal couldn't let the poor girl be fooled any longer. She leaned down to their level and tried to speak in her clearest French possible. 'I regret to say that that ring belongs to someone else.'

With that, she plucked the jewel out of the girl's fingers and flew off before things got even more awkward. *Golly this is some ring,* she thought as she inspected it. It was a platinum band, a bead of coffee balanced on the large, cushion cut diamond. *This looks like a few carats; no wonder Clementina was so distraught to have lost it.* She polished the ring dry on her left sleeve, held it abreast, lengthened her neck and re-entered the auditorium.

All heads snapped in her direction. She couldn't help but curl the corners of her mouth up in a little smile. She halted a few yards in front of Clementina.

'Excuse me, Clementina, but your ring came off with your tight gloves,' Opal said and cleared her throat which due to her nerves sounded like a rusty flute. 'When the waitress handed them back to you by the tips, the ring fell into an empty cup on the trolley. I saw a sparkle when it happened.'

'Oh, *ma chérie, merci,* thank you so much!' The cabaret queen exhaled, took the ring and slipped it on her engagement finger again. She then took Opal by the shoulders. She planted a violet-scented kiss on each of Opal's cheeks. Opal felt highly pleased with herself. Her cousin would have to approve of her now.

'You must have a very sharp eye, *chérie.*'

'Oh, it's no problem,' Opal said, 'and, yes, I do. I'm always finding things for people. Papa used to call me "Bins", short for "binoculars", when he went birdwatching. I'd always be the first to spot any life amongst the forest canopy.'

'What was your name, young lady?' Leon Dumoulin asked, stepping forward and encasing Opal's hand in his palm.

'Opal Laplume.'

'And you're English?'

'Yes, she's from London,' interrupted Clementina. 'She is

my cousin. The Honourable Opal Laplume. I told you I had aristocratic lineage, did I not, Monsieur Dumoulin?'

Opal's stomach clenched. She felt eyes blink at her from every direction as if the air was disturbed by their lids batting. Her mother made her promise not to reveal that she was related to the showgirl. It was strictly a secret and the story was that Clementina was hat shop clientele. But Clementina seemed proud to be announcing this information. Opal inwardly shrugged it off. She guessed it was too late to deny it.

'Yes, yes, you did tell me!' The American *diamantaire* nodded in reminiscence of some champagne-sozzled conversation he'd had with Clementina. 'Your grandfather was Baron Laplume and your mother ran away to Paris...'

'We don't need to disclose all of the grizzly details,' Clementina whispered, nudging him with her balloon sleeve. 'If we go on, the rejected auditionees will have a little tale to sell to the papers.'

Leon Dumoulin's eyes swelled with annoyance and closed his mouth.

'Yes, I am from London,' Opal interjected to paint over the awkwardness. 'And I'm here to make feather headdresses. I hear a lot of help is needed.'

'From the sound of gunshots and squealing from the atelier, I think you're right,' chortled Mr Dumoulin.

Clementina looked at him sideways with slitted eyes. 'That's an inappropriate joke seeing as someone died, don't you think?'

He shrunk down into his collar and nodded his head at both Opal and Clementina as if to give up on the conversation.

'Excuse me, but it's getting late. We need to decide on a dancer,' said the choreographer, Monsieur Blanchett.

'*Oui, oui,* I agree,' Clementina said. 'But what about the girls we haven't seen?'

'Bad luck for them,' Monsieur Blanchett said, deadpan.

Opal slowly shrank down into a red velvet seat so as not to eavesdrop on their adjudication. She glanced up at the stage to see dozens of hopeful faces. She felt terribly sorry for the ones who didn't get to show their ability.

The judges huddled together with their notepads and whispered numbers argumentatively, and things like, '*Are you mad? She walked like a rugby player.*'

Monsieur Blanchett eyed the candidate 229 with his chin in his hands. She was raven-haired and slender, and smiled like a proud cat, as if she knew she was being discussed.

'Fine, have it your own way! I need to get home for my dauphinoise potatoes.' M. Blanchett folded his arms and minced away along the front row of seats. He stepped over the slumbering greyhound, Yvette. She didn't move but emitted a low growl in response to the man's unpleasant aura.

'I agree, I think 229 is a winner,' said Mr Dumoulin to Clementina, if only to make himself feel included in the decision.

'Alright, girls, thank you all for today.' Clementina spoke very loudly and addressed the girls assembled on the stage. 'We have made our selection. Number 229, Mademoiselle Wang Mei Ling. Everyone else... *merci et bonne nuit.*'

From the wings came moans and huffs. Mei Ling seemed to drink up the jealous remarks as if they were the upmost compliments and slunk off into the wings, chin high.

Clementina's voice cut above the ruckus onstage as she looked down at Opal in her seat. 'Opal, if you can make it to rehearsals tomorrow at eight o'clock in the morning it would be *magnifique.* I'm going home now but we will get better acquainted tomorrow.'

Opal felt herself nod and smile at the magnificent woman above her.

It seemed like a dream to be finally meeting her. Clementina's figure seemed smudged as if it were filtered through deep water as she walked away. The diva's pet greyhound followed her out of the auditorium, a slight flick of the paw at the end of each step, as though the legs themselves were too refined to simply *end* the step but rather must *finish* it.

But then, from behind a pillar, a blond man stepped out, stopping Clementina in her tracks. In the low light the only things about him that were visible were his white shirt collar, perfect teeth, a shaving cut on his chin and the notepad he held under the light.

'Detective Inspector Prosper Delacroix.' Clementina nodded at him. 'Have you interviewed everyone you needed to today?'

'Yes, except I haven't spoken to that lady over there... who is she?'

'Oh no, no. That's my new millinery assistant, Opal Laplume. She's only arrived today.'

Opal nodded and did a little wave. Prosper lifted his trilby at her and then slunk out of the auditorium behind Clementina.

Up on the stage, Zsa Zsa poked her head out from the left wings followed by Napoleon's curious conk. She beckoned Opal excitedly.

SIX

A PRICK OF INTRIGUE

'One of the stage managers said you would be staying at the Reinette Hotel with me!' Zsa Zsa said joyously when Opal had come to meet her up onstage.

'Oh... yes! Jolly good, I'm so pleased. We can play late night games of piquet and rummy, I brought cards with me!'

'My card education stopped at snap, I'm afraid,' Zsa Zsa replied. 'But it will be good to have a chum down the corridor.'

Opal felt awash with excitement. Had she set the wheels of a friendship in motion?

She felt someone squeeze her wrist and lift it up to warm lips. She whipped her head around. It was Leon Dumoulin, the American impresario.

'Welcome to our theatrical family, my darling.' His veneers radiated before he kissed her hand.

'Mr Dumoulin, thank you,' Opal said, quickly pulling her hand back. 'I'm so relieved that everyone is so... friendly.'

'We'll look after you. And your millinery career will reach new heights!'

'Well, I do hope so. And what more beautiful theatrical headwear than a Parisian cabaret dancer?'

'Quite right. I see you've kitted your critter out in a bicorn hat.'

'Oh yes, this is Napoleon.' Mr Dumoulin reached down to pet the pooch, but was met with a growl. 'He can be a bit confrontational with strangers,' Opal quickly said. 'He's terribly protective of me, the darling.'

'You have a soldier. Appreciate the forewarning,' Mr Dumoulin replied and retracted his hand. 'Ah, you London girls will have a great time together I bet.' Leon beamed and swooped Zsa Zsa's mink sleeve under his.

'We certainly will.' Zsa Zsa looked at Opal. 'We will be part of the grandest and most extravagant show that the world has ever seen.'

'It certainly will be,' Leon Dumoulin agreed. 'I've put enough cash into it. I've even got the dancers wearing my beautiful diamonds.'

'Really?' Opal asked, a bit taken aback by the man's boastful tone.

'Yes. You see, this is my first time producing a show. My real business is diamonds. I own the fine jewellery brand Dumoulin, my grandfather founded it.'

'Oh gosh. I've seen models wearing Dumoulin jewellery in *Vogue* magazine,' Opal said, impressed.

'Yes, but you see I want our brand to grow beyond the pages of magazines. In fact, that's why I'm here. I'm entering a design competition, part of the International Exposition of Jewellery and Goldsmithing, here in Paris. I'll be submitting a spectacular necklace with a diamond worth *twelve* million francs.' Opal gasped at the enormous amount.

'It's called the Apolline Diamond, and it will be displayed around Clementina's neck during her performance. What better way to show my designs off than on the most famous showgirl in the world? I just had to whip out my chequebook to pay for it all.' His front veneers jumped onto his lower lip in a cheeky grin.

'He loves his chequebook.' Zsa Zsa rolled her eyes up at him, and Opal found it hard not to do the same.

'Very true.' Leon clapped his hands together. 'Now, let's go and put you both in a car. And, of course, Napoleon, I didn't forget you.'

Opal followed Leon and Zsa Zsa out through the main foyer onto the street. She was just adjusting her hat in the breeze when she heard car doors slamming and fast conversation.

Suddenly, a blinding flash came from behind the railings with the tinkle noise of a shattering bulb. Then another flash, then another a little further along the railings. Opal blinked rapidly and protected her face from the staunch light with her hatbox. Napoleon yapped after each explosion of the cameras.

'Is this girl the replacement for Valentine Beaumanoir?' They repeated the question over and over, like a bunch of hyenas.

'*S'il vous plaît!*' Leon waved his hand at them. 'This is *not* the girl. We will send out a press release tomorrow, please leave us alone.'

They ignored him and carried on clamouring.

'Do you know who murdered Valentine?'

'Is there a suspect yet?'

'Aren't you terrified a killer is at large and after the showgirls?'

The bulbs continued to flash in Opal's face, and she felt she had to smile – if they got an awful picture of her, it would only be worse.

'Beautiful hat, where is it from?' One of the paparazzi attempted to engage with her.

Opal's eyelashes fluttered like an excited butterfly, and looked at him in inspiration. This could be a great way to advertise mother's hat business.

'It's Laplume Millinery, we're based in London,' she said. Then pulled her brim forward for an angled shot.

'We will send you a press release tomorrow,' Leon carried on resolutely. 'Just get in the car, darling.'

Opal gladly ensconced herself on the smooth leather seat of the streamline black Renault. Zsa Zsa entered the car after her, her lipstick a little smudged from Leon's zealous goodbye kiss.

'Gosh, that's going to be all over the papers tomorrow,' said Zsa Zsa.

'I should think the real new dancer will be vexed to see a picture of me instead of her,' Opal said guiltily.

'Well,' exclaimed Zsa Zsa as their driver pulled away, 'we did tell them it wasn't you.'

'How did you get the part in the show, Zsa Zsa?' Opal enquired, gazing up at a beautiful gas street lamp through her window.

'Monsieur Blanchett, the choreographer, had been in London a few months ago and came to Grosvenor House. I was in a fun double act dressed as a cockerel. You should have seen my feather tail, it was like someone had lit my *derrière* ablaze.' She giggled at the memory. 'He approached me after the show saying he was scouting for girls to appear in Clementina's revue in Paris. I believed him because it was obvious that he was interested in my talent and not my underpinnings. You know, because it's obvious he prefers the company of gentlemen. He paid for my Golden Arrow ticket to Paris shortly after and Valentine and I got the parts.'

After a moment's hypnotism from the scintillating lights on the Seine, Opal straightened up in her seat and pulled Napoleon onto her lap. She was very curious about what Zsa Zsa had revealed earlier. She wanted to hear about the murder and the fact that Zsa Zsa had accused Christophe Tasse of it. Christophe was going to be Opal's new boss. She needed to get as much information as she could.

'I do hope you aren't feeling too cut up about what happened to Valentine...' Opal opened the conversation.

'Well, it's a complete shock, but I didn't really know Valentine. She pretended to be fond of me for the camaraderie of backstage. But my French isn't very good and her English was nil. She was a bit of a pain in the buttocks for the few weeks I did know her, but it's a dreadful thing to have happened and some of the chorus girls in the show seem traumatised. Clementina is also very upset. She knew Valentine for years. She was kind of Clementina's protégée you know.'

'Can I ask exactly what happened?'

'I heard the entire thing. I was in the room below her. She started to shout for help, demanding that Christophe Tasse get off her. I heard those words crystal clear. We managed to break the door down and we found the room empty. She'd been hurled from the balcony. But no way for the killer to have escaped the room. It was locked from the inside.'

Zsa Zsa sighed, a sad look passing over her face.

'Nobody believes me when I say I heard Valentine scream Christophe's name. His alibi is solid. He was still at the theatre when it happened, working late. He was with his seamstresses who vouched for him. Ironically, they were working on Valentine's costume. Clementina vouched for him also.'

Zsa Zsa shook her head.

'I don't know though, Opal... I just think he may have manipulated his workers into giving him an alibi. I mean, he's their employer, what would they do without him? The unemployment wave is veering west and there's been an influx of seamstresses to Paris from all over the place looking for work.'

'That is something to think about,' mused Opal. 'Did any of the other guests in the hotel hear Valentine shout Christophe Tasse's name?'

'No, they just heard muffled yells. I guess I could hear clearest through the floorboards above me.'

Opal believed her completely. She sounded sincere, and what reason could she possibly have to fabricate what she heard? Unless she was trying to pin it on the man for some unknown reason.

Opal massaged Napoleon's head in circles while she pondered. 'Could there be another person named Christophe Tasse? Or the killer disguised themselves as Christophe for some reason?'

'Not impossible, but I highly doubt it.' Zsa Zsa shrugged.

'Or the killer could have been trying to get information from her and Christophe Tasse was the answer they were looking for?'

'No, no, the way she shouted it... she was shouting *at* him.'

'Could she have been on the blower?' Opal's eyes lit up as she thought about the telephone.

'The police inspector asked that... but she said the words "get off me", so you wouldn't say that unless someone was touching you.'

'Are the police getting anywhere with it?'

'They questioned everyone in the theatre cast and crew. They wanted to know if anyone had any reason to want Valentine dead. They didn't come up with anything. I mean, everyone knew that Christophe and Valentine fought. They were lovers but tormented each other. She didn't like how his costumes fit and they would squabble about that. Then he started to get keen on Estelle, one of the chorus girls... he was asking Estelle for one too many "fittings". Valentine got wildly upset about that and ripped one of her costumes, accidently on purpose, to make him redo it.'

'Not a match made in heaven then. Do the police have any other suspects or leads?' Opal enquired.

'No, I asked the inspector how a girl could be arguing and pushed by someone who was seemingly never there and all he said was: *I don't know.*'

'Well that's sounds rather inept. I do hope they are taking it seriously.'

'One would hope. I think Paris is a little overrun with crime, seeing as the Depression is looming.'

'Quite.'

Opal blinked slowly in thought and then turned to her window. They came up to a flamboyant gothic church, its great bulk blackened as if blasted with soot. Huddled up against the railings was what looked like sacks of butcher's waste. It moved and as they drove closer Opal realised with sadness that it was a group of benumbed vagrants, bottles in their hands, bedraggled on the pavement. The Depression was indeed imminent in Paris.

They turned a corner and a giant billboard for their show 'Clementina Lalonde La Grande Revue' appeared up ahead. Valentine was still the third dancer on the advertisement. Opal's stomach squeezed. Something about this entire situation was just so terribly unsettling. *What kind of a thing was she getting caught up in, if Christophe, her new boss, was truly a murderer?*

'Everyone in Paris is talking about our show,' said Zsa Zsa, noticing the billboard. 'We have huge posters in the Metro and Clementina's talking about it in all the magazines.' She paused for a moment and lowered her tone. 'The press has been talking about the show even more since Valentine was killed. It's actually been very good publicity for it. Horrid, I know, that we should be benefitting from it.'

'*Voilà, l'hôtel Reinette*,' the driver said, interrupting Zsa Zsa.

The car came to a halt and Opal looked out of her drizzle-speckled window. The pavement was glistening, and a piece of rope dragged in a puddle. The rope led up to some bollards that squared off a section of the pavement close to the hotel. Inside the section was a white chalked outline of a body. It was smudged somewhat due to the drizzle, but Opal could see the waist of the body was very tiny as if the person who'd been outlined had been cinched in a corset.

'That's where she fell,' Zsa Zsa said sombrely over Opal's shoulder. Zsa Zsa cracked open the heavy car door and a gust chilled Opal's calves.

'The police only thought it necessary to close off the top floor to investigate, so I'm still in the same room. I would have moved but all the other hotels are full because of the Exposition of Jewellery and Goldsmithing. The only other option Mr Dumoulin gave me was to stay at *his* apartment, but I wasn't going to do *that*,' Zsa Zsa said, then sighed. 'So here we are.'

Opal's lashes batted sporadically as she studied the chalked pavement. Perhaps she could have a snoop at the crime scene by somehow persuading the police to show her. She always noticed things that nobody else did. Perhaps she would be able to help? It would be a relief to find the real killer and not to worry about Christophe being a murderer. The pointed tip of her nose twitched with the temptation. *What was it that the police were missing? Why couldn't they figure out how the killer managed to vanish out of the room?*

SEVEN

L'HÔTEL REINETTE

Inside L'Hôtel Reinette, the girls' heels sounded like castanets on the marble floor, which was so shiny Opal could see the cherubic chandeliers reflected in it. Napoleon gazed as his mirror image swirled by on a floor vase spilling with Albertine roses in all the pastel shades.

Ahead was a wooden spiral staircase. It had a narrow lift in the centre that was evidently designed to go up inside the spiral. To the right was a doorway labelled 'Salon de Petit-Déjeuner' and to the left was a long reception desk laden with more pastel blooms. Behind the desk was a tired-looking, plump woman hunched over a novel.

'*Bonsoir*, madame!' Zsa Zsa said, her cockney slipping through slightly on the '*soir*'.

'*Bonsoir*, mademoiselle,' the receptionist replied with a reptilian croak.

'Clementina Lalonde said she had reserved a room for Opal Laplume?'

'*Oui, oui.*' The receptionist leaned over the desk and handed Opal a mortice key. 'You are lucky we 'ave a room. Someone left because they were upset about ze murder. You will be next to Mademoiselle Zsa Zsa in room 406 on ze fourth floor. Someone will bring your luggage up... Oh! The top floor is prohibited. Nobody is to go up zere.'

'*Merci*, madame. I just have to mention that I have a little poodle.' Opal lifted Napoleon's head above the desk, hoping the bicorn would charm the madame.

The woman looked at the pooch with a deadpan expression, then up at Opal, saying nothing. She smacked her lips and looked Opal directly in the eye, seeming to enjoy the suspenseful look on Opal's face.

'Have you got any francs?' Zsa Zsa broke the silence, looking pointedly at Opal's purse.

'Oh, oh, of course, how silly of me.'

Opal riffled through her purse and produced a note on the table. She hadn't a clue how much it was.

The woman craned her neck forward to peek at the banknote and rested her gaze as if she were expecting it to grow.

'Bit more,' Zsa Zsa said out of the side of her mouth.

Opal sifted two more notes from her wad onto the desk. The receptionist's chubby fingers slapped over them and dragged them away.

'*Oui*, Clementina mentioned in ze booking you 'ad a dogue. It is not protocol but Clementina is a special client.' The lady smiled contently and shrunk back into her novel.

Opal thanked her and nodded. But she had no intention of obeying the lady about the top floor. She would simply *have* to do some nosing. Perhaps she'd have to play the 'silly card' and pretend she had got lost up there.

A golden plaque glowed on the oak door. *The Marquise de Vintimille Suite* it read. Opal opened the door and her right eyebrow shot up. The suite was so luxurious you'd think it was made for a real marquise. Or Marie Antoinette, even.

She clambered onto the four-poster bed and buried her face into a pile of cushions that looked like a mountain of giant macarons. Above her, silk dupion fabric was gathered into a glorious chandelier.

'No, no, Napoleon! The tassels are not titbits!' Opal reprimanded her poodle. Zsa Zsa patted him off them and opened the French windows for a cigarette.

The balcony. Valentine fell from one of these. I must take a nosy. Opal slid off the duchess satin sheets and almost stubbed her toe on the claw-foot bath that was perched in the centre of the room.

'I say! A bath in the centre of the room? I've never seen anything so decadent,' Opal said, clutching her beads.

'Oh yes. This is Pariiiiis!' Zsa Zsa threw her arms in the air. '*And,* you can watch yourself bathe in the mirror opposite.' Opal blushed a little at the thought.

'Is that identical to the balcony Valentine fell off?' Opal asked, joining Zsa Zsa under the French windows.

'Yeah it is,' Zsa Zsa replied, the amber tip of her cigarette glowing like an amber ring on her figure.

Opal curled her fingers around the balustrade, gripping it tight. It came up to just below her waist. She imagined she was Valentine, standing in front of it before tumbling off, and a shiver shot from the base of her spine to the nape of her neck.

It was not very high, so it would be easy to push someone over it, especially if they were tall, or in high heels. She looked to the right and left, to see whether there was any chance the killer could have shimmied along the wall to the next balcony, but it was just a dead drop down the obsidian black façade. Nothing with a foothold.

'Which balcony was Valentine's?' she asked.

'It's above and to the left,' replied Zsa Zsa, pointing up.

Opal leant forward over the balustrade, pressing her pelvis against it, the plumes on her hat flopping forward.

'Careful, you bedlamite!' yelled Zsa Zsa.

Opal craned her neck and looked up, trying to see the underside of Valentine's balcony, but her view was blocked by the overhanging arch. *Drat.*

Zsa Zsa's voice seemed to get the attention of a man below on the street. He was standing by a mud-splattered Citroën and smoking a sagging cigarillo, ribbons of smoke twisted around his weathered trilby hat. Opal noticed a scar that ripped his left cheek down to his jaw in a 'T' shape. It looked old, and so deep it had never lost its reddish coloration. On his sloping shoulders hung a thick Ulster coat in a camel shade. There was something about him that made Opal feel uneasy.

He was looking up at Opal's balcony, but when he caught her eye, he immediately flicked his cigarillo onto the pavement, stooped into his car and accelerated away. Opal blinked anxiously and followed the car with her eyes up the Rue de Rivoli.

He left as soon as he'd seen I'd noticed him. Opal thought, a touch of fear rising in her belly. *Who was he, and what was he doing at the hotel?*

EIGHT

ILLUSTRATIONS IN LIPSTICK

'Tell me all about your society love life,' Zsa Zsa said when she returned to Opal's room having gone to change into a more relaxing butterfly embroidered kimono. 'It'll be like reading *Tattles* or *Tatler* or whatever you lot read.'

'Oh... my love life consists of my mother trying to set me up with a viscount named Turkey. Viscount Cecil Turks-Leyton is his full title. It's like pulling teeth trying to tell her I'm not interested.'

'Turkey!' Zsa Zsa laughed. 'Think of the headlines: *Society Wedding a Roast Success – Bride Carved Out a New Life!*'

'It's my mother's way of marrying her way back up the ranks again, through me. You see, she "married down" when she married my father, a baron. Her father was the Viscount Oulton of Jacksands. But there just aren't enough viscounts, earls and dukes to go around.'

'There aren't enough normal nice blokes to go around since the war as it is! So, what's wrong with this Turkey then? Does he gobble nervously whenever commitment is mentioned?'

'Well, he's just so terribly fuddy and old-fashioned. I mean, he dresses like a gamekeeper from the 1880s and his only hobby is hunting, which I despise. And I'd just really love a man with more artistic interests who is as keen as I am to see more of the world.' Opal giggled. 'You'd get on so well with my father. He makes jokes about Turkey too.'

'Oh great... when do I meet Lord Laplume?' Zsa Zsa said, now doing a plié, her cigarette hanging from her teeth.

What an interesting way to smoke, Opal thought. She continued to watch Zsa Zsa do a full forward bend, flattening her back like a tabletop. Opal felt an artistic twitch of desire to draw her. She riffled in her handbag.

'What are you doing? Don't avoid my question,' Zsa Zsa said, upside down with her nose to her knees now.

'I want to draw you, but I've got no pencil.' Opal kept looking through her handbag and found an old lipstick. Perhaps she could use it as a crayon?

'You like drawing?'

'Well, I like fashion illustration for millinery. I love to draw people and illustrate a whimsical hat on them.'

Zsa Zsa straightened up, stubbed out the cigarette and positioned her feet like a ballerina, accentuating the curve of her hips.

'Good,' Opal said, then lounged back on the bed to get a good angle. Napoleon joined her and sat up straight as if in an art lesson.

Opal twisted the lipstick up and put the red waxy substance to paper. It would have to be impressionist style with thick strokes as it wasn't a fine pencil, but Opal felt it was rather apt to draw a showgirl with lipstick.

After Opal had finished Zsa Zsa's silhouette, she tried to imagine what kind of hat she'd put on her. She'd never designed a voluminous twinkling cabaret headdress before. Her drawing hand fizzed with delight.

'What's your act like?' Opal asked Zsa Zsa for some inspiration.

'I'm an English Rose. I have a giant petal skirt, and the narrative is that I'm the rose that is pinned to a man's button-hole and I come to life.'

'How splendid.' Opal bit the gold case of the lipstick like it was a pencil as she blinked quickly in thought.

With a dozen or so flame-like licks around the head of the illustration, Opal produced a velvet rosebud headpiece for Zsa Zsa. For stage-scale prominence she added some cascading strokes leaping from the centre of the bud. These could be long green pheasant feathers.

'Let me see... this is brilliant, Opal,' Zsa Zsa gasped. 'Don't breathe a word of this to anyone but I think your designs are far better than Christophe Tasse's.'

Opal felt a warm glow wash over her and a proud smile lift the corners of her mouth. 'Thank you... It is what I want to do with my life. Design and make hats. Perhaps even become as famous as Chanel one day.'

'Opal... you don't mind me asking something?'

'Depends on what you're asking,' Opal replied, closing her sketchbook.

'I thought *you* lot, you well-to-do folk... didn't *work*. I mean, don't you just play bridge in tiaras while the lords go off chasing foxes and things like that? I'm surprised that you've got a trade and whatnot.'

'Oh!' Opal raised her eyebrows and yawned. 'If you want to know our riches-to-rags story, I'll tell you. But it may have to be tomorrow. I've had an awfully long day and I'm about ready to turn in.'

Zsa Zsa looked a bit forlorn. 'Actually, Opal... Can I sleep in here with you? It's been giving me the creeps these past nights staying in my room alone, thinking about the murder.'

'Of course. The bed is large enough, certainly.' Opal removed her hat and smiled. 'I thought I was going to be alone here in Paris. I really am grateful to have some company.'

'Hold your horses, love. You might find I'm more trouble than I'm worth,' Zsa Zsa chortled.

NINE

TWO BIRDS WITH ONE STONE

Napoleon, Opal and Zsa Zsa, in that order, were tucked under the thick marshmallow of bedding. Napoleon had been fed and brushed. Opal had wrapped her hair in a silk scarf to protect her marcel waves and Zsa Zsa had a layer of cold cream on her face as thick as cake-icing.

'I must say, your kimono has inspired me to jazz up my nightwear, Zsa Zsa,' said Opal.

'But who's going to see you in your bed chamber if you haven't got Lord Turkey Leg?' Zsa Zsa chortled.

Napoleon made a huff noise in a protective manner over Opal's mockery.

'I'd rather be in the company of frilly nightdresses, thank you.'

'You seem to prefer clothes to human beings.'

'I find it hard to make friends. But indeed, marrying a floating fedora could be easier.'

'I'm the opposite to you really. I've had many beaus in my twenty-five years. I've courted a bus conductor, a costermonger, a rag-and-bone man, a barrow boy...'

'Oh gosh...'

Zsa Zsa sighed. 'I'd keep stringing them all along until they fell in love with me but didn't give them as much as a peck. I *am* wicked. Mr Dumoulin is starting to grow on me though. And I've shared the odd kiss. Though it might just be the diamonds that are catching my eye.' Her eyes sparkled deviously.

'Oh yes, Mr Leon Dumoulin. How did that start out with you two?' Opal asked.

'He took me and some of the chorus girls to an amazing seafood hall called La Coupole. I saw *Picasso* in there! We ate *fruits de mer* and got plastered. The other girls slowly got tired and filtered away until there were only three of us: Mr Dumoulin, a chorus girl and me. When driving us home he asked his driver to drop *her* off first. After she got out of the taxi he said, *"We're not going home I was just getting rid of her."* And took me to a very saucy club.'

'What happened next?' Opal and Napoleon both fluttered their eyelids as they craved for more.

'Oh, he tried to get me back to his apartment didn't he, *the devil*,' said Zsa Zsa. 'Even if I'd wanted to, I couldn't, really, could I? He's the producer of the show. I can't meddle with that.'

'I understand what you mean,' said Opal, going slightly pink. 'You can't risk your career.'

Zsa Zsa yawned. 'I can't wait for the opening night. Clementina will be wearing the Apolline Diamond in the finale of the show. It's one of the rarest and most expensive diamonds in the world. I'm sure it'll win first prize, which is what Mr Dumoulin wants. And imagine all the affluent people who'll be wanting to buy it after that... Russians, Americans, all kinds of foreign princes...'

'I have always wondered why someone would spend millions on jewellery,' Opal mused. 'My grandmama, Viscountess Oulton, had beautiful pieces. They were rarely worn, only at State Banquets or Court presentations.'

'Oh goodness. Did she have a tiara?' Zsa Zsa leant up on an elbow.

'Oh yes. I have one too. It has an opal as its centre stone and seed pearls intertwined around its silver frame. Grandmama presented it to me as a baby. She said to my mother, "*What striking blue opalescent eyes this cherub possesses! You simply must call her Opal, and she must have my opals.*"'

'She sounds very grandiose.' Zsa Zsa gazed up into the chandelier in the canopy. 'What other jewellery did she give you?'

'Oh, bits and bobs. Some very nice pieces. But we had to sell some of ours, you see...'

'Oh yes, you were going to tell me your riches-to-rags tale...' Zsa Zsa rolled onto her stomach and rested her cheeks in her hands. 'I mean not exactly rags but it's more fun to put it like that.'

'Well, thank you kindly!' laughed Opal. 'It's not uncommon these days for peers to be learning a trade or doing the odd thing in secret for some income. Mother grew up on a big estate in Norfolk called Jacksands Park and her papa was Viscount Oulton. When he died, everything went to my uncle, who lives there now. Then Mother met Father. It's quite a sweet tale really.'

'Do tell.'

'So, my papa is an ornithologist—'

'What in 'eaven's name's that? Someone who flogs 'orns?'

'No, it's a person that studies birds. He is Baron Edmund Laplume, and he wrote a famous book called *Paradisical Birds: A Field Guide*. He travels around the world looking for new species and studies their behaviours.' Opal yawned. 'Mother was always terribly fashionable and would design hats for herself and her circle of friends. One day, she'd been reading a scientific journal that her father had left lying about. My father had written an article about a rare bird with iridescent gold feathers my mother had wanted for a hat. She wrote to him and asked if she could meet to talk about the feather specimens he had. They went for tea and she asked him if she could buy a feather from him for her hat so she could show off to her friends. My father gifted it to her and their romance blossomed.'

'He killed two birds with one stone then,' Zsa Zsa said.

'A jolly good quip. But just so you know, Daddy doesn't kill birds. He only forages for feathers, like the ones you'll see in my hats.'

'Alright, alright... what happened next?'

'Well, they married and moved into his estate, Copperfields Hall in Suffolk, where I was born. Daddy would be away for months at a time on adventures with his ornithologist friends. Copperfields was quite a handful to keep going with the gardens and grounds to take care of and he didn't have a lot of money, apart from the actual house.'

'Sounds big for only three people,' Zsa Zsa said.

'Mother did get rather lonely but continued her love for designing hats. She thought with a name like Laplume it was just fate for her to start her own family millinery business. She invested in a shop in Marylebone and then wanted to open one in New York.'

'She was very *ambitious*.' Zsa Zsa yawned.

'A bit too ambitious. Without asking Father she bought a huge amount of stock... straws, monogrammed hatpins, velvets, chiffons, ostrich tips, egret, paradise feathers, silk and taffeta flowers, glass beads and cabochons, and put it as cargo... on the *Titanic*.'

'No.' Zsa Zsa sat up and the covers flung down.

'Yes, she did. *And* she didn't insure it,' Opal said.

'Crumbs!'

'Indeed. She had prepaid the rent for the New York shop for an entire year which she couldn't get the cash back for either. We lost nearly all our money. In fact, we had to sell

Copperfields Hall... to a... *mustard factory*.' Opal shivered at the memory. 'I was about eight when we had to move above the London shop. I've been used to a more humble lifestyle for a long time. Mother still never dresses herself. But I do.'

'You're pulling my leg – a mustard factory!'

'No, no, I'm not. And a penny-pinching label at that.' Opal shook her head slowly and imagined her old bedroom, now with bright mustard-yellow walls and the scent of spicy mustard seeds. The noise of a bottling machine, its intricate gears and pistons humming. With graceful swoops, it descends upon each luminous yellow jar, imprinting labels as they twirl past her old window.

'What did your father say when he found out she'd squandered all the family dough down the Atlantic plughole?'

'He laughed actually,' Opal scoffed. 'He didn't care much for Copperfields because he was never there, and he found the upkeep of it a big strain. He couldn't wait to be off on his next field trip. A bit of a nomad, if you like. His sister, who is Clementina's mother, was similar. Ran off to Paris and...' Opal stopped short when she realised she was going too far.

'Oh, the story gets sweeter and sweeter.' Zsa Zsa rubbed her hands together like an excited old codger.

'I can't say any more. It is a scandal. Even though it happened in the 1890s it's still rarely spoken about even in my family. It almost killed my grandpapa Laplume. *Grand-père*, I called him. He was French.'

'Oh, do tell, Opal...'

'Well there's not much more to it. She ran off and had Clementina.'

'Who with?'

'We don't know,' Opal lied. 'And my mother made me promise not to even reveal I was related to her. I was just supposed to be an acquaintance in the hat world. But

Clementina blurted it out anyway, so I guess it's not really my fault.'

'What's your mother so worried for?'

'Just gossip on the London circuit. She's had enough embarrassments. Having to sell her estate to a cut-price condiment factory, while her brother lords it up in Jacksands Park. She wouldn't want them to know she was related to a *danseuse de cabaret*.'

'But it is the thirties, now. Anything goes!' Zsa Zsa said, flipping her curls.

'Oh, believe me, Mother is stuck in the 1890s. And my neck will be stuck in this ninety-degree angle from talking to you unless we go to sleep soon.'

'Oh, alright. You still don't mind if I stay in your bed with you tonight, Opal?' Zsa Zsa asked.

'Why, of course. But don't get all that cold cream on the pillows. Oh, and we need to wind an alarm clock.'

Opal let Napoleon straddle her head like a warm woollen wig and closed her eyes. All the talk of her mother set her mind racing and after half an hour of trying, Opal couldn't sleep. She felt like a whirling dervish was trapped in her skull.

Is Christophe going to find my skills disappointing tomorrow? Should I be more worried about the fact he may be a murderer? If not, then is there a killer in this hotel? Who was that suspicious man outside the balcony? And why did Mother banish me from London in such a frenzy?

Zsa Zsa clearly also couldn't sleep. 'You know,' she whispered. 'There was one very strange detail about Valentine's murder. She *didn't scream* when she was pushed off the balcony. I almost wish she had, because there would perhaps be some closure for me. You know, like an end to it all. But there was just silence.'

'Hmm?' Opal's lashes fluttered with intrigue. 'I agree that's odd. You would naturally scream the split second you'd been hurled over a balcony. Even if it was for half a second before you hit the ground.'

'I also can't get over how they managed to vanish from a locked room. If it was one of the guests, or one of the hotel workers who knew about a secret passage or something, they could easily get us too.'

'Did the police find any passages?' Opal asked.

'No, they didn't. But I just can't relax about it until I know what happened.'

'We must try and sleep. At least we have Napoleon to protect us.'

The poodle was now curled up on a macaroon-shaped cushion which was the perfect size for him, and kept one eye open as if he knew his exact duty.

Opal finally started to relax as sleep found her in the dark. Before she drifted off, she thought how grateful she was that she'd perhaps finally made a friend.

TEN

MISTAKEN IDENTITY

A tinny bell sound hammered on Opal's eardrums. *Oh, crikey, it's the morning.* Her arms shot up by her head, creating an avalanche of cushions. She crawled out of them and switched the alarm clock off. *Six o'clock!* Her brow ached as though she had been frowning as she slept.

She looked over at Zsa Zsa who was still fast asleep, lying like Hera in a Grecian myth painting, with one arm framing her face and her knees swooped up onto one side. *Trust her to exude the poise of a goddess even as she slumbers!*

'Zsa Zsa. It's six o'clock. The morning has broken.'

The maiden stirred, pouted in protest and moaned from the back of her throat. 'Okay,' she croaked. 'I'll get up. I'm going to my room to get ready. See you down at breakfast in an hour.'

Opal scrubbed herself in the bathtub, careful not to get her hair wet and lose her perfect wave set. She then put on her lingerie and petticoat and sat at the dresser. She got out the small makeup pouch she'd brought with her. She'd have to try her hardest to look like someone who knew a thing or two about showbusiness. The best impression of her abilities would shine through her presentation.

She started by powdering her skin, and to add colour to her complexion she daubed a peony pink in the apples of her cheeks.

She sharpened a dark eyebrow pencil and accentuated her thin arches. With a steady hand she drew a dramatic Cupid's bow over her top lip with a lip liner in a cinnabar red. She continued the line under her bottom lip and filled the centre in with lipstick. Lastly, concentrating on her favourite feature, her eyes, she applied an oyster-silver eyeshadow over her lids to bring out the blue. A long flick of black liquid liner at the base of her lashes defined her blink. Generous helpings of mascara came next, spanning her eyelashes out like wings in flight.

With a comb and some fingers dampened with setting lotion she neatened the waves that she'd had set in her hair for the past couple of days. *Not my absolute best, but I could believe I was a costumier if I saw me on the street.*

She swivelled on the pouffe and reached into her hatbox. *Oh fig*, she thought, *what should I wear? My polka-dot shirt-waist dress with Juliet sleeves? Or perhaps, as it's my first day, my tea dress with the orchid print and bell sleeves would make the best impression?* Opal bit her lip. *Perhaps I had better consult Zsa Zsa.*

She concealed her modesty with her overcoat, swiped her key from her bedside table and left the room, locking it behind her. She consulted Zsa Zsa who was half asleep at her dressing table and waving a marcel curling iron around. The verdict was the flamboyant orchid-print tea dress which would help her stand out among the seamstresses in their drab uniforms. Opal smiled, happy at the thought that she now had a sisterly ally to help her deliberate over dresses.

On her way back to her room, she heard someone heavy-footed creaking up the stairs behind her. Turning her head, she saw a tall, ash-suited man walking towards her with a stoical expression.

His eyebrows were thick and blond like his hair and moustache. He had a healing shaving cut on his chin. Opal recognised him from the auditorium, where he'd spoken to Clementina.

She fumbled with her key, stabbing it in the lock, but it was awkward and stiff. *Damn it. It wasn't this difficult last night.* She was conscious that she looked a berk stabbing and twisting the confounded thing. She looked over her shoulder to see the man grin amusedly.

'*Bonjour.*' Opal smiled, leaving the key in the lock and smoothing down her overcoat.

'*Bonjour,*' he replied with a polite nod.

Opal wanted him to continue past, but he stayed put. With a swallow she turned back and continued to jab and contort the useless piece of metal. *Oh please, please open, damn door, this is humiliating.*

'Do you need 'elp?' he asked after a few moments, obviously detecting her English in her greeting.

'Oh... errr ... yes, it's a little stiff,' Opal said, sidestepping and looking up at him sideways.

The man tried. His amber cufflinks jangling.

'You're right.' He looked at her down the middle of his dimpled chin. 'It is a bit stiff.'

Opal scrunched her toes nervously and waited with her hands clasped behind her back for him to try again.

'*Voilà!*' he said, pushing the door ajar.

'Oh! *Merci*, monsieur!' Opal clapped her hands twice.

He held out her key. She took it gratefully. The man's chin lifted in a slightly conceited smile and he carried on up to the top 'prohibited' floor.

Opal's eyes flickered as she watched him ascend the stairs. Perhaps he was an '*agent de police*' and could show her the murder scene? It might be good to make friends with this gentleman. She patted her hair in place and entered her room.

She got out her case of hat pins and corsages. She had adorned them all with her most precious treasures from expeditions with her father – feathers of all kinds: pheasant, scarlet ibis, pheasant, quetzal, flamingo and, of course, birds of paradise feathers. Many were plumes she'd collected as a child that she'd foraged from the forest floors. The paradise birds would shed and regrow their feathers every year so it was quite often she would find them when out with her father in Northern Australia, and once in Papua. Today she felt drawn to the red bird of paradise plumes that she had secured around a bright-green bead. She pierced it into the Petersham ribbon on her fedora securely.

She pinned the matching corsage to the left lapel of her coat and faced the mirror. Pulling the brim down over the left eye she gave herself a pep talk: *Be confident today. It will all go swimmingly. If not, you can just flee and board the next train to the Riviera and get a job in a millinery shop on the seafront. Catering to the Russians and Americans that go there. I bet they need lots of hats to go with their sunsuits, ballgowns and cocktail pyjamas.*

Napoleon was sitting proudly at Opal's feet, gazing up at her through the mirror, his paws neatly together.

'I'll be back up soon with some bacon rashers for you.'

Opal descended the spiral staircase to the breakfast room. A continental buffet was spread on a long table in front of the vast windows. Orangish morning light spilled over baskets of pastries including pain au chocolat, brioche, palmier, croissant aux abricots and croquettes. Opal quite greedily took one of each to try. She could always pop one in her handbag for later. Thankfully there was a hot fork section with some bacon for Napoleon.

Zsa Zsa, looking like an elegant black widow, was already in the room, sitting at a table for two under a giant portrait where Opal joined her.

'I met a man in the corridor. He had blond hair and a moustache. He was rather kind, helping me unlock my door, which was jammed.'

'Really?' Zsa Zsa paused in cutting a sausage.

'Yes. I think he might have been a policeman, because he went up to the prohibited floor.'

'Oh yes...' Zsa Zsa pointed her fork in the air. 'I know who you mean... was he about six foot three with a shaving cut on his chin?'

'Yes.'

'That's the gumshoe. Detective Inspector Prosper Delacroix. Dashing, but a bit of a cad, I reckon.'

'Hmmm, yes, I got a hint of that, I suppose,' Opal agreed.

Opal looked across the breakfast room dotted with circular tables with white linen and saw an old man with his tongue between his lips, concentrating hard on a newspaper. On the page he was holding up was a huge picture of Opal and her Laplume hat.

It read, *Remplacement pour Valentine Beaumanoir.*

'Oh gosh,' Opal hissed to Zsa Zsa and nodded in the newspaper's direction. 'I'm in the rag. Great angle of the hat. But the paparazzi didn't listen to us when I said I wasn't the new dancer!'

'Oh yes, so you are. It'll be all over London too by the afternoon, I reckon. The *Evening Standard* were following the story, weren't they.' Zsa Zsa nodded and munched. 'Though I still haven't received that kind of press, perhaps after the premiere I will.'

'Crikey! I have friends at home who will see my picture.' Opal suddenly thought and stretched her lips in an awkward strain. 'Mother won't be happy about it saying I'm a dancer. But there's a wonderful photo of our hat, so perhaps that will soften the blow a little bit.'

Zsa Zsa shrugged, and Opal thought she detected an air of envy because of the press she had received.

Opal felt a slight panic. As soon as she'd made a chum she was turning icy on her. *Blithering fig! She'd rather have her friend than be in the blasted newspaper!*

Opal recalled a friendship she had ignited with a fellow schoolgirl, Isadora, during a heroic escapade involving the rescue of an injured sparrow. But when Opal's fashion drawing talents catapulted her to the front page of the school gazette, Isadora, who also fancied herself an artist, promptly withdrew into a huff and ceased all communication. Opal had never been more heartbroken. And now, it was happening again!

'I'm sure you'll be so plastered over the papers by the end of the month, Zsa Zsa, that everyone and his dog will know your name.'

Zsa Zsa's eyebrows made a doubtful jump. She was obviously still vexed.

The Renault dropped Opal, Napoleon and Zsa Zsa off outside the Casino de Paris just before eight a.m. Opal felt so dreadfully skittish about meeting Christophe as she followed Zsa Zsa's confident stride along the street to the stage door. But before slipping inside, Opal's lashes gave a rapid tremor as she noticed a familiar automobile up the road.

It was the mud-splattered Citroën. Opal squinted. Through the greasy-looking windscreen, she could see the man with the T-shaped scar. *Hmmm. Rather fishy that he was outside the hotel last night and now he's here again today. Hopefully just a coincidence.* She shivered and went inside the theatre. *Perhaps Paris is small,* she justified. She knew it was much smaller than London. But still... She quickly took out her sketch pad and once again found herself without a pencil. She found the lipstick she had used last night to draw Zsa Zsa and scrawled the reg plate of the car down. She then relented to Napoleon's tugs on the leash which was latched around her elbow and went inside.

ELEVEN

FIRST DAY NERVES

Opal was once again in awe of the magnitude of the ruby auditorium. Lots of people were already there. Some pretty girls Opal assumed to be the chorus dancers were stretching onstage. A dozen or so other dancers were sitting in the auditorium seats, their feet up on the ones in front. One was practising dance moves in the aisle and another was reading a magazine while munching on a paper bag of apricots. Opal blinked and frowned concernedly at a blonde-haired girl who was crying with her arms folded on the seat in front of her.

'Some of the people who knew Valentine are very sad, and aren't in the best mood today. But some others don't seem to give a damn,' Zsa Zsa said, noticing Opal's concerned face.

A man walked briskly up to Opal with a wooden metre stick in his hand. He was lank and so thin that his corduroy trousers and rolled-up shirt seemed full of air rather than flesh.

'*Bonjour*, Zsa Zsa,' he said, then addressed Opal. 'Who are you?'

'I'm Opal, I'm the new *plummasier*.'

'Oh, well, looking at you, you certainly know a thing or two about feathers. And English too. Lovely. I'm David, the set designer. I make all the backdrops and props.'

'Lovely to meet you,' she replied, and noted his accent was also London, similar to Zsa Zsa's, veering east.

'If you need anything, anything at all, I'll be absolutely honoured to help you,' he said, and pressed the metre stick to his chest in an earnest fashion.

'That *is* kind.'

'Some of the headdresses you'll be fixing are as large as the props themselves so I guess I might be able to come in handy there. I mean one of them is as tall as an elephant!' He gestured upwards with his metre stick.

'Oh golly.' Opal gulped and scrunched her toes nervously.

'I'm only pulling your leg. But honestly, anything you need.'

What a sweet man, Opal thought. He was suddenly elbowed out of the way by a rotund young woman, a clipboard brandished in front of her.

'Opal, wonderful to meet you, I'm Claudette, the stage manager.' The woman puffed, her whisky-brown pin-curls stuck to her forehead with setting lotion.

'Oh, good morning, lovely to meet you.' Opal kissed her on both cheeks.

'Thank God you're here, you have so much to catch up on. The costume atelier is a bit of a... how do you say? A shambles.'

'Don't worry I'll do my best to help,' said Opal, biting her lip. 'But I am rather nervous.'

'Don't panic. But you will have to work very hard. The format of the show will be quite different to anything you will see in London. It's the traditional French theatrical format, *La Grande Revue.* No storyline, just huge props and scenery with multiple acts of dance and live music. Our star is Clementina Lalonde and supporting her will be the beauties Miss Zsa Zsa and the new girl... err... Mei Ling. In the background there will be eight chorus dancers, a trio of tap-dancing crooners, and a full live orchestra.'

'Oh, that sounds top-notch!' Opal said, never had she seen anything of this kind in her life.

'I think I'd better introduce you to the cast and crew to start off with!' Claudette said.

'I'd be delighted.'

'Zsa Zsa, could you follow us, I need to give everyone today's briefing.' Claudette beckoned them over to the cluster of seats further back where everyone else was congregated.

She bellowed at the dancers on the stage, waving her clipboard in the air. They rolled, slid and slunk off the front like supple cats and joined their colleagues.

Claudette scanned the assembly frantically and frowned, squashing her features down to the bottom half of her face.

'Where is Estelle? *Zut!*' she cursed.

'I am here!' A brunette head popped up over the seats a few rows back from everyone else. Opal's eyes ballooned as she noticed the girl and blinked in surprise.

Gosh, she looks exactly like me! Opal thought. An uncanny resemblance to Opal, Estelle had a rounded jaw and the same ripples of dark hair. She had a similar small, pyramidical nose. Her marine-blue eyes were not as piercing blue as Opal's and didn't have the same aquiline sharpness. And unlike Opal she didn't wear a striking hat, just a sleek and simple mauve cloche, but still, quite a strong resemblance.

'*Bon*. Alright, everyone. Opal Laplume here will be responsible for your headwear. If you have any problems with it, go to her. She has come all the way from London to help us. We are very lucky to have her, so everyone please assist her with any questions she might have.'

Opal's lips twitched into a nervous smile. The two dozen eyes slid from Claudette on to her like they'd been tipped sideways in a marble game. Some eyes were bright and warm, some cold and a little mean. *I hope, they like me and the headpieces I'll make them,* Opal thought. She imagined them all adorned in a rainbow of cascading plumage and her fingers twitched in excitement.

'You were in the paper this morning. The paparazzi thought *you* were the replacement for Valentine,' Mei Ling piped up from amongst the crowd, her arms folded, her nails indenting her flesh like a pincushion. There was a slight jealous tinge to her voice.

'Oh yes, I saw.' Opal gulped. 'That was a silly mistake, wasn't it? I guess they will correct it on press night.'

'Okay, Opal, we have eight chorus girls who will be in various tableaux who will be wearing the same headdresses. They are Stephanie, Bernadette, Daisy, Rumba, Chloe, Anne-Laure, Rebecca and err... Estelle.'

The gaggle of girls flapped their twig-thin wrists at Opal. They all looked identical in weight with long necks, but facially all very different, like an assortment of cherubs on the ceiling of Versailles.

Claudette then pointed out the lighting designer and various other rope pullers and crew members. Opal nodded at them, her fedora slipping further forward. Her cheek muscles started to ache a little, she was smiling so hard.

'That's pretty much everyone apart from the musicians who aren't here at the moment. Christophe Tasse the costumier is in the atelier, and of course Clementina, who must be upstairs somewhere also.'

'Merci, madame,' said Opal and perched her bottom on a seat next to Zsa Zsa.

Claudette cleared her throat and continued with difficulty to be heard over the chatter that had swelled.

'Okay everyone, so back to the new schedules, I've added extra rehearsals so we can get Mei Ling up to speed. We will need to go over the finale and for some of the numbers that need far more *attention*.' Claudette's eyelids flared open wide on that last word. She proceeded to call people's names out and hand them their personal schedules on stapled sheets of paper.

Opal peeked over at Zsa Zsa's sheet. The schedule ran for two weeks from today, the 21st of April, to the 3rd of May. They'd be opening on the 4th. Opal inwardly gagged. That was very, *very* soon. *Cripes* she thought, *I hope I'll be fast enough for Christophe. Why did I take this on?* She went to nibble at the nail of her little finger but thankfully her gloves stopped her from conducting this indelicate habit.

She put her finger down and in the corner of her eye noticed something mauve flourish by. It was Estelle, the chorus girl who looked just like Opal. She was rushing through the seats in the direction of a side door. In the doorway stood the dark silhouette of a man in a very elegantly cut suit.

Once Estelle reached the figure, she kissed him on the lips and he put his hand on the small of her back. A tape measure dangled from his wrist.

Could that be Christophe? Zsa Zsa had mentioned in the taxi that Estelle and Christophe were now lovers after Valentine's death. And it didn't seem like they were being discreet about it at all...

TWELVE
BACKSTAGE

'Opal, you need to go upstairs to meet with Christophe now,' Claudette said. 'Zsa Zsa, could you please take her up there and hurry back?'

Zsa Zsa clamped her arms to the sides of her body. 'I'll show her up but I'm not going to go near Christophe, and you know why.'

'Zsa Zsa, we are a company, there's no avoiding anyone. Now, please show Opal upstairs.'

'Fine, but I'm not going to go near him,' Zsa Zsa repeated and went off ahead, her hips whipping from side to side with more passion than usual.

Christophe and Estelle had disappeared from the doorway. Zsa Zsa went through and her shoes clonked as they went up various sets of stairs.

'Zsa Zsa?' Opal asked in a cheery tone as she followed her up. She was desperate to dispel the silence and get back on chummy terms with her. Opal's newspaper coverage seemed to have really ticked Zsa Zsa off.

'What?' she replied shortly.

'Why is it called Casino de Paris if it's not a casino but a theatre?' Opal asked, wildly trying to think of a conversation starter.

'I asked Leon that question. He said the word casino didn't always mean what it does today; it used to mean, *house open to the public.*'

'Oh, what a twit I am, I should have known that,' replied Opal, thinking that Zsa Zsa still sounded churlish. She hoped this wouldn't last long.

They came to a wooden double door with what must have been a security guard standing in front. *Gosh, he's easy on the eye*, Opal thought. His build reminded Opal of a Victorian wrestler; his arms clasped behind his back accentuated his massive shoulders. He had thick black hair that unfurled in shiny waves with lots of Brilliantine. His pencil-thin moustache was oiled also. His chin bore a distinct dimple, a dark stubble emphasising its depth. Her lashes nervously flittered and she felt herself blush as he caught her eye.

'*Bonjour*, Augusto,' said Zsa Zsa florally, switching out of her mood. 'This is Opal, the new milliner. Opal, this is Augusto, Clementina's bodyguard.'

'How do you do?' Opal said, patting her hat into position.

Napoleon yapped almost the same syllables, as if to assert his own bodyguard-ship for Opal.

'Nice to meet you,' he said with a heavy Spanish accent and an absent expression. No smile, just a quick glance at the dog. Opal assumed he had to stay stern for the job, but she felt slightly miffed that he didn't smile at her. There was something about this man that she found instantly magnetic. She'd have to try a touch harder.

'Is it pleasant being Clementina's bodyguard?' she asked, brushing the feather in her hat aside and looking up at him. 'Do you have to brawl with many stage-door Johnnies?'

Augusto blinked as if having seen her for the first time and smirked at her question. 'What is *stage-door Johnny*?'

'That's what we call men in London who wait outside stage doors with flowers for the female stars. Hopeless fools.'

'Oh, we do get those. Clementina asks me to receive the flowers for her but then we use a secret exit when it gets too crowded.' He spoke the first half to Opal but resumed the end of the sentence looking at the wall ahead. Frozen like a toy soldier.

'Come on, Opal,' Zsa Zsa said. 'Stop flossing.'

Opal went red, half with embarrassment and half with annoyance that Zsa Zsa had accused her of flirting with the gentleman.

'Well, delighted to make your acquaintance,' Opal said, with a nod.

'*Encantado*,' he replied, nodding back to Opal. His eyelashes dipped to look at Napoleon and his chin-dimple became an apostrophe as he smiled. *He obviously likes the dog more than he likes me*, Opal thought.

'I wasn't flossing,' she whispered to Zsa Zsa when they carried on round the corner.

'Naturally! I imagine those fluttering lashes were due to the dust particles flying around in here?' Zsa Zsa smirked sideways at her.

A wave of relief swept over Opal. Zsa Zsa had clearly left her bout of envy behind and was back to her usual banter.

Next they entered the quaintest dressing room. It had honey-coloured, satin-padded walls. There were two dressing tables with arched mirrors studded with glowing bulbs.

'Oh!' Opal sighed. 'A theatrical dressing room! I always fantasised about having my hair done in one of these.'

Opal plonked her handbag down onto the left side of the dresser. The right side was littered with Zsa Zsa's makeup products and on her mirror was a postcard she'd had printed of herself with a tower of roses on her head and fringed scarf draped over her body.

'I shared this room with Valentine before it happened,' said Zsa Zsa, picking up some rhinestone heels from under the dresser. 'My God she was a prima donna. She wouldn't let me borrow her lipstick because she said it was a vector for germs, even though a minute before she'd told me about kissing a stranger on the train to Paris. Double standards, if you ask me.'

'Well, yes, it is a bit,' agreed Opal.

'To be quite honest, I wasn't fond of her, and I'm sure others in the cast weren't either. I mean, some of them are crying but it's only because death turned her into this *angelic victim*. When she was alive, she was pretty unbearable.'

Gosh, she is becoming rather cut-throat, Opal thought. But Valentine could really have been unbearable. And I mustn't forget, she had been Zsa Zsa's competition.

'Her things are still in this drawer. Her mother has been and taken everything she wanted.' Zsa Zsa sighed.

Opal's lashes quivered briefly as she eyed the gold knob of the drawer in question.

'Oh, I've already looked in there, it's just rubbish,' Zsa Zsa said when she noticed Opal's eyeline. She then opened the drawer to prove it.

Opal riffled with one hand casually through the things. There were some laddered silk stockings. A small bottle of Chanel No. 5 with only a drop left. Hairnets and bus tickets. French fashion magazines. They could be very inspiring for Parisian hat trends and ideas. Opal took them and glanced through them.

What's this?

Inside the centrefold of one of the magazines was a slim sketchbook. Inside were beautiful hand-painted designs for cabaret costumes. They looked quite familiar. *How interesting,* Opal thought.

'Do you think I can keep these rags if they're going to get binned?' Opal asked, waving them in the air.

'I should think so. I think Mei Ling will be using that dresser next and will want it cleared,' Zsa Zsa replied, inspecting her brows in the mirror. 'I might actually take that empty Chanel No. 5 bottle and pour some of my cheap perfume in it as it is a nicer bottle. That's what we do on Petticoat Lane market to flog 'em. We *are* wicked.'

'Oh... how astute,' said Opal, not quite sure what to say. 'Where do I find Christophe then? I'm rather anxious to get the day started.'

'If you follow the corridor round to the left, you'll go past a row of dressing rooms. At the very end is the costume atelier. You'll know when you've found it as it's full of miserable seamstresses,' Zsa Zsa said and took a practice leotard out of the cupboard. 'Sorry that I can't introduce you... I'm trying to stay as far away from that man as possible.'

'That's understandable,' Opal replied calmly. 'Shall we meet for elevenses?'

'Elevenses? Oh, we don't even get lunch. Its scoff-a-croissant-at-noon-and-go, I'm afraid, queenie... you'll see.'

Opal bid her friend farewell till later and followed the directions to the atelier. Napoleon stuck his nose inside messy rooms that were ajar on the way. A swell of female French gossip came from behind the door at the end of the corridor, mixed in with the rustle of fabric, sheering of scissors and the puff of a steam iron. Opal drummed on the door twice with her knuckles, her anxious hand contributing a few more raps. The swell of chatter lowered a fraction and the door swung back.

'*Oui?*' a small lady said with pins sticking out of her gritted teeth.

Behind her were a dozen girls at various workstations. Three were applying pleated gold ribbon onto the bottoms of ruched skirts, one was sorting through a box of beads, others were cutting satin with large silver scissors, and a few were puffing a steam iron. They all had something in common. Eyes that sagged with exhaustion. Opal had the suspicion they had been here since dawn.

'*Excusez-moi*, mademoiselle. Where can I find Christophe Tasse?' Opal asked as politely as she could.

The girl replied that she thought Christophe was with Clementina but would be back shortly. Opal carefully moved a stack of tasselled bustiers off a wooden chair and into a box and sat down. She gave Napoleon a rawhide chew to keep him occupied and away from the delicate creations. He made contented grumbling noises as he got to work on it.

Opal blinked in awe as she looked up at the shelves lining the walls. They were spilling with the most flamboyant and beautiful headdresses. Plumes cascaded from them in all diverse arrangements; sprays, spikes and pom-poms in both pastel and vibrant dyes.

The seamstresses' tongues went back to rapidly rolling in *français*. Opal couldn't understand exactly what they were saying, but got the vague gist that they were being catty about their boss, Christophe. He certainly worked them too hard. She wished she could understand their exact words.

'Do you need help?' Opal asked a girl struggling to curl a pheasant feather. She thought if she was kind, it would be more likely they would let her in on the chatter. She took one of the feathers and a pair of scissors, opened them and used the blunt side to whip a perfect spiralised spine.

'*Merci*... thank you,' sighed the girl.

'I'm Opal, I'm going to be helping with the headdresses.'

'Oh, thank God. We've got to have this whole pile of feathers finished in two hours,' the girl replied and pointed to a thick bundle of the plumes, standing up in a larder jar.

Opal gulped. That was *a lot* of feathers. At least she knew exactly what to do with them though. After small introductions and comments on the workload, Opal thought she'd try a question about the murder.

'Such awful news about Valentine, isn't it? Who do you think could have killed her?' she asked.

'We don't know, but we're not surprised.' A girl with an iron replied and blasted a huge puff of smoke. 'We didn't like her here in the atelier, she was very demanding and rude. *Zut!*'

The girl realised she'd burnt a hole in the chiffon sleeve she was ironing. A few other seamstresses came rushing over to inspect the damage. The girl with the iron then parted a rail of clothes behind her. She unlatched a small door and threw the offending piece of fabric out. She then locked the door again and pulled the clothes back in front of the door.

Opal blinked in fascination. The girl whom she was helping with the feathers piped up.

'If we ever make a mistake or do anything wrong, we throw it out of that old door. We don't want Christophe to see we've made a mistake. He checks the bins in here and is furious if he finds anything. When we throw things outside they fall down to the rubbish bins outside the kitchen. It's an obsolete door that has a spiral staircase down to the kitchens. They used to use it to bring champagne up for the stars. But now the stars just keep a bottle iced in their dressing rooms.'

'Oh, I see. Augusto mentioned a secret door that Clementina would use when she didn't want to be seen by fans or paparazzi,' Opal mused. 'Is that also the same door?'

'*Oui...* I think I've seen Clementina use it, yes.'

Opal went back to her work and frowned in thought. *Was there a tiny hole in Christophe's alibi the night Valentine died? He could have slipped out of this exit, attacked Valentine and then slipped back in again. He would be unseen by Clementina or others in the theatre apart from his seamstresses, who would surely cover his tracks for him – their jobs depended on it, after all.* Opal watched the ladies work. Their hands scrabbled to keep the speed up as if their fingers were in a kind of miniature Olympic games. She had a feeling they were all very scared of him. Why else would their eyes be so red-rimmed and fraught with anxiety?

Opal looked back over at the door. *I wonder what secrets it really holds.*

THIRTEEN
CHRISTOPHE TASSE

Opal had finished ten pheasant feathers. They looked like artist's brushstrokes, fluid and intentional. She was most pleased. *But where was Christophe?* He may have forgotten she was here. It would be prudent to seek him out.

Opal took Napoleon from the lap of a very enamoured seamstress who'd added a blue bow to his bicorn. She exited the atelier with her pooch and floated down the corridor to where Augusto stood guard. He noticed her but kept the same stoical expression as before. Opal felt her heart rate rise a little and she scrunched her toes in her shoes. She parted her lips and was about to enquire as to where Christophe was when the dressing-room doors swung open, almost hitting Augusto in the back.

In the doorway stood a tweed-suited, medium height man, his arms holding both doors open, one knee cocked inwards. A tape measure dangled around his neck and his slitted eyes snaked up and down Opal's body.

'Opal Laplume?' He raised an eyebrow in question.

'Yes, how do you do?' Opal replied, tweaking her hat. 'Are you Christophe Tasse?'

'Yes, I am,' he said. 'Thank goodness you're here. We have

twelve more headdresses to make and only two weeks to make them. Sod the dress rehearsals, they probably won't be ready for those.'

'I can't wait to get started.'

Christophe seemed distracted with something over Opal's shoulder. Mei Ling had come up the stairs and was standing with her neat dancer's feet together, one hand clasping a makeup box. Opal stepped aside.

'Ahh, Mei Ling, you're here for your fitting?' Christophe clasped his hands together.

'Yes. Is this a good time?' she answered.

'It's never a good time, my dear, but I guess you're going to be hogged by Monsieur Blanchette in rehearsals so I will utilise you while I can.' He then stood for a few moments cognitively measuring her, demanding she turn to the right and left.

Opal tilted her head so she could see past him into Clementina's dressing room. There was a bar stocked with Dom Pérignon champagne and a table laden with colourful bouquets and packages tied with liquid-shine ribbons.

She could see Clementina in the reflection of a stand-alone mirror sitting on a pouffe in a translucent dressing gown. Her fire-opal curls fell over one side of her head and a telephone was to her ear on the other.

Her eyes, usually emerald sparks, were clouded, the weight of tears drooping her lower lids.

'Joshua, I just can't do it... I can't have this transatlantic, ridiculously long-distance relationship anymore. I need you here *right now*.' Her voice cracked. 'One of my dearest friends, Valentine, has been murdered, I need you here!'

Augusto, Christophe and Mei Ling also heard the commotion. Augusto ushered Christophe out of the doorway and closed the doors to protect his client's privacy.

'I tell you all, Clementina can do better than that Mr Joshua Davenport,' Christophe confided quietly.

'Oh dear,' Opal said. 'Was that her beau she was on the phone to?'

'Yes, her fiancé. He works for some film studio in New York and the long-distance game isn't Clementina's style. She is such a romantic. Clementina is very upset about Valentine's death and wanted him to come and support her through this difficult time, but he won't take the time off work.'

'That's a shame,' Opal replied. 'I do hope she has someone to console her.'

'She will be fine. I can't understand people who do romance across towns, let alone continents.' Christophe sniffed. 'I've told her to get rid of him, but she won't listen to me. Alright, Mei Ling, let's do your fitting. Opal, you can come and assist me, please.'

Christophe glanced down and narrowed his eyes. 'I am not having a dog anywhere near my costumes or atelier. Augusto, you will have to take this *thing* for a while.'

Opal had no choice but to hand over Napoleon's lead to Augusto. She brushed his knuckles by accident while transferring him the leather loop. She looked up, his dimpled chin at her eyeline. The indent leant sideways in a smile as if to say he would take good care of Napoleon. They looked a very smart pair indeed, standing guard with pulled back shoulders and puffed out chests.

'I'll be back soon, my dear!' Opal called over her shoulder.

Christophe, Mei Ling and Opal entered a side room off the atelier that was reserved for fittings. There were various black-lacquered Chinese screens to change behind.

'Please get undressed to just your chemise. I'll be back in one moment,' Christophe requested of Mei Ling as he popped out to check on his seamstresses.

Opal listened to him berate them and could hear a pair of

scissors snip vigorously. 'Let me do it. Honestly, my arthritic grandmother could work faster than all of you put together!'

Mei Ling came out in a mint-coloured chemise. Opal noticed an interesting tattoo on Mei Ling's thigh – three small squares overlapping each other diagonally. The tattoo was far too high to be seen in any costume, so Opal figured it was a secret. She was about to ask about it, but then decided it may be too impertinent.

'Is that the new... whatsit called... *rayon* fabric? It's delightful,' Opal enquired, eyeing Mei Ling's chemise, hands clasped together.

'Yes, I bought it last week,' replied Mei Ling, softening from the compliment.

Christophe entered, brandishing his tape measure with both hands. He whipped it taut and looked Mei Ling sharply in the eye. He proceeded to measure her all over, scribbling the measurements down in his notebook. He made violent tutting noises when measuring her waist and hips, which Opal felt was rather rude. Mei Ling's fists clenched in fear.

He then sidestepped over to the costume rail. He pulled out what must have been Valentine's costumes. He hung them from the top of the screens.

'Oh, I forgot to ask what shoe size you are? You look a thirty-seven.' Christophe eyed Mei Ling's feet. 'Urgh, I'll have to tell the girls they'll have to rhinestone another two pairs of shoes for you as you won't fit into Valentine's.'

He grabbed a white costume, paused and looked back over his shoulder at Mei Ling.

'If you let the doves poop on this costume I'll wring their tiny necks.'

'Doves?' Mei Ling asked, utterly perplexed.

'Don't tell me they haven't explained what you'll be doing in your act yet?'

'No one's told me anything,' Mei Ling said, shrugging. 'They just said I'd be dancing with feather fans.'

'To start off you'll be dancing with doves, trained ones. They will fly away with part of your costume. Please tell me you don't mind birds.'

'My word! That sounds fantastic,' Opal chimed in.

'It sounds like a challenge, but I can do it,' Mei Ling said confidently.

'Opal, can you help dress Mei Ling, please. Go behind the screens.'

Opal nervously obliged and after ten minutes of tugging, wincing, lacing, cursing and clasping, Mei Ling was ready.

'*Voilà*. Look at yourself in the mirror,' Christophe said, his chin in his hands and his eyes slitted in a kind of analytical satisfaction. 'The only thing that is missing is the grandiose headdress of ostrich plumes which Opal will be making soon.'

Mei Ling turned to the large oval mirror in the corner of the room and eyed herself up. She appeared luminous in brilliant-white, her willowy physique clasped inside a corset embellished with feathery down, like a dove's breast. The plumage rose and fell as she breathed in awe. Opal could tell Mei Ling was very happy indeed.

Suddenly, Opal realised something. She'd seen this design in the beautiful sketchbook she'd found in Valentine's drawer.

While Christophe tweaked and plucked at Mei Ling, Opal riffled in her handbag for the sketchbook, flipping carefully through the delicate watercolour pages until she found the design. The hat was a beautiful yet simple design of three towering ostrich plumes, in a fleur- de-lis shape. Opal appreciated the interesting style of the drawing, with flicks and criss-crosses for texture. The artist had a unique way of drawing feet in heels, tiny like a cat's paw. She glanced at the bottom of the page, there was a signature '*R.S. 1934*'. *That's odd*, thought Opal. *Surely it would say 'C.T.' as Christophe Tasse was the costume designer?* All the other pages had the same 'R.S.' signature too.

'Is *this* the hat I'll be making?' Opal asked, holding the dove costume page up for Christophe.

Christophe, who was bent down at Mei Ling's knees with a pin, stood up abruptly like he was on a spring. His eyes were slitted almost shut and his mouth puckered into a tight prune.

'Where did you get this?' he said curtly and snatched the sketchbook out of Opal's hands.

'I... I... found it in Valentine's dressing room. I'm ever so sorry if I wasn't supposed to take it. I thought it would help me reference your designs.'

'I have reference drawings especially for you,' he said, and buried the book inside his suit jacket.

Opal felt a little nauseous. She didn't want to do anything to get on the wrong side of Christophe. Had she really done something wrong? Or was there something about the sketchbook that had bothered him?

'Well, it is the most beautiful costume I've ever seen,' said Opal, trying to redeem herself, clasping her hands in front of her as if praying.

'I agree, it's one of my favourites designs!' Christophe lightened his tone and crossed his arms with pride. 'Normally my costumes are covered in rhinestones, but we only want the Dumoulin diamonds to sparkle onstage so the costumes will have no sparkle to draw away from them.'

'Do I get to try on the jewels now?' Mei Ling asked excitedly.

'*Non*, don't be stupid! The Dumoulin collection is worth a fortune. We can't have them in the building without security. We won't be putting them on until the first dress rehearsal of the show.'

Mei Ling made a sudden frown and grasped her back, her shoulders curling forward.

'Are you alright?' Opal asked.

'I think we tied the corset a little tight,' Mei Ling replied.

'Oh, I'm terribly sorry.' Opal flushed.

Christophe sighed. 'Look here is a trick if you are on your own with nobody to help you.'

Christophe whipped a pen from the spiral-spine of his note-book and handed it to her.

'After you undo the bow, just tuck the pen inside the centre laces and waggle it to loosen them. You can use anything actually – a pen, cigarette holder, whatever you have nearby.'

Mei Ling followed the instructions and it worked. The blood that was caught in her upper body seemed to fall away as her cheeks resumed a normal colour. Opal helped her tie the laces again but with more slack this time.

'Can you move and dance now?' Christophe asked with his arms folded, in a way that seemed to imply it was tough if not.

'I don't know all of the choreography yet, but I think it's fine now, yes,' Mei Ling breathed.

'*Bon*. Valentine really did kick up such a scene with this corset. I made it to fit her perfectly, but all she did was complain and she had me make a new one. The one you are wearing was her original. God knows what happened to the other one.'

Christophe sighed.

'I've been working with Clementina for fifteen years on her costumes and I know the score.'

'Wow that's a long time,' Opal said. 'You must be good friends with Clementina.'

'Yes, we are,' Christophe said sincerely. 'We're extremely fond of each other. I say exactly what I think and that's why she respects me. If I see a blemish on her skin when she is onstage, I tell her and the lighting is changed. If she sees a man I don't like, I tell her what I think of them and I'm always right. You see, Clementina has too many dishonest people kissing up around her. Valentine was one of those people. But if Valentine could have ruined Clementina's career and taken over, she would in an instant.'

'Oh... I see, it must be hard for Clementina, being top dog.'

'Mark my words, Zsa Zsa is even worse than Valentine. Anyone that stands in her way she will try to eliminate. You know she tried to have me arrested for Valentine's murder? Saying she heard Valentine scream my name. She made the whole thing up...'

Christophe looked sideways at Mei Ling who was also listening intently, then back at Opal. 'I tell you why. She overheard me discussing her dancing ability with the choreographer and she's had it in for me ever since. It is because I said she did not have good stage presence. She is too vampish with her movements... too aggressive.'

'I'm sure it was all a terrible misunderstanding,' Opal stammered, rather intimidated by the furious way Christophe was gesticulating. He breathed in sharply through his nostrils to calm himself. 'That girl Zsa Zsa, I am telling you, is one to *watch*.'

FOURTEEN
MURMURS

After two full days' work in the atelier Opal was not feeling confident. It was after midnight, and she sat on her hotel balcony with Napoleon on her lap. She stroked his warm fur all the way to his pom-pom tail tip. She reflected on her slow progress with Mei Ling's headdress. She was supposed to have had it all done by the end of the night but she'd been helping another seamstress who'd been crying over some difficult beadwork.

Napoleon jumped off her lap to watch a Parisian pigeon on the next balcony. Opal folded her arms flat on the balustrade and laid her head sideways on them, looking down at the street below.

Her stomach dropped. The mud-splattered Citroën was parked outside the hotel again. She could make out the man with the T-shaped scar inside. *Who was he? Was he there to spy on someone?*

Through the windscreen, she watched him for a couple of minutes. He seemed to be half reading a newspaper and half nodding to sleep. She could see from the headlines on the rag that it was a London paper. Was he an Englishman? He then rolled it up and chucked it back onto the seats behind him. Opal's imagination started to brew up the picture of an East End racketeer that was after Zsa Zsa. Could it be someone from her past with a debt to settle?

He then reached inside his coat's breast pocket and pulled out a black object. Light gleamed across the object's shaft. *A pistol!* Opal's breath started to quicken.

He opened the chamber and inspected it, then put it back inside his coat and looked up at the hotel. Opal quickly pulled her head away from the edge to make sure he didn't see her and retreated inside.

'Napoleon! Get in!' she hissed, whipping the French windows shut behind the dog as fast as she could.

Opal felt exceedingly nervous. What should she do? Should she mention it to Leon Dumoulin, or perhaps Augusto? She blushed at the thought of him. The past few days all she'd been able to do was mumble a thank you when he took Napoleon. She perched on her bed for a moment. Perhaps she should make a telephone call... But it was much too late now. She decided it would have to wait until tomorrow.

Lying down in the dark, uneasy thoughts jumbled in Opal's mind, stopping her from drifting off to sleep. She couldn't help but feel that her arrival in Paris and the man with the gun were connected somehow. And why did this stranger feel... a little familiar?

Opal jumped so violently that she woke herself up. An awful feeling in her gut confirmed she must have been having a nightmare. About the blaggard outside, she'd wager. Blast it! She'd been so exhausted she'd nodded off despite her anxious thoughts.

Opal grasped her throat and tried to calm her breathing. She hadn't had a nightmare in years. She assumed she'd been repressing her anxiety the past few days being so busy, and the demons had been crawling out in her dream.

She was glad it was morning and she didn't have to worry about going back to sleep.

A creak sounded out on the floorboards in the corridor, and Opal blinked in concentration when she heard two male voices murmuring in French. Her eyes darted towards the door. It sounded like that gentleman's voice, Detective Inspector Prosper Delacroix.

She got up and glided to the door. She pushed her door open a crack, just enough width for her right eye to glare out, feeling her lashes brush the door frame.

It was Sylvain Leclerc, the hotel manager, scratching his head, looking up at Prosper who had his arms folded, the shaving cut in his chin the darkest point of his face. *He looks quite arrogant,* Opal thought, exhaling as quietly as she could.

From what Opal could understand, Sylvain was asking when he could open the top floor to guests again. The hotel was in high demand due to many tourists coming to see the Jewellery and Goldsmithing Exposition and he needed the rooms to be available. Prosper muttered something about it all being wrapped up tomorrow.

Tomorrow? Opal bit her lower lip. She'd have to make her move and try to see the crime scene before he left. It was now or never. She wanted to try and get to the nub of the matter once and for all! She was sick of worrying whether she was working for a murderer and for the safety of all the other girls, as well as herself.

She waited for Sylvain to bumble down the stairs. Then she flung the door open, smoothed her pillow-frizzed hair and floated over to Prosper.

'*Bonjour,*' she said, going on tiptoes to kiss his cheeks in the French fashion.

'Oh, good morning, Miss... err, I'm sorry, I've forgotten your name.'

'Opal.'

'Oh yes, Opal. Off to the Casino de Paris today?'

'Yes, my third day today.'

'*Très bien.*'

'So, how is the case going? Have you found out who did it?' Opal asked him, cocking her head to the left.

'What do you mean, who did it? We believe there was no murder.' Delacroix turned to leave, but Opal stopped him.

'But Zsa Zsa swore she heard Valentine scream for help. And Valentine was pleading for someone to take their hands off her. Are you calling Zsa Zsa a liar?'

Delacroix swivelled around again and looked Opal straight in the eye. 'You shouldn't know any of this. But, for your information, we think that Zsa Zsa simply heard another guest shouting from another room and that Valentine fell or jumped shortly after. It's the only feasible explanation for the door being locked and no one found inside.'

Opal put her hands on her hips, her eyelashes dusting him up and down.

'Did you find another guest that said they had been shouting at that time then?'

'No,' he replied curtly, and glanced towards the staircase as if he wanted to make a move and not discuss it further.

'I don't think you're being very thorough,' Opal persisted.

'I'm a detective, I know what I'm doing,' he replied, shaking his head in both an amused and arrogant fashion.

'I think you're wrong. I think you are lackadaisical and don't truly care.' She had become a tad ruffled by his sheer nonchalance towards the case.

'Well, I'm sorry that you think that of me, but I can assure you, mademoiselle, we have come to the correct conclusion.'

'You've only come to this conclusion because you can't find

out how a killer could leave the room with it locked from the inside. I think you're missing something.' Opal knotted her arms, puffed her chest up over them.

'Well, how do you suggest they did it?'

'I don't know. But you know, people who know me ask me to look out for things. I just happen to notice everything. I even managed to find Clementina Lalonde's engagement ring when she lost it at the theatre, just from being watchful.' Opal decided that flirting a smidge couldn't hurt. 'You know, perhaps I can help if I saw the crime scene?'

Prosper looked back up at her eyes and his chin swung to the side in amusement. Clearly, her tactic had worked. 'Well... if it concerns you this much, I can meet you this evening, perhaps in the hotel lounge to try and reassure you that I'm right?'

'Okay, what time?' Opal said, sticking her chin up.

'Err... say eight?'

'Splendid.' Opal immediately followed up with what had been haunting her since last night. 'There is one other thing I think I should mention. There is a man who I believe may be following me or Zsa Zsa. I've seen him a few times, outside the hotel here or in the street outside the Casino de Paris. And last night I saw he was carrying a gun.'

'I see.' Prosper clasped his chin. 'Has he approached you or been threatening in any way?'

'Well, no, but it's a bit of a strange coincidence he always seems to be wherever I am.'

'Only these two places and you've seen him a few times?'

'Yes.'

'It could be a coincidence but I will look into this for you.'

'Is it illegal in France to carry a gun?'

'It is without a licence. So, if he has a licence and he does not approach or threaten you, then I will not be able to do anything. But as I said, mademoiselle, I will investigate this.'

'I have his registration number,' Opal said and pulled her sketchbook out of her pocket. She ripped out the page she'd written it on in lipstick and handed it to the detective. 'It's a filthy mud-splattered car. And he's always here or the Casino de Paris so I'm sure you'll be able to find him.'

'*Parfait*. Have a great day at the theatre, mademoiselle.'

Opal floated back to her room and stopped at the doorway. She turned back to him, gave him a last reprimanding glance as if to say *I'm counting on you* and slipped inside.

FIFTEEN

THE UNDERWATER DANCE

Mei Ling's headdress was finally finished. It was a triumph. It floated above her head like white-feathered sails of an ethereal galleon. Opal watched her rehearse wearing it from the wings, her eyes glittering with pride. But she suddenly jolted as a clatter and bump echoed around the stage. Opal gasped.

Mei Ling had tripped and was lying at the bottom of the Bakelite staircase. It was lit from behind and looked like a stack of giant gold ingots. The dancer looked like a trampled pigeon at the bottom, her headdress lopsided. *She didn't look too hurt, thank the Lord.*

'Imagine doing that on press night!' M. Blanchett said, his nasal cavity exhuming all the words. 'The critics would say "Mei Ling – the only bumps and grinds we saw from her was when she fell down the stairs!"'

It had been her first run-through in full-costume and she had started off very confident. But now her pride had been assassinated by her stumble and she retreated backstage, holding her thwacked hip. Opal thought she'd better go after her to check that both the girl and the pristine headdress were okay.

She found Mei Ling in the sanctuary of her dressing room. She was lying face down on the carpet with her head in her arms. The headdress was propped on the dresser, still intact in all its glory. *Phew.* Opal leaned on the door frame and tried to think of something to say to cheer her up.

'At last, some peace away from the sound of Monsieur Blanchette's nasal screeching! Gosh it still rings in my ears,' said Opal. 'I say, Mei Ling, old girl, I trust your descent wasn't too Shakespearean? No broken limbs or tragic soliloquies?'

Mei Ling grunted in both appreciation and pain but didn't move. At that moment, Opal spotted Zsa Zsa, who was also in the dressing room, munching on macarons and guffawing at a naughty note Leon had written her.

'You sound happy, Zsa Zsa. How did your rehearsal go today?' Opal said, trying to signal with her eyes for Zsa Zsa to say something to cheer Mei Ling up.

'Oh *terrible*.'

Mei Ling instantly sat up against the sink. 'Oh, no? Why's that?'

'An awful costume malfunction. I'm back here because Christophe is repairing it for me. I had to get Augusto to relay the message and handover the costume because I'm still not speaking to Christophe.'

Zsa Zsa held a pistachio macaroon to Mei Ling's nose, who took it eagerly.

'I do a split at a crescendo point in the music,' Zsa Zsa continued. 'And almost every time, the press studs at the back of my dress come undone. It looks so amateur.'

Opal glanced at her watch. 'Do you want to watch Clementina's underwater act? I think she's practising it now.'

'Oh yes, please! I haven't seen that one yet and I hear it's spectacular,' Zsa Zsa replied.

'Did you say you were watching the underwater dance?'

asked a pointed nose, poking through the door. It belonged to Estelle, the chorus girl who had an uncanny likeness to Opal.

'We are indeed, come and join us, Estelle,' Opal replied with a warm smile.

'I'm going to stay here, my hip is still hurting,' Mei Ling said, pressing her hip with both hands.

'What's that?' Zsa Zsa said, pointing at Mei Ling's upper thigh.

'Oh, it's just a tattoo.' Mei Ling blushed, pulling her costume back down over it. 'You girls go, you're going to miss the rehearsal.'

Opal, Zsa Zsa and Estelle left to go down to the auditorium. Opal was glad Estelle wanted to hang out with them. She hadn't got acquainted with any of the chorus girls so far.

'So, where are the other chorus girls?' Opal asked.

'Urgh, I don't know. I think they went to dine out together,' she muttered. 'I'm not pally with them.'

'Is that so?' Opal asked. 'Why's that?'

'They've been rather catty since I've begun to see Christophe.'

'Oh,' sympathised Opal. Though she was more occupied with the mystery of Christophe's appeal. First Valentine, now Estelle. Perhaps it was his status as the famous costumier, or more likely his hold over Clementina and her casting whims.

'I heard that Christophe and Valentine split up because he was soft on you,' Opal pried, with the air of one trying to sound casual but failing spectacularly.

'Excuse Opal, she's a dreadful gossip queen!' Zsa Zsa nudged Opal with her mink elbow. 'Should be a tabloid writer, but she was born a few centuries too late for pamphleteering.'

Estelle, looking as though she'd bitten into a particularly sour lemon, said, 'I only saw Christophe *after* he broke up with Valentine.'

Opal felt her cheeks flush. 'Please forgive me, I'm not trying to stir the proverbial pot.'

'Did someone suggest,' Estelle pressed on, 'that Christophe was seeing both Valentine and I at the same time?'

'Oh, heaven no! Just a terrible misunderstanding, I'm sure,' Opal stammered, nervously gnawing at her lower lip while casting a desperate sideways glance at Zsa Zsa for rescue.

Zsa Zsa rolled her eyes and with a grand sweep of her hand, flung open the double doors to the auditorium as if she were unveiling some great theatrical spectacle.

They chose seats in the centre front. David Miller, the set designer, was already there. He was wearing a soft, brown corduroy suit with red neckerchief and had his wooden metre stick resting over his crossed legs. His mouth stretched at the sight of Opal and she sat down next to him.

'Oh, good heavens,' she gushed as she took in the stage set, her eyes widening to large marbles. In the centre of the stage was a ginormous prop, about the size of a double-decker bus. It was an underwater castle, shimmering gold, with walls and turrets built from giant twisting shells. A huge scallop shell was set in the front of it like a drawbridge.

'That's Salacia's Castle. Salacia was Neptune's wife from Roman mythology,' David leaned sideways and announced proudly to his audience of girls.

'Hasn't David done an amazing job!' Estelle breathed, pressing her hands to her chest.

All three girls sighed in their seats as Clementina waltzed onstage. She was encased in an embellished bikini, the top resembling a conch shell, twisting up over one shoulder and shooting a waterfall of chiffon down her back. Streams of chiffon were attached at her hips and waist also, like a rare jelly-fish. She tweaked the conch-shaped turban on her head with regal arms that were taut in opera gloves.

Christophe appeared behind her and fiddled with the skirt fastidiously. Next to fuss over her was Leon, who walked over to her wearing white gloves, carrying some black velvet boxes. He opened one and Opal was blinded by the sparkle of the diamonds inside.

'We have to test how the diamonds will look in the water. I'm so glad you're not going to be wearing the twelve million one underwater. That piece is only fit for the finale.' His piano teeth chattered while clasping a very heavy pearl and diamond choker around her neck, affixing some matching earrings and clasping a brooch into the centre front of her turban, very gently. She turned in a circle to the approving nods and hums of Christophe.

'Salacia!' he said, admiring his own costumier skills.

As the cabaret queen turned, she noticed the three girls in the audience. She put her hand over her brow to try and see past the glare of the lighting.

'*Qui est là?*' she asked.

'It's Opal! Zsa Zsa, Estelle and David are here too!' shouted Opal. 'We just wanted to watch your act!'

'Oh! Opal! Just one moment!' she shouted back.

Clementina walked down the stairs on the side of the stage, chiffon billowing behind her. Opal's heart started to pound; it was so thrilling that her celebrity cousin was coming to speak to her. In the manic days she'd been here, there hadn't been a chance to speak.

'The guys up there are fiddling with technicalities of the water tank so I've got time to chat to you girls!' she said sweetly, sitting down on the other side of Opal. 'Opal, how are you getting on?'

'Oh, splendidly, thank you,' Opal said. 'I've been learning so much about how to create headdresses. I feel so much more of a well-rounded milliner already!'

'Is the water cold in the tank?' Zsa Zsa asked.

'That's what they are adjusting for me now,' Clementina replied. 'There is something at the bottom of the tank that heats it slightly for me, but I don't really know how it works.'

'Thank God it's not freezing!' Estelle piped up.

'Well, I have to get into the tank at the interval before the curtains open, then wait inside for twenty minutes while the dancers perform around my castle. I wouldn't want to look blue when I began!' She laughed a delicate and controlled laugh.

'Where is the tank?' Opal asked, blinking at the stage.

'It's inside the castle prop. You see the front panel of it comes down and inside you see my underwater palace. I do some water ballet. I have furniture; a chaise longue and a dresser resting at the bottom under the water... you'll see.'

'I'm so eager to see,' Zsa Zsa said, crossing her legs and grabbing hold of the chair arms.

'We all need to get together for tea or something for some pep talk before the show starts!' Clementina addressed them all as she stood up. 'Co-stars need to have camaraderie because it will truly shine through onstage!'

The girls agreed that would be wonderful. But as Clementina returned to the stage, Opal wondered whether the busy celebrity sincerely meant it. She had thought she'd be seeing a lot more of her cousin, but so far it just hadn't happened.

Clementina ascended a ladder at the back of the castle set and waved at the girls at the top.

She slipped down into the invisible tank. Her entourage and technicians left the stage and sat down to watch. M. Blanchett put his hand up to signal for the music to start and the theatre swelled with dramatic strings. David yelled at the rope pullers and the whole front face of the castle started to lower down like a drawbridge to reveal the water tank inside.

The walls of the water tank were only transparent from the front, the inside walls were decorated like the inside of a water goddess's palace; gold panelling and vases, a chaise longue, dressing table and screens all sat underwater.

Clementina was deep in the centre, underwater. Her skirts swirled around her like an exotic jellyfish. The Dumoulin diamonds she was wearing twinkled blindingly through the liquid. She somersaulted four times with one leg bent in front like an arrow the other pointed out behind.

'I can safely say, in all my life so far, this stage set might be the most outlandish and wonderful thing I've ever seen,' Opal said to David.

'Thank you, Opal. It is my pièce de résistance of my set design career, I must say,' David replied. 'I owe so much to Clementina for all these opportunities. I was just a stagehand when I met her. She saw my sketchbook by chance and asked me to start making her things. I have a crippled brother and I've been able to look after him, thanks to her.'

'Well, that is lovely. From the impression I get, many people seem to be very fond of my cousin.'

'That they are.'

Clementina was currently mid-act, exhaling air bubbles, and her body descended until she lay on the chaise longue. Opal noticed she seemed to be under the water for a long time. She mentally counted and it was about a minute and a half before she swam up to take a breath. *Very impressive indeed, especially for a smoker*, Opal thought.

With a climatic saxophone solo she swam to a gold pillar at the centre back of the tank and stood up on it in her final pose, her arms a curved 'V' shape above her head. Simultaneously fountains of water sprayed up in a glorious display. The curtain lowered. The music rounded up. The small audience clapped with the energy of a full house.

'*Magnifique!*' M. Blanchett screeched, as the curtain rose

again and Clementina climbed out of the tank. She was met by a dresser who raced out of the wings to wrap her in a large towel.

'If I had those props and that costume... I'd be the headliner,' Zsa Zsa whispered in Opal's ear, then raised her voice and addressed Estelle. 'It's almost time for our car now. Do you want to leave with us, Estelle?'

'Oh, I'm going to wait for Christophe to finish taking the diamonds off Clementina. We're going for oysters later,' she replied and shivered. 'It's so cold in this theatre.'

'Oh... well... have my coat,' Opal said, taking her blue trench coat off. 'I've got my angora cardigan, I'll be fine.'

'Oh really? Thank you so much. You are kind.'

'It's alright, give it back to me tomorrow.'

Opal trotted upstairs to collect Napoleon from the ever-patient Augusto. When she returned to the foyer, a spot of drama was unfolding. Christophe had Estelle cornered against a pillar, wagging a finger at her like a bad-tempered schoolmaster. His eyes were reduced to slits, while Estelle, chin tilted upwards, was tossing about that familiar insult, '*Salaud*'.

Christophe, perhaps sensing he'd lost this particular round, retreated a few paces. Seizing the moment, Opal tiptoed by, confident Estelle had the situation well in hand.

'I'm going to have a smoke while we wait for our car,' Zsa Zsa said, leaning on the glass doors of the entrance, her black fur squashing into a large ball around her.

Napoleon yapped, straining on Opal's lead, his pom-pom tail batting back and forth. His gaze was transfixed on something forty yards up the street. Opal let him drag her towards the railing and looked. There it was again. The mud-spattered Citroën, and the hulk of a man moving around inside. He angled his scarred cheek upwards in the rear-view mirror and daubed a kind of ointment on it with his handkerchief. The glass tincture bottle had a label on it that read *Marylebone Medicinals.*

Holy fig on a hobby horse, thought Opal. *He is from London – and not only London; my neighbourhood, I know that pharmacy.*

SIXTEEN

DETECTIVE INSPECTOR PROSPER DELACROIX

Napoleon padded out of the lift of the Reinette Hotel, his paws quite equestrian in their proud movements. Opal kept in tow, her fedora topped off with an orange bird of paradise feather like a firework. *Quite a firecracker*, she thought as she eyed herself in the opulent mirror opposite the lift. *I had to make a bit of effort if I was going to try and convince the detective to let me go upstairs.*

She stopped behind the doorway to the hotel lounge and pulled her shoulders back, feeling a little timid. She wasn't soft on the arrogant detective but, as a young lady, she was nervous he would not take her seriously. She fiddled with the angle of her fedora, then stepped inside.

Nobody was there. Her shoulders fell as she meandered through the pastel armchairs and chaise longues. Napoleon leapt onto a tasselled pouffe that he assumed was made especially for his bottom.

What should she be doing when he came in? She might as well pour herself some wine. *Le Clos du Serpent* was the name on the label with an etching of a monastery. She poured herself one from the decanter on the mantel and tilted her head towards the bookshelf.

It was stocked with deteriorating volumes on Louis XV's mistresses, their scandals, love letters and biographies. She pulled out an old volume about the Marquise de Vintimille as her suite was named after this historical figure.

Just as she was reading the first sentence, a robust voice sounded behind her. 'You didn't pour any wine for me then?'

She snapped closed the book, swivelled on one heel and leaned the other up against the bookshelf. She whipped him up and down with her lashes.

Detective Inspector Prosper Delacroix, hands in his pockets, walked towards her with a faint swing in his upper body. The shaving scar on his chin stopped about a foot in front of Opal's eyeline.

'Detective Inspector Delacroix. Thank you so much for coming to meet me. I must ask you to put my mind at rest first off. Did you manage to investigate the man in the muddy Citroën with the gun?'

'Not yet, mademoiselle. I have been wrapping things up here. I also did not see him this morning when I left the hotel. Nor just now when I arrived.'

Opal's shoulders drooped in disappointment. 'Well, I saw him again outside the theatre this evening. I'd appreciate it if you could get on to this tomorrow, or have one of your men on the streets, please. He has a gun and I am frightened,' the Honourable Opal Laplume said in an assertive tone, the way she may have spoken to a policeman in London who knew and respected her status. But this French detective did not know or care.

'I will do my best, mademoiselle. But the good news is, if he hasn't approached you already or done anything by now, then it's not likely he will at all. I also would find it hard to convict him if no harassment has taken place. Only if his gun is not licensed.'

'Do you not think he could be connected to Valentine's case?'

'No, I do not,' he said, and sniffed as if that was concluded. 'You have poured yourself some wine, mademoiselle. I would also like some. We can speak and I hope to calm you down.'

'Really, Inspector, I'm as calm as a cow in clover,' she said, giving him a smile as thin as a razor's edge. 'I was only worried that your, shall we say, leisurely arrival time suggested a certain... lack of urgency on your part!'

'Me? I'm never late,' he said, shaking his head. 'I'm a man of the law. I can do what I like.'

'How reassuring,' Opal said, and with a dramatic *thunk*, she slid her book back into place on the bookshelf. 'I'm sure that's precisely the attitude that wins hearts in the world of law enforcement.'

'I have an *impeccable* attitude,' he replied, puffing out his chest in the manner of a pigeon trying to impress a statue.

'Like making a languorous decision about a murder investigation that you're not clever enough to solve?' Opal shot him a sidelong glance, her lips curling into a smirk.

He raised his eyebrows in a challenging manner.

Opal floated past him with balletic grace and made a beeline for the wine decanter. As she bent over to pour him a glass, her fedora tipped forward. Another example of a hat not keeping pace with its owner.

'Not clever enough?' His voice rose, his chin now taking the lead in this conversation.

'Oh, Detective, let's not pretend.' Opal poured his wine with a flourish that would've impressed a sommelier. 'There's more to this case than your clumsy "accident or suicide" theory. Honestly, I've seen more plausible conclusions drawn from a deck of tarot cards.'

'Well, Opal Laplume, tell me what *you* think happened?'

'I can't give a solid judgement without seeing the crime scene with my own eyes,' she replied, her eyes glinting.

'You know, your eyes are the most striking blue I've ever seen.' His initial effort to charm her seemed to turn into genuine fascination. He looked at them for a prolonged moment.

Oh, here we go, Opal thought. *The inevitable moment where the detective mistakes my intellectual superiority for physical charm.*

'Don't change the subject, I want to see the room, please,' she said, cutting through the compliment like a pair of shears through a rose stem. 'Your wine. Perhaps it'll help your *focus.*'

'*Merci*, mademoiselle,' he said, taking it. He then spoke in a more serious policeman-like tone. 'It is not possible for you to enter the crime scene. I'm sorry.'

Opal looked him straight in the eye, knowing she had the upper hand. 'Prosper, you came to meet me to reassure me that your conclusion for Valentine's death was the right one. You can only do that by showing me the evidence. I can help, I promise you.'

'I'm sorry, mademoiselle, but it is against procedure to let you in there.' Prosper took his hat off and placed it onto a side table. He then sank into the armchair next to it.

'Nobody will know,' Opal said exasperated.

'*I* will know,' he said, his voice baritone, seeming to express the fact that he was not to be bossed around.

Opal blinked three strong blinks and gave him her most commanding look, and perched on the armchair in front of him.

'Well, there are some things I picked up at the Casino de Paris that were a little off that could point to Christophe Tasse. I found a sketchbook of his designs in Valentine's dresser drawer. The signature in the corner of the drawings was not his. He snatched it from me when he saw that I had it. Perhaps he did not design the costumes and Valentine was blackmailing him?'

'Motives are nothing without any physical evidence at the crime scene,' Prosper said, his dimpled chin twitching disinterestedly.

'Secondly, his alibi. All the seamstresses say he was at the theatre at two a.m., still sewing. I'm not sure how reliable that is since he is their employer and they are all scared of losing their jobs.'

'Casino de Paris staff and Clementina said he left for home around three a.m. and they saw him go. Nobody left before then and he'd been in the theatre all day.'

'I know, but there's another exit, you see,' Opal said. 'An obsolete doorway that leads out of the atelier to the kitchens. He could have left from there without anyone seeing. It's about a thirty-minute walk to here from the Casino de Paris, so he could have come here and gone back through that door and told the seamstresses to keep shtum.'

'The hotelier did not see him arrive at the hotel that night. And how would he get in and out of her room with the door still locked from the inside?'

'That is the ultimate question. And that is why I would like to see the room.'

'Not a chance, mademoiselle.'

Opal exhaled through her nostrils. She noticed the glass of red wine balanced next to Prosper's hat on the side table.

It was a homburg hat in light grey and speckled like bone-ash. The smooth dent in the top resembled a molar tooth. The Petersham band was a lovely contrast in eau de Nil green. Her respect for him rose a teensy-weensy bit, but not enough for what she was about to do.

Her eyeline moved to Napoleon under the table and her lashes flickered in inspiration. The dog tilted his head on its side, his devoted shining coals for eyes ready for any command.

'Have you met my dog Napoleon, Detective?' Opal asked, eyes still transfixed on her canine. She then made a quiet click noise with a pocket in her cheek and signalled with her eyeline to Napoleon. He understood his instruction instantly and sprung up onto the dinky table. The glass of wine teetered on its axis and spilled its contents all over the beautiful hat.

'*Zut!*' spat the detective and lifted the hat, drips of burgundy alcohol dripping from the rim.

'Oh goodness, I do apologise, he is a tad clumsy,' she said, stroking Napoleon's head to let him know he was a good boy. 'Goodness, that's beaver felt. That's not going to come out unless...'

'Unless what?' Prosper said, mopping at the hat and table with a hanky.

'Don't mop it like that! The fabric is porous, and it'll absorb! I'm a milliner, you know, I deal with these kinds of stains all the time.'

'My wife bought this for me last week for my promotion. She's not going to be happy,' the detective said. 'How do I get it out?'

'Well, I could certainly clean it for you. We should hurry, we've got about an hour until it sets in. Perhaps that's enough time for me to see the crime scene, then go back to my room and fetch my special cleaning elixir. I'll get it looking brand new again.'

Prosper put the hat back on the table and sighed like a balloon had been burst inside his chest, then shook his head. 'Mademoiselle, if my wife wasn't so ferocious I would not be even considering this. If you want to see the room that badly I will show you. But please let's be quick and then get this stain out of my new hat.'

'I knew you'd come around.' Opal smiled and sprang to her feet.

SEVENTEEN

VALENTINE'S ROOM

Prosper twisted the mortice key to Valentine's room with a metallic ratchetting sound.

'*Merci*, monsieur!' Opal said as she slunk inside the crime scene and flicked on the light.

'Always happy to oblige, mademoiselle,' Prosper said reluctantly. But before he could step inside, Napoleon dashed in front of him.

The poodle trotted around the edges of the room with a commanding presence, his paws tapping lightly against the wooden floor like precise hoofbeats. As he reached the French windows he paused, nostrils flaring in assessment.

Opal followed him, using her knuckles to tap the walls, listening for any hollow sound or indication that there may be a hidden door within the panelling. There was one in the library at her uncle's estate, Jacksands Park, so she knew exactly what to listen for. But alas, there was not.

Gosh. Valentine was a messy girl, she thought as she blinked irregularly and surveyed the objects that Valentine had left behind her.

A handbag lay open on the bed, its contents flung around it.

An assortment of setting lotions and Brilliantine cluttered the dresser with combs and hairpieces, a wind-up gramophone sat on the corner of it. General things a young woman would carry about. On the floorboards were some snakeskin heels and... a *broken pencil*. Napoleon sniffed at it and looked up at his mistress.

'Hmm,' Opal muttered, her lashes fluttering as she squinted at it.

'A pencil breaking is a pretty mundane occurrence, mademoiselle.'

'Have you fingerprinted it?' Opal asked.

'Yes, we've dusted every object in the room.'

Opal pointed her pyramidical nose towards the French windows and glided to them. She stretched out her hand to the door handle, hesitated and took it back.

'I guess I'm not allowed to touch anything in here?' she said over her shoulder.

'As I said, we've already dusted and fingerprinted so it's alright.' He sighed, already bored. 'Go out on the balcony if you want.'

Opal stepped out into the frigid air. She held onto the balustrade and concluded that if Valentine was tall or had heels on, it would be easy to be pushed over it as it only came up to her pelvis.

'How tall was she?' Opal asked.

'She was tall; five foot eleven, if I remember from her records,' Prosper said, arms folded.

'And was she wearing high heels when she died?'

'Yes.'

Opal did a quick scan of the balcony, holding her hair away from her face in the breeze. She came to the same conclusion as when she checked her own identical balcony; there was no way for the killer to have escaped, not without the witnesses below seeing anyway.

'Does Detective Opal think the killer flew off the balcony with bat wings?' Prosper teased her, his pencil moustache curled up in amusement.

'Well, it's about as silly as *your* conclusion,' Opal retorted, slipping past him back into the room.

She stood at the dresser and gazed at the mess on it. She guessed there could have been a struggle here, seeing as some of the objects were knocked over. But then again, a lot of glamorous girls she knew were messy. They were pristine on the outside, but it was as if they expected imaginary servants to come and do all their cleaning up.

'Pray tell, what precisely did the medical examiner report as the cause of death?' she asked, opening and examining the drawers.

'A cervical fracture. In other words, a broken neck. She also had a hip fracture and trauma to the skull from the fall.'

'No signs or marks on her body from a struggle before she fell?'

'*Non*... but if Detective Opal needs every last detail, Valentine had a fingernail that broke off inside the centre front opening of her corset.'

'Ah, quite intriguing, wouldn't you say?' Opal said, closing the last drawer.

Prosper sighed with impatience again, swung his torso out of the French window and lit a cigarette. Opal pointed her nose downwards in the direction of the waste bin below the dresser.

There was a clear cellophane box that had been opened. Inside the box was a withering white rose, resting in pink tissue paper. There was a handwritten note that Opal picked up. She tried to decipher it, but she wasn't as good at translating written French.

'What does this read?' Opal stuck the card under the smoke billowing out of Prosper's nose.

'"*Dear Clementina, Inhale deeply the sweetest smelling rose in Paris. An eternal fan."* Then it's the address of the florist on the other side,' he explained in a flat tone.

'That's queer.' Opal frowned. 'Why did Valentine have a rose addressed to Clementina?'

'Clementina gave it to her because she had too many flowers from fans in the dressing room and she wanted to cheer Valentine up after an argument with Christophe,' Prosper said. 'That's the last interaction they had, from what Clementina told me.'

'Oh,' said Opal, looking down at the curling petal lips. She'd found the note interesting and wanted to ponder over it a bit more. She placed it back beside the rose and closed the cellophane lid. 'May I take this and keep it in my room please, Detective?'

'Yes, yes whatever you like, but can we just take our little party out of here now, mademoiselle. You said you would fix my hat?'

'I haven't had a nosy in her handbag yet,' Opal said and hovered over the bed.

It was a green snakeskin box handbag. Tipped out of it was an array of red lipsticks, wooden toothpicks, a purse crammed with coins, a mother-of-pearl business card holder and a spare pair of fresh stockings. Opal then brushed her hand over the bedside telephone.

'We first thought that Zsa Zsa could have heard her arguing on the phone but that wasn't the case,' Prosper said.

'Of course it wasn't the case. She had shouted *"get off me"*, you wouldn't say that to someone on the phone.'

'Exactly,' Prosper said, his syllables expressing puffs of smoke. 'But we can't always trust a witness's ears to get everything accurate.'

'Let's see about that,' Opal said and sat smugly on the bed with her hands clasped on her lap. She then opened her mouth wide and shouted, 'Zsa Zsa! Zsa Zsa, can you hear me down there?'

A moment passed and Prosper rolled his eyes and looked out at the sky.

'Opal? Opal? Are you upstairs? In Valentine's room?' Zsa Zsa's response was muffled but clear.

'Yes, I am indeed, my dear. I am trying to prove the reliability of your ears. Can you repeat after me please the following words... Detective Inspector Prosper Delacroix is remarkably indolent.'

There was a few seconds silence in which Zsa Zsa was probably chortling, then she shouted back, 'Detective Inspector Prosper Delacroix is remarkably indolent!'

'There!' Opal beamed proudly over at Prosper.

He looked back at her over his shoulder with his chin protruding in an intimidating fashion. Opal looked down at her feet. Perhaps she had gone a smidge too far.

Prosper flicked his cigarette stub over the balcony and closed the doors.

'Now, I have done as you have asked. Please, please get this mark off my hat and be done with it. If I don't get scolded for the hat, I will get scolded for being late.'

'Alright, give it to me, please. I'll sort it out in my room and meet you in the lounge in ten minutes?'

Back in her room, Opal felt a bit nervous. When she said to Prosper that she could fix his hat, she may have told a tiny fib. There was no magic elixir to get the wine stain out, and she'd have to come up with a solution, fast.

She'd gotten some vinegar from the hotel's kitchen, which luckily worked a treat on the felt, turning the wine into a kind of invisible ink as she daubed and patted it.

'*Voilà!*' Opal smiled and eyed her work.

Napoleon padded on the bedsheets towards the hat she was holding abreast. He sniffed it and grumbled.

'Oh...' Opal sniffed it also. 'It does reek of vinegar now. Perhaps French vinegar is extra strong. Oh well, it can't be helped.'

Napoleon nuzzled his nose inside her handbag and pawed at the bottle of perfume that was inside.

'Good idea, darling boy.'

Opal spritzed the homburg heartily with Chanel No. 5, her idol's iconic fragrance. Then left her room to head down to the lounge.

'Here you go... good as new, old chum.' Opal handed back the homburg to its surly owner.

'Thank you. But what is that smell?' Prosper's dimpled chin twitched upwards as he wafted the hat around his nose. 'It's not Chanel No. 5, is it?'

'Yes, sir. I thought I'd mask the scent of the vinegar. It's my favourite perfume.'

Prosper looked crestfallen. 'It was also my ex-girlfriend's favourite perfume! She tried to break us up! I cannot go home with this.' Prosper pinched the centre part of his nose as if he was getting a headache.

'Please, please find a way to clean it off. I will be by the theatre to collect it sometime soon. I will have to tell my wife I left my hat at work.'

'Oh gosh,' Opal said, taking the homburg back. 'I do apologise, Detective. I will do my best. Well, goodnight and thank you kindly for showing me the crime scene.'

Opal bit her lip in deep thought. *What is the significance of the rose in the cellophane box and why was there a broken pencil in the middle of the floor? What is the link between them?*

EIGHTEEN

A MISSING CHORUS GIRL

An umbrella poked out of the girls' drop-off cab outside the Casino de Paris. It expanded with a spray of water droplets and swept over the head of Zsa Zsa. The unlit cigarette that was cushioned on her lips lifted upwards with her distasteful grimace as she peered at the sky.

Opal slid out of the car after her and Napoleon splashed down onto the cobbles, surrounded by little moats of rainwater. Opal squeezed under Zsa Zsa's umbrella and shuddered, her arms wrapped around her waist.

'No good deed goes unpunished, eh?' Opal groaned. 'Why did I think it would be fine to lend my coat to Estelle in this dreary weather? I didn't see her yesterday to get it back, and now I'm both cold and wet.'

At that exact moment, the stage door burst open with all the force of a dam giving way. Clementina emerged with her greyhound, Yvette, by her side, her brolly shooting up like a parachute. Her usually pristine red hair was unkempt like she'd just pulled at it.

'No! No!' she shouted. 'It cannot be happening again. Not to another of my girls!'

Detective Inspector Prosper Delacroix dashed out after her with his arms out wide, as if he'd been trying to stop her leaving.

'What is going on?' Opal rushed forward and demanded.

'I'm afraid that one of the chorus girls, Estelle Dufour, has gone missing.'

'No!' said Opal and Zsa Zsa in unison.

'It's been more than thirty-six hours,' the detective continued. 'If you'll excuse me, I have to organise interviews. I will be speaking with you soon.'

Opal hung her head and looked down at Napoleon. He whimpered, rainwater streaming down from his chin.

'Let's get inside,' said Zsa Zsa.

Detective Inspector Prosper Delacroix had set up the green room to conduct the questioning of the cast and crew.

'*Entrez s'il vous plaît,*' he called through the open door.

Opal was leaning with one heel up against the backstage corridor wall. Finally, after nail biting for two hours, it was her turn to be interviewed.

Prosper was sitting cross-legged on a leather chesterfield at the back. His blond head rose expectantly. The clinical brightness of the fluorescent lights bleached his skin, making his eyes and moustache darker in contrast.

'*Bonjour,* Mademoiselle Laplume. Have you got my homburg?'

Opal tweaked her fedora lower over her left eye, abashed. 'Well, no, monsieur. I'm dreadfully sorry but I'll have to bring it to you another day. I was airing it out on the balcony and it was working splendidly, except this morning...' She paused and gulped.

'What happened?' he asked with dread in his voice.

'We had a rather unfortunate case of what the French call... *pluie.*'

Prosper went slightly pink with vexation. 'Ploooie? What is ploooie?'

'Sorry, sir, it's a difficult word for the English to pronounce. Rain, monsieur, rain.'

Prosper pinched the bridge of his nose for composure, then resumed in a calm voice. 'Is my homburg ruined?'

'No, monsieur. I can dry it out and reshape it. Leave it with me.'

'You don't seem to be the expert milliner you fluff yourself up to be, Mademoiselle Laplume.'

Opal flashed her eyes at him and she felt the plumage in her fedora stir like embers. *How very dare he.*

'I'm not sure *you* could detect a sneeze in a pepper factory, monsieur,' she retorted. 'Pray, have you found anything useful out about Estelle, or have you simply drawn a blank like you did with Valentine's case?'

His moustache fell flat as he resumed that lawful, stoic expression and pretended not to notice her cheek. 'No advancements on Estelle yet. She's not been seen. She's not contacted her family. She hasn't left a note. Nothing.'

Opal rolled her eyes. She perched on the other end of the settee, then said, 'Fire away with the questions then.'

'When did you last see Estelle Dufour?'

'I was with her in the auditorium the night before last.'

'Yes, that's when she was last seen.'

'Estelle, Zsa Zsa, David, the set designer, and I were watching Clementina practise her underwater routine from around six o'clock. Zsa Zsa and I left around seven thirty. Estelle said she wanted to wait for Christophe Tasse to finish work, they were to go out for oysters. I gave her my coat because she was chilly. I saw her arguing with Christophe in the foyer on my way out. I could only hear her calling him a *"Salaud"*. Zsa Zsa heard Valentine use that insult also before she perished.'

Prosper lowered his chin. 'Christophe said they had a lover's quarrel and that Estelle stormed out of the theatre shortly afterwards with a blue coat on, cancelling their evening plans to go for oysters. Since it was your coat she was wearing, can you describe it for me?'

'It's azure in colour, made from one hundred per cent wool. About knee length, padded shoulders, long sleeves, double-breasted with winged lapels. Six big buttons about the size of an English penny. Here, let me sketch out the shape.'

With large strokes she did a quick outline with the lipstick on her sketchpad and gave it to him.

'Thank you,' Prosper said, surprised at her effort.

'Can we be certain Christophe did not leave with Estelle?' Opal asked.

'Christophe was seen leaving alone at nine by the front of house staff.'

'What did Christophe say the fight was about?' Opal asked.

'Apparently Estelle had heard that there'd been a crossover from when he'd started dating her and finished dating Valentine,' he replied.

Opal gulped guiltily. *I was the one who told Estelle that!*

She blinked fast and stared down at her scarlet manicure in thought. Valentine and Estelle had both been Christophe's lovers. They had called him a '*Salaud*'. Could there be a connection to both mysteries there?

Prosper continued, 'Is there any reason you might think Estelle would want to leave town abruptly, or know about anyone she was on bad terms with?'

'I barely knew her at all. I'm sorry, Detective.' Opal shrugged.

'Well, if you think of anything else, you can reach me at the police station.'

'Actually, you know, there is something,' Opal said. 'Did you manage to speak to the man in the Citroën with the pistol?'

'One of my men did indeed, mademoiselle. I'm sorry I didn't keep you up to speed with it. It's all okay, the man *does* have a licence to carry his firearm, and he said he frequents both the street outside this theatre *and* the street outside your hotel because he lives and works on them. Coincidence, I know.'

'Did he give any proof of this? It seems like he's simply lurking, not going about a day's business.'

'We saw his firearm licence. And I am afraid lurking isn't a crime, mademoiselle. He has not harassed you.'

Opal scrunched her fists and seethed. She had to bite her tongue from uttering the words, *Your detective horsepower couldn't pull a pea across a table.* But instead said, 'Well, he is jolly well harassing my sense of safety. But I see I'm not going to get much help from you.'

She then stood up, and without looking at him said curtly, 'I've got stitching to do in the atelier. *Au revoir,* Detective Delacroix.'

She exited the room, and came nose to nose with Zsa Zsa, who was next to go in and give her statement.

'I say, I don't often get on the sauce but I think after today I am in need of a hefty sundowner,' Opal said, and Zsa Zsa groaned in agreement.

At that moment Clementina swished past in her transparent, voluminous dressing gown. Keeping in tow with her was her greyhound, Yvette, with her rhinestone choker. Curling rags swung on Clementina's head as she turned to look at them, her cheekbones dewy as if she'd quite got over the shock of Estelle's disappearance.

'Did I hear you girls say "sundowner"?' she said, halting.

'Yes,' Zsa Zsa replied, clasping her hands in excited prayer. 'We need to get together and make a plan to find Estelle!'

'Indeed,' Clementina said. 'Come to my apartment tonight for *l'heure verte.* The green hour. To drink absinthe for an hour – or two? We can brainstorm.'

Though the reason was maudlin, Opal was delighted to at last be invited to her cousin's abode. 'Splendid idea, cousin. We must get to the bottom of this. That detective is lamentably inept.'

'Did you say absinthe, Clementina?' Zsa Zsa pouted. 'But I thought absinthe was banned?'

'*En France, oui.* Yes. But I get mine on the black market from Catalonia. It's magnificent stuff, Pernod Fils. It's going to be just a handful of us... and Yvette, of course! *Ma grande fille glamour.*' She addressed her darling beast at the end of her speech, bending down and scooping its chin in her palm. It glanced up at its owner dopily.

Opal was pleased. At last she would get a moment with her cousin. Perhaps she would finally get a quiet moment to ask her about Mother and why she'd wanted Opal banished to Paris so abruptly...

'Cousin...?' Opal called after Clementina. 'Will Augusto be coming?'

'Why?' Clementina looked Opal up and down with a tiny smirk. 'You want me to invite him?'

Opal blushed when she realised how transparent she was being.

'Oh, no, no,' Opal backtracked, her cheeks scarlet. 'Only if you were going to invite him anyway. I just thought he might have a good plan of how to find Estelle, that's all.'

'I'll invite him and let's see what he says. He is a dark horse that one, so I can't predict whether he will or won't.'

Opal pulled her fedora down over one eye in a determined fashion. First Valentine, now Estelle. If they didn't make haste and get to the bottom of all this, then who would be next?

NINETEEN

THE ABSINTHE SOIRÉE

Clementina's apartment made Opal feel a little on edge. It was beautifully equipped, but the furniture was a matching suite of pieces with mirrored panels and surfaces. It was like a narcissistic maniac lived there who needed to be able to see themselves in mirrors every way they turned. The screens, coffee table, dining table, cupboards and worktops were all made from mirrored panels. It turned the room into a kaleidoscope of guests – Clementina, Zsa Zsa, Leon, Christophe, and David were duplicated on every surface and swaying in time to the lively gypsy jazz blaring from the gramophone.

Opal sat alone and gazed at the absinthe fountain on the cocktail table. She watched a drip of condensation collect on the outside of the fountain's glass globe vessel, swell and slip down the side.

'When I am blue, I drink the emerald liquor,' Clementina said, downed the rest of her glass and placed it down on the mirrored centre table. She then straightened up, hands on her hips, the bat wings of her dress billowing. 'Round two?'

'Oh, I will refrain, thank you. I find the taste a tinge too liquorice for my palette.' Opal winced and smiled at the same time. 'Are we going to make a plan of how to find Estelle?'

'Oh, I can't bear to speak about that yet.' Clementina brushed away the subject with a bejewelled hand, then pointed at the centre table. 'You haven't even tried the absinthe atomiser! It's such a delight. It looks like a pretty perfume bottle and you simply spritz it at the back of your throat. Or try the absinthe pipe, perhaps? You add the ice into the reservoir here...'

'No, thank you, cousin,' Opal declined politely. 'I'm still somewhat of a novice in the world of spirits. I don't want to get squiffy.'

Clementina lounged back next to Opal on the chaise longue and spritzed the atomiser, directed at the back of her throat. Yvette, the greyhound, floated past like a sleek grey cloud, and curled beneath her mistress on the floor in a giant snail shape and closed her eyes.

'This is Paris, *ma chérie*. When all this mess is over, I'll show you the café culture. We drink all day long. You are a young flower – are you not only twenty?'

'I'm twenty-two,' Opal replied. 'I'm not sure Mother would approve of me drinking plonk all day long, but I would love to sample the artists' cafés one afternoon.'

'Why are you thinking about your mother?' Clementina grimaced. 'She is not here.'

'Quite right, I shouldn't be,' Opal replied. 'Though I always feel a twinge of guilt when I do something she wouldn't approve of, even if she remains unaware. It is rather daft, I concur. I wonder why I feel that way.'

'It is about growing up. Evaluating life for yourself. Your mother, Lady Phyllis, is terribly Victorian and dogmatic. Well, I never met her but that's what Mamma said. Her brother, your papa, married her to please our *grand-père* Laplume, I think.

Mother did the exact opposite, ran away to Paris and had me. An illegitimate child with a penniless artiste.'

'Actually, Clementina, I have been wanting to ask you something.' Opal shuffled more upright. 'Now that I have a moment, was there any particular reason why Mother wanted me to come to Paris so urgently? It was quite out of character for her to ask, considering her previous reluctance for us to meet. She said it was to assist you in the atelier, but with the throngs of seamstresses flocking to Paris in search of work, you could have asked anyone. It feels as though she *needed* me to leave London. It all seemed terribly frantic.'

Clementina placed the atomiser in her lap, the liquid inside glowed like a crystal ball brewing a green storm. She took a moment to devise what to say. 'There is nothing more to it that I know of, *chérie*. I contacted her because I knew you were a skilled milliner. I also know your father would be pleased you are here with me. It was a good opportunity for you to spread your wings. We needed you urgently, so she sent you.'

Opal wanted to believe Clementina, but the fact she kept glancing down at her lap as she spoke could be read as dishonest.

'I also am still very surprised that she wanted to visit Papa in Papua. She vowed never to put herself through another one of his *rainforest rampages*. And yet she has, leaving our shop in the hands of very questionable management to boot.'

'I think she may have realised that a marriage is a marriage and being away from each other for so long all the time is not in anyone's interest.'

'You mean Father wants to spend more time with her?' Opal scrunched her features in perplexity. 'That's a bit off the rails!'

'I have no idea. Perhaps it is lonely out there.' Clementina shrugged.

'I'm not even sure Daddy is capable of loneliness. How else could he stand being away from us so much?' Opal sighed. 'How often do you and Daddy keep in touch?'

'Every year or so. I or Mother will get a letter and Christmas cards, of course, usually with pheasants on the front.'

'We usually correspond fortnightly by airmail, or he'll send the odd silly telegram to tell me he's fed a saltwater crocodile a scone or something daft. I have no idea whether it's true or not.'

'English tea with a croc,' snorted Clementina. 'He is... how do you say in English, a bit of a *twit*?'

'Yes.' Opal chuckled. 'You could say Father is a bit of a twit. He would probably prefer the term eccentric though.'

'Ah yes, the eccentric Laplumes. Tchin tchin.'

'I wonder if our eccentricity is the reason we're lone horses. I've always felt alone and have found it difficult to make friends.' Opal got a bit misty-eyed as she said this, but turned her face away so her cousin wouldn't see.

'I suffer from this too, yes.' Clementina nodded and spritzed her throat again.

'Do you think it's the reason you pursue fame? The more people who know who you are, the less you feel alone?' Opal pondered, now blinking her tears away at the ceiling.

'That could be what draws me, yes. But I'll tell you something,' Clementina said rather gravely. 'It doesn't work. Thinking fame will fulfil you is like thinking a louder gramophone makes a song more beautiful.'

On that rather gloomy note, Clementina sat up and splashed some absinthe into her shaped glass. She took a silver perforated spoon and balanced it on top of the glass. She then put a white sugar cube on the spoon. She watched the water pat onto it, crumbling the cube like a tiny avalanche. The absinthe clouded with every drip of sugared water to a denser mint-green.

'Now this is how we used to drink it in the belle époque.' Clementina then got up to speak to David over by the mantel, leaving Opal alone on the chaise longue.

Opal swayed to the gypsy jazz record and stared at the ornate floor tiles. Even though they had gathered to discuss what to do about Estelle's disappearance, she was a bit miffed that Augusto had not shown up. She looked over at herself in the grand mirror hanging over the mantelpiece. She admired the way her hat cast a huge shadow on the wall behind her in the candlelight.

The flat, pillbox top of her hat was stabbed with dozens of red feathers, fanning out, creating its huge brim, a magnificent two foot in diameter. It made a scarlet halo, like Saturn's rings, around her head, punctuated with her bright eyes in the centre.

Just then, Christophe Tasse sat down next to her and sucked on a glass absinthe pipe, the crushed ice and liquid in the reservoir draining with a bubbling sound. He then offered it to Opal, but she politely brushed his hand away.

'Christophe, you seem rather chipper in the light of what's come to pass. Are you not distraught over the disappearance of Estelle?'

'This is how I behave when I'm upset, dear girl. I overcompensate in order to carry on. Besides, I don't believe she's gone for good. I think she was just sick of the show and has done a runner.'

'Did she give you that impression when you squabbled?' Opal asked.

'Yes. She said she had nothing to look forward to. Nobody she could trust. She was upset that she'd heard my relationship with Valentine had crossed over with ours.'

'Where would she go if she ran away? She would have to get some sort of work somewhere to keep going.'

'Another theatre somewhere, perhaps in the south. I'm sure

she would change her name, so it would be impossible to make enquires.'

Opal got the impression that he had given up already. Meanwhile, Zsa Zsa slid onto Leon's lap in the armchair with the atomiser. Her black dress draped over Leon's knees and made a puddle of velvet on the floor.

The liquid swirled violently in the atomiser as Zsa Zsa and Leon fought over possession of it, snatching it from one another. Opal couldn't believe that the little throat spritzer had gotten them so well-oiled.

'I thought we were supposed to be concocting a plan to find Estelle?' Opal said in a slightly scolding tone to the playmates.

'Yes, yes, I know,' said Zsa Zsa guiltily, lowering the atomiser to her lap.

'That chappy, Prosper Delacroix, seems to be on the case though,' Leon said, rather cross-eyed.

'He couldn't detect an elephant in a telephone booth,' Opal said, thoroughly disappointed that her friends were getting bleary instead of proactive.

'I remember now what I meant to tell you, Leon!' Zsa Zsa said and her eyes twinkled. 'I could get Mei Ling banned from the theatre!'

'That's rather wicked of you. How are you going to manage to ruin my show so close to opening?'

'Mei Ling has a tattoo. Monsieur Blanchette says we're not allowed them.'

'Does she now?' Leon opened his eyes wide in mock-shock. 'We must throw her in the clink. What is this tattoo and where on her body is it?'

'It's on her upper thigh. Rather an eyesore. Three squares overlapping each other diagonally.'

Leon shut his veneers away behind his lips and jerked his head upright. He frowned as if he'd misheard something Zsa Zsa had said.

'Describe the tattoo again for me, please,' he said in a serious tone.

'Three squares diagonally overlapping. Really dull. Nothing like I would choose. I'd get a tiger on a chaise longue with—'

'Can you draw Mei Ling's tattoo for me, please?' Leon said deadpan, and looked around for a sketching implement.

'What's wrong?' Zsa Zsa said hazily.

'I'll draw it for you,' said Opal, and produced her sketchbook and lipstick crayon.

When she'd finished scribbling Mei Ling's geometric tattoo design, she held her sketchbook up.

'Yes, that's it. Boring thing. Wonder what it means?' Zsa Zsa jabbered.

Leon shifted Zsa Zsa off his lap, his eyes transfixed on Opal's sketchbook. The sight of it seemed to sober him up completely.

'Do you recognise the symbol?' Opal asked him. 'Is there some significance to you, Mr Dumoulin?'

'No,' he said, shaking himself out of a daze. 'It's just an interesting design.'

'Are you going to throw her out of the show?' Zsa Zsa's eyes flashed jokingly.

'I should think even a giant tattoo of a Lindy Hopping Komodo dragon on Mei Ling's back wouldn't cause us to sack her. We're so close to opening now and we've had so many setbacks.'

Zsa Zsa sprayed a minute amount of absinthe from the atomiser in Mr Dumoulin's ear. He twitched in shock. Then flashed his veneers in a lionesque manner at his aggressor and they play-fought.

Opal left them to it, snapped her sketchbook away in her handbag and looked around the room. Clementina and David appeared to be in an intense conversation. Opal was quite taken aback at how well they seemed to know each other. She'd previously thought that David was just the scruffy set designer and wasn't really part of Clementina's social circle. David also seemed to know Clementina's apartment pretty well. He'd been scurrying around most of the night, fetching things from the kitchenette, selecting records, arranging candles and lighting them, like he was well acquainted with the whereabouts of her things.

At that moment they were chattering very soberly, almost nose to nose as though their conversation was both intensely private and deeply serious. Clementina had her hands on her hips, her heart-shaped cheekbones sculpted by the candlelight as she pouted in concentration. David's lanky shoulders curled inwards, revealing his introverted side.

A 'tonk' noise sounded on the marble floor. Clementina straightened up, her eyes scanning the ground. The greyhound's fur tulip of an ear twisted in the direction of the sound. The guests, in varying extremes of drunken delayed reaction, bent forward to look also. Opal quickly realised what the noise was.

Clementina had had a brooch pinned on her chest earlier. Opal had noticed this when the driver had dropped Opal and Zsa Zsa off outside and they ran into Clementina coming back from the shops. Clementina was carrying a paper bag full of cocktail ingredients, and Opal distinctly remembered the half-moon, rhinestone brooch affixed to Clementina's dress.

'It's your brooch,' Opal said. 'I think it went under the coffee table.'

'It probably fell off because of all that shaking you did while you were making cocktails,' Christophe remarked, the only one not bending down to look.

'I've got it...' Zsa Zsa said on all fours, her black velvet bottom shuffling back from beneath the coffee table. 'Oh... I think its broken, the pin is bent and rusted. What a shame, it's so pretty.'

'You keep it, *chérie*,' Clementina said. 'I remember you complimented me on it. I don't get the time to get my things fixed. It's only an old costume brooch.'

'Oh! Thank you ever so much! How kind.' Zsa Zsa beamed, slipping it into her clutch bag.

Leon Dumoulin lounged back in the armchair. 'Never wear any jewellery that's not real,' he teased, tutting at Zsa Zsa.

She slapped him on the knee. 'Those teeth aren't real!!' she guffawed.

He bared his pearly veneers, unabashed.

'Stick that in your pipe and smoke it, Mr Dumoulin!' Christophe joined in, extending the absinthe pipe.

'That reminds me, I want my cigarettes,' Clementina said.

She flicked the light on, killing the mellowness of the candlelight. Opal watched Clementina enter a room in the far corner, probably to look for her smokes.

A few seconds later a scream sliced the air, cutting everyone silent. The greyhound lifted its head and her ears swung forward. Opal felt as if someone had thrown the icy water from the absinthe fountain over her. Only the gypsy jazz record could be heard playing, the music now feeling rather sinister.

Leon shoved Zsa Zsa off his lap and spilled some of his frothy mint mixture on the floor. He scurried into the room, followed closely by Christophe.

Opal's eyelids trembled, adjusting to the shift in her perception, trying to listen intently. She couldn't hear over the record so she switched it off.

'What in heavens name could be the matter?' David clasped his face, mouth stretched in deep concern.

Opal couldn't stand not knowing what was going on any longer and flew to the bedroom to see if Clementina needed help.

What on earth is going on? She peered over Leon's shoulder to see what he was examining. Scratched in crude, thin lettering into the dark mahogany headboard was the phrase:

Ne dormez pas seule. Vous serez la prochaine à mourir.

Leon read it aloud, completely tonelessly, 'It says, *"Don't sleep alone, you'll be next to die."*'

TWENTY

A HYSTERICAL TURN

'I don't know whose sick joke this is but it's not funny,' asserted Christophe, massaging Clementina's back.

'It's not a joke,' Clementina said, gazing at the floor, eyelids stitched open. 'Ever since Valentine's death I've felt like someone wants me dead too. I don't have any proof or physical evidence, I just feel it.'

'Well, you've got physical evidence now,' Christophe said, peering closer at the markings made on the ornate headboard.

'Christophe, can you telephone Augusto and get him to come here now, please.'

'Of course,' Christophe said, and disappeared back into the lounge.

'When were you last in this room, Clementina?' Opal asked, eyes flickering, photographically memorising the bed markings.

'When I was changing into my dress around eight o'clock, just before I went out to get cocktail ingredients. The message wasn't scratched on the headboard then, I would have noticed it straight away. I haven't been in this room since I've been back, as you know, Opal. You and Zsa Zsa have been with me since I got back. I'm guessing it was while I was out.'

'Are there concierges here at night?' Opal asked.

'Yes, there are,' Clementina replied quietly.

'We'll have to ask them if they saw anyone suspicious, and we need to call the police. If this is connected to Valentine, or even Estelle, in any way, then it's got to be looked into,' Leon said, standing up, twisting a cufflink in fast jerks.

'I can't sleep here tonight,' blurted Clementina.

'Of course, you can't, darling,' said Christophe. 'We'll sort you out a hotel, or perhaps you could stay with one of us.'

'I think I'm going to have a... hysterical turn,' she said in voice that ironically sounded calm. 'I need my vapour, I won't be able to sleep without it.'

Opal wondered what kind of 'vapour' she was talking about. Clementina grabbed the knob of her dressing table drawer and yanked it open with a maraca sound that indicated it was full of pill bottles. She moved her hand around inside frantically.

'*Nom d'un chien!*' she cursed. 'It's not here.'

She stood up and scurried out of the room. Christophe and Leon followed her, leaving Opal alone with the message on the headboard.

The note had been scrawled viciously with something sharp and thinner than a knife blade. The dark varnish was jagged and sticking up in parts. Opal peeled a piece of the varnish off, dropped it in her handbag and then snapped it shut.

Inspecting the bottles of medicine in Clementina's drawer, Opal raised her eyebrows. They seemed to be all sedatives and sleep aids. Chloral hydrate, veronal. Clementina was evidently some sort of insomniac.

Opal blinked involuntarily, as though trying to grasp the full weight of what she'd seen. At face value, it seemed very likely that this death threat was connected to Valentine, not only because of the wording used in the threat but the circumstance in which it was executed. The killer had entered and left locked premises, like a ghost. Estelle also was missing, of course, but nobody knew if she was even alive or if her disappearance could be connected to the case.

A waft of air whipped past Opal. David had rushed over to the bed. He was looking at the note, frowning so much his features screwed themselves into a jagged cluster. He muttered something inaudible to himself as he slunk out of the room again.

Opal could tell he was very genuinely shocked. Everyone had seemed to be. She didn't feel that she could pin this on anyone at the party. She joined them all in the living room, where they were congregated around the coffee table.

'Clementina, should I get you a drink?' David asked timidly, as if worried that the reply would be hysterical.

'*Oui*,' she replied absently and sank into the armchair.

'I think someone is trying to sabotage the show,' he continued. 'Don't let them scare you, Clementina. The show must go on.'

'Don't let them scare me? *Mon Dieu!*' Clementina's cheekbones contorted. 'They managed to get into and out of my flat seamlessly without a key and knew exactly when I would be out! If that's not scary, then I don't know what is.' She took a large gulp of absinthe and continued in a calmer voice. 'I'm so sorry, everyone, to end the night like this, but I'm going to have to pack if I'm staying somewhere else tonight. Leon, do let me know what's going on with the concierge. I think the rest of you have to leave... I'm so sorry.'

'Of course,' Opal said. 'Zsa Zsa and I will go and hail a cab, but do let us know if there's anything we can do!'

Clementina disappeared into the bathroom without answering. She was cursing under her breath about her lost 'vapour'.

'Goodnight, girls,' David answered for her. 'Don't worry

about anything, just concentrate on the show and this mess will all sort itself out.'

Opal's hopes for the evening, to devise a grand plan to find Estelle, had been promptly overshadowed by the panic surrounding Clementina's predicament. Had a stranger really slipped into Clementina's apartment to deliver that horrid little note? Or... Opal's spine prickled. Was it remotely conceivable that the culprit was in fact an insider? Could she have been mingling with them that very evening?

TWENTY-ONE

THE OYSTER TRICYCLE

Sea salt and citrus perfumed the air. A glimmer of mother-of-pearl winked from the oyster shell cradled in Opal's palm, while the seafood vendor, with all the finesse of a man milking a cow, squeezed a lemon over it with his fist. He had parked his tricycle outside the Casino de Paris gates, no doubt calculating that a troupe of performers might be susceptible to a mid-day mollusc. It could be their last chance seeing as the season was almost over. His instincts had paid off, roping in Opal, Zsa Zsa, Mei Ling and the stoic Augusto. Napoleon was curiously resting his paws on Opal's knees, sniffing the oyster with the air of a gourmet connoisseur.

'Not for pups,' Opal said curtly and devoured the marine delicacy, smacking her lips.

'Only for the glitterati of the glove-and-garter brigade,' Zsa Zsa said, lifting her shell out of reach from the dog.

'And then the exception... Augusto,' Opal smirked.

The Spaniard was on his fourth sea creature which he'd dowsed in an onion vinaigrette. He knocked it back with gusto, as if it was a kind of obscure sport.

'Am I not glitterati of the glove-and-garter brigade?' he asked with mock devastation.

'Hardly. You didn't come to the glitterati gathering at Clementina's, did you?' tutted Zsa Zsa.

'I did... at the end of the evening when... she was distressed.' Augusto resumed a more serious tone.

Suddenly a black Bugatti swerved cleanly into a space nearby. Through the veil of Zsa Zsa's smoke Opal saw a man step out of the passenger side. He rose up to an average height, a sleek mackintosh hanging on his boyish frame. His face matched his childlike physique, his highly set eyebrows giving him a naïve sort of look.

At that moment, the stage door thwacked open. Clementina, swathed in chinchilla, rushed over to the man and flung her arms out. Like a circus artist leaping off a trapeze, she fell into him. He embraced her with a gentle encirclement and planted lingering kisses on her cheekbones.

'I'm assuming that's Joshua Davenport, her fiancé,' Opal whispered into the fronds of Zsa Zsa's fur collar.

'Yes, I guess after the death threat he got on the next plane,' she whispered back, small dots of smoke emerging from her lips.

The lovers stood nose to nose; their hands buckled tight together. Opal gestured to Zsa Zsa to shuffle sideways so they could be in better earshot of their conversation and get an idea of how genuine this diehard romance really was.

'I got here as soon as I could, you wouldn't believe how hard it was to get away,' Joshua said, his voice deeper and more commanding than you'd expect from someone who looked so boyish.

'I know, darling. I feel terrible dragging you away from work, but I just need you here. I'm so shaken up.'

'I won't leave your side for a second. Whoever the blaggard is that left you that threat, he's not going to get close to you.'

'*Mon Dieu*, it's so good to see you,' Clementina gushed, grabbing his head with her red nails.

Zsa Zsa sucked on her cigarette longingly as she watched the lovers delve into a relentless kiss. They weren't even disturbed when a blast of chorus girls cannonaded out of the stage door, shrieking with gratefulness that the tricycle was there.

'This is a beautiful image,' Augusto said, eyeing up everyone gathered at the seafood oasis. He rummaged in his trench coat pocket and pulled out a thick sketch pad and a sharp artist's pencil. He walked back a few metres to frame the scene and started to map out the silhouettes of the girls around the stall.

'Do you draw, Augusto?' Opal asked him in surprise.

'Yes, Mademoiselle Laplume. It is my favourite pastime, in fact.'

'Oh, you're just made for each other,' whispered Zsa Zsa into Opal's ear with a short snorting laugh.

Opal blushed and whipped Zsa Zsa with her eyelashes to silence her. She tossed her empty oystershell back onto the tricycle pile and went to go and see.

'Don't move until I say!' Augusto commanded with a pencil. His dimpled chin rose authoritatively.

'Oh, I do apologise,' Opal said, going pinker, and standing still for a moment.

'I've finished your pose, you can look now if you like,' he said.

Opal stood behind him while he drew the rest of the scene. There were chorus girls sitting on the kerb. Some begging for another free marine delicacy at the trike, Zsa Zsa gossiping with Mei Ling in a smudge of grey smoke and then Opal.

'I'm not happy with this one... I can do better,' he said, pointing his chin to the right.

Opal's lashes fluttered, absorbing the details of the artwork. *Not bad.* Bold strokes and delicate flecked markings. He was good at capturing noses and hands. She had no idea how she got the confidence to do this, but she cracked open her handbag, pulled out her lipstick crayon and leaned over the sketch pad.

She gave everyone in the picture a red hat, swirling halos and turbans with feather centrepieces. The oysterman she gave a red drooping beret. Opal's heart pumped. Surely Augusto wouldn't be furious. After all, he'd grumbled about not liking this particular creation. She glanced up at him, smiling sheepishly.

'Opal Laplume,' Augusto said, his dimple dancing in his chin. 'You have defaced my art in the most beautiful way.'

Opal pulled her hand away from the drawing and let herself breathe with relief. Her audacity had paid off splendidly.

'Are you a drawing double act?' asked Mei Ling, who had come over to see.

'We are *now*.' Augusto smiled and brandished the grey-and-red artwork out in front of him, proudly gazing at it.

Opal felt her knees give, like butter sliding down a plate. Was he saying that he'd like to make more illustrations together like this? Or was he just being polite? Probably the latter, seeing as he was a gentleman.

'Where did you learn to draw then, both of you?' Mei Ling asked, swallowing a mouthful of mollusc.

'I taught myself, *en España*. The earth is chalky where I come from. I used that chalk to draw my mother and her friends who were weavers, sitting around with their looms.'

'Gosh. I'm surprised. Your technique looks like you went to a prestigious art school. You've used dissection lines to get the proportions of the oysterman,' said Opal.

'I read some books,' Augusto said shortly.

'Well, I'd love to see your chalk creations,' Opal said, clasping her hands behind her back and looking sideways up at him.

'You can't, I'm afraid. I used to draw on the pavement or

walls. Paper was expensive, still is. Look, I've been scrubbing out half of these pages.'

'Oh yes, decent artist paper like that.'

'What about you, Opal? Where did you learn to draw?' Augusto asked, shutting his book and clasping it behind his back, shoulders broad.

'I had a lovely governess as a child at Copperfields Hall. She was always making me draw still lifes she'd arrange from bric-a-brac. Perhaps because she could nap while I did so. But still, it really brought out a joy in me. Then I would copy Mother and design hats. I look at a lot of fashion magazines and try to emulate the techniques of the illustrations.'

'Can I see?' Mei Ling enquired.

'Oh yes. I always carry my sketchbook.' Opal plucked it out of her bag and before she could help it the pages fell open on the page on which she had sketched Mei Ling's tattoo.

Mei Ling gasped when she saw it.

'What is that?' Mei Ling said accusingly.

'Oh, I'm so sorry, Mei Ling,' Opal said, flustered. 'I was inspired by your tattoo I saw in the dressing room. Very interesting geometric pattern. What does it mean?'

Mei Ling narrowed her eyes and looked back and forth at Augusto and Opal.

'I don't know what you're talking about. I don't have a tattoo.' She spun on her heel and her shiny bob flew outwards. She tossed her rocky shell onto the tricycle with a clatter and marched off.

'Oh dear,' said Augusto. 'Perhaps she is worried. I heard the dancers aren't allowed tattoos.'

'I think there's more to it. Like it's some sort of insignia that reveals something about her... about her past.'

'Well, that is the theatre for you. People escaping from all kinds of plight. Everyone has a secret.'

'Do you have a secret?' Opal asked before her mouth could stop.

'Do you?' He raised his chin as he shot the question back like a little tennis game.

'I'm an open book!' said Opal. 'Ask me anything.'

They were interrupted by a whirlwind of chinchilla as Clementina handed everyone another ocean treasure.

'These are the best in town. Pierre often treats us!' she said, and gave her New York fiancé another passionate kiss.

Zsa Zsa approached and eyed Clementina and Joshua up cravingly.

'My lips burn for a kiss like that,' said Zsa Zsa quietly to Opal. 'I don't fancy Mr Dumoulin enough to give him a real passionate one like that.'

Opal consumed her fruits de mer and wondered whether she would ever get to kiss Augusto like that. She gave her hat a brisk, corrective tweak. Of course not. Such a notion was utterly absurd, and more to the point, thoroughly inappropriate. She'd never be able to present him to Mother. Lady Phyllis Laplume had firm views on these matters; no title, no ancestral pile, no deal, and as for a foreigner? Well, that was simply beyond the pale. Opal let out a breath. Why could she never rid herself of this voice of maternal disapproval, nagging in her ear like a loose shutter on a windy night?

TWENTY-TWO
OPENING NIGHT

The Casino de Paris was roused in all its showtime glory. The lights behind its vast stained-glass window were switched on, weeping multicoloured rays onto the red carpet lining the pavement below.

Twelve security guards stood along the carpet, feet wide, shoulders pinned back. A couple of beautiful hostesses stood at the guest-list post, arms folded, shaking their bobs apologetically at a guest. This guest was wearing a tuxedo and top hat and had a vicious-looking T-shaped scar on his left cheek. He was trying to get in without an invitation.

He was persistent, his purple scar twisting frustratedly as he pleaded. He asked if there had been any cancellations. One of the hostesses rolled her heavily made-up eyes and ran her finger down her list, then nodded – there had been a cancellation. She would let him in because they didn't want to have any empty seats on opening night. It would look bad. She told him his seat number and his shoulders moved with the current of tuxedos through the glass doors.

Inside the foyer, a magnificent emerald cuff clasped a Russian woman's wrist. Close by, a marquise-cut ruby dangled from a much-revered earlobe. Its deep pavilion glittered in a red flutter as Coco Chanel turned her head. Across the room, a blue topaz baguette adorned the finger of Josephine Baker, curved around a champagne glass, twinkling with the lights of the chandelier above. Every piece of treasure glinting in the foyer at the Casino de Paris had something in common; the designer was Dumoulin.

The main topic of discussion was how excited people were to see the multimillion-franc necklace on the delectable Clementina. Would the necklace win the first prize at the Exposition of Jewellery and Goldsmithing?

Beyond the bustling foyer and red universe of the auditorium, the cast, crew and musicians of the Clementina Lalonde La Grande Revue gathered in a corridor behind the stage. They had been summoned by Leon Dumoulin for a 'pep talk'. There was a distinct void without Estelle in their little congregation. The chorus dancer who had replaced her looked almost cross-eyed as she attempted to run through all the moves in her head.

Opal stood on tiptoes and, manoeuvring her head like a meerkat, checked all her headdresses on the performer's heads. *Splendid, nothing out of place.* Once satisfied, she patted her own turban and arranged her skirts. The purple taffeta fabric burst like a waterfall into Spanish frills from her dropped waist.

Leon cleared his throat. 'It was Clementina's idea that I show you all the Apolline Diamond necklace before the show begins. It's a magnificent piece and I agree you should all be able to see it up close for good luck.'

Opal pulsed her eyes at Zsa Zsa in excitement.

Leon parted his veneers. 'Firstly, I'd like to thank you all for being in this show. It won't only be an amazing spectacle, but it will also give my necklace a greater chance of winning.'

He paused for a moment and ran a finger over the top of his champagne glass. 'I'd like to take a moment to talk about diamonds. Indeed, they are beautiful, but it is where they come from that fascinates me. Diamonds stem from deep inside the earth's mantle. They've only become accessible through volcanic activity bringing them up to the surface. That is why, to me, they are the deepest and most secret treasures of the earth. And this year, one of the largest and most flawless diamonds in the world was found in Papua in the Taritatu River.'

Gosh, Opal thought. *I know that river. It's close to where Daddy studies the birds of paradise. How uncanny.*

Leon went on. 'And this very diamond, which I have named Apolline, is now yours to behold behind me in this dressing room.'

He pointed to the door behind him. 'This fascinating piece of history can be yours to own after the Exposition is over, should you have twelve million francs to blow. Anyone got that much dough?' His veneers chattered as he laughed.

He then resumed his seriousness, raising his chin. 'But truly, it is a once in a lifetime experience just to behold it. Now, if everyone would like to queue up, we are letting groups of ten into the dressing room.'

Clementina, standing by the door, circled her finger in the air and counted the heads of ten people first to enter the room. It included Opal and Zsa Zsa, Mei Ling, David and six of the musicians.

Opal smiled delightedly. There was something exhilarating in the prospect of being close to something so inconceivably expensive, though she knew it was the 'gold goggles' effect. When an object is tagged with a princely sum, it wears an almost magical veil, making it seem far more desirable than it has any business being.

'He told me it weighs one hundred and six grams in total. Imagine having that around your neck!' Zsa Zsa whispered.

Clementina clasped the gold knob of the door and pushed it inwards and Opal entered the dark chamber.

A spotlight fell down from a singular chandelier in the centre of the room. It encircled a black plinth on which sat a black velvet bust. Clasped around the neck was the Apolline Diamond. It appeared as a blurry, scintillating halo of gold as Opal first regarded it.

When her sight managed to focus on the blinding object, the anchor of the necklace became visible in all its faceted glory. The size of a fat plum, its pavilion was sliced as deep as an infinity mirror. Its colour changed like rippling water from a rich honey to an acrid, champagne yellow.

The chain of the necklace was affixed with hundreds of oval-cut diamonds, ending in the formation of a lady's delicate hand, the fingers coming to a pinch, holding the grandiose yellow diamond between thumb and middle finger. *It's so exquisite! This isn't jewellery, it's art! This has got to win a medal!* Opal was completely bedazzled.

When all ten guests had surrounded the plinth, Clementina shut the door. Everyone inside was silent. Opal gawked at the jewels and it felt as intense as if she was staring deep into a flame. She didn't know how long she'd been there, but Clementina opened the door again and it was time for everyone to leave the dressing room.

Opal was the last to leave after Zsa Zsa's huge petal costume had managed to squeeze through the door frame. She turned her head to get one last glance at the necklace. *Goodbye beauty, you certainly are worth twelve million francs.* Once she'd ducked her hat under the door frame, Clementina pulled the door shut, leaving the necklace all alone and safe inside.

'Guess I'd better go and warm up now,' said Zsa Zsa, and Opal followed her to give her headdress one last primp.

They got to the end of the corridor when a loud scream could be heard. It sounded like it was one of the chorus girls. Shouting followed. Opal spun around. Everyone was looking inside the room with their hands plastered to their cheeks, mouths gaping wide.

Opal darted back to the chamber and looked inside. She blinked rapidly and rubbed her eyes. The Apolline Diamond was gone. Tiny particles of dust fibre from the velvet bust floated in the spotlight, as if to imply that the necklace had simply gone 'pouf'.

TWENTY-THREE
GONE

Opal froze amongst the sea of gasps and yells. *How in God's name could it be gone? Who out of the people who went inside the chamber with her could have taken it?*

Opal's arm was brushed as Mr Leon Dumoulin pushed to the front of the doorway. His jaw was shut so hard the muscles around it quivered. His eyes ballooned with a kind of devilish rage. He marched inside the room, followed by three members of his security team.

'The people who were just in this room, come back inside now!' his voice boomed.

Opal, Zsa Zsa, Mei Ling, David and the six musicians obeyed, heads bowed and arms folded.

'Shut the door behind us!' Leon yelled at Clementina. She slammed it shut.

One of Leon's arms was clenched tight around his waist, the other propped his head up. His eyes pierced the bare velvet bust with a stare that could have cut the bust in two.

'I've told my head of security to call the police and to lock the main doors of the theatre. All the guests have arrived now. The thief won't be able to get out. We will only let the police in,' Leon said in a far more serious voice than he had ever used. 'Now, I'm not insinuating any of you are responsible for this, but you will all have to be searched. You understand.'

'Yes, of course,' Opal said, along with a chorus of others.

Two of the white-gloved security guards got to searching people, while another walked around the edges of the room, looking high and low. There was nothing in the chamber apart from the plinth, the bust and the chandelier above. The walls were bare.

The security guard asked Opal to lift up her turban and next to pry open her bag. Her skirts were patted down. Once she was cleared, she decided to inspect the room herself.

She moved her nose close to the bust and scanned her eye over its surface. There were little indents in the velvet where the weighty diamond had made an impression. Moving her eyes down onto the plinth, she noticed something.

It was a cotton thread, about three inches long. It was dyed red at the tip, then changed colour to white and then to blue. A rapid flicker of her eyelids passed, her focus sharpening in response as she stared at it for a few more seconds. She then ducked and peered under the plinth. Nothing else strange. She stood up and eyed the walls of the dressing room. It didn't seem like there were any secret passages. She looked up, but the ceiling had no hatch or any means for escape.

Once the security guards had finished searching David and Zsa Zsa, they moved on to the musicians. One even had to dismantle the saxophone he'd brought in.

David was looking from the naked bust to Leon and back again, his linear mouth sloping in dread. Zsa Zsa rubbed Leon's back, who didn't seem to notice her at all.

'I just don't understand it,' Opal broke the silence. 'I was the last out of the room and it was still there when I looked! It's just vanished into thin air.'

'It reminds me of all the other crimes that have been

committed recently. Valentine's killer vanishing into thin air, the person who wrote the death threat on Clementina's bedstead disappearing like a puff of smoke. It's like there's some evil revenant doing these things.' Zsa Zsa put her hands on her cheeks, her eyes filling with tears.

'Zsa Zsa, be quiet,' Leon said in a dead tone. 'I'm trying work out what to do next.' He then stumbled and fell to his knees, beads of sweat oozing on his forehead.

'Leon?' Zsa Zsa cried. 'What do we do? What about the show?'

'Will the show go on?' Mei Ling chimed in, throwing her arms apart while being patted down.

'We've got twenty minutes until the curtain,' David summarised, looking at his watch. 'You've locked and manned the exits of the theatre. No thief can escape. Why don't you just let the show run while we and the police search for the necklace backstage? It might be found before the finale and Clementina can go on as normal.'

'You're right, you're right,' Leon said, looking barely lucid. 'Clementina can just wear another necklace for the finale if not. We'll find it. We have to. I couldn't bear the embarrassment of telling the exposition committee that it's been stolen.'

Opal exhaled. She was relieved that the show would go on, but she wasn't sure if Leon was thinking straight enough to handle this situation properly. He looked utterly spooked.

TWENTY-FOUR
CLEMENTINA LALONDE LA GRANDE REVUE

The auditorium was as red and full as the inside of a pomegranate, each ruby seat settling with a *derrière* of importance. In the centre of the front row were the judges of the 1934 Jewellery and Goldsmithing Exposition's Committee, crossing and uncrossing their legs expectantly. Chanel whispered something wicked to Josephine Baker and they tittered into their silk gloves.

The lights dimmed. A spotlight swung across the closed velvet curtain in time to the sweeping music and landed in the bottom right corner.

It encircled two chorus girls, their elegant limbs glowing a lilac-white. The girl on the right breathed and a psychedelic scintillation of diamonds peppered her beige leotard. The other chorus girl was wrapped like a spool of ribbon in a blue banner. Her partner held the end of the banner with one arm, the other arm she unfolded balletically above her head.

The strings in the pit spiralled upwards in a vortex and the banner-girl unwound herself, spinning on her heels in whipping chain turns across the stage, all the way to the other side. The banner's gold lettering was revealed as she did to read *Clementina Lalonde La Grande Revue.*

The heavy curtain lifted as the girl spun back, winding the banner up and departing with her partner. The Bakelite staircase was slowly revealed and gleamed like it had been built out of thirty slices of scorching sun.

A bloom of strings reversed the tone and quietened the audience's applause. A figure emerged at the top of the Bakelite staircase. It was Mei Ling.

She looked as if she was a new species of bird of paradise, with her feathered crest a blinding white. The eight doves seated on her arms cocked their heads up at her as if she was their avian sovereign.

She floated to the bottom of the steps, her Dumoulin jewels pricking her neck and ears with prisms. With a booming crescendo in the music, the doves flapped and flew to their gilt cage at the right of the stage as Mei Ling's chiffon gown fell to the floor.

The chorus girls flooded out from the wings and created a half-circle around Mei Ling with four-foot ostrich feather fans, swooping, ruffling and making synchronised patterns, their toes scurrying on white pointe shoes.

Opal was watching from the wings with a handful of hairgrips in her hand and some in her mouth, ready in case one of the girls came off and needed reinforcement of the heavy sculptures on their heads. She could see the right side of the front row if she craned. It was highly unprofessional to be seen by the audience but with the darkness it was unlikely anyone would see her.

The front rows were dim, and Opal couldn't quite make out the faces, until she saw a familiar one. Her breath caught in her throat.

She'd caught the glimpse of a blackish-purple T-shaped scar

on one of the faces. Her heart palpitated. *Why was he here? Did he have something to do with the stolen necklace?*

When Mei Ling's act was over, the curtain thudded onto the stage floor. Mei Ling's head fell forward with what looked like relief and ecstasy, and the stage manager, Claudette, ushered her off the stage.

Mei Ling glided shakily into the wings and was confronted by the white gloves of a security guard. He plucked the Dumoulin jewellery off her ears and throat and snapped them into a box. Opal helped Mei Ling off with the snowy avalanche of plumage that was her headdress. Mei Ling rubbed the sides of her neck in gratitude and departed into the blackness of the wings.

Zsa Zsa's headdress, the blooming rose about the circumference of a dinner plate, popped up behind the diamond handler's shoulder.

Opal grabbed her by the upper arms and hissed, 'T-Scar's in the audience.' She only realised she was shaking when the shakes transferred onto Zsa Zsa's arms, making the giant rose hat tremble.

'What?'

'Shhhhhh!' the stage manager hissed from the darkness of the wings.

'He's in the third row, eighth seat in from the right,' Opal said in a lowered tone. She knew she only had a few seconds to speak to Zsa Zsa before she went onstage.

'Are you sure?'

'Certain. Can you see if he's still there when you go on?'

'Okay, okay... just stay calm. I'll try, but I'll be dancing. Just remember this place is teeming with security and police, nothing can happen to you.'

'Yes, yes, I know...' Opal exhaled, realising she needed to be rational.

'I've got to go...'

'Oh, oh yes, of course... break a leg, Zsa Zsa!'

Zsa Zsa rustled away in her magnificent costume like a flower-nymph.

Opal crept quietly to the front end of the wings, to try and peer out and watch her friend. Since seeing T-Scar, she just wanted to stay as close to Zsa Zsa as she could. The lights had flooded the stage with a reddish hue, the music had become a snazzy bump-and-grind number with oboes and snare drum.

The backdrop was a painted mural of a giant tuxedo jacket. Standing in the bottom right corner was Zsa Zsa, the buttonhole rose. Her legs were together, representing the stalk of the flower, her head down, the headdress appearing as the epicentre of the bloom of her voluminous petal skirt.

She came alive with the strum of a harp. She came forward, swaying the huge circumference of her petal skirt to the timpani beats. The strings made withering, falling sounds as she plucked a petal that had been attached at the hip and threw it into the air.

When the act was over, Opal helped Zsa Zsa back up the stairs to their dressing room.

'You were amazing, Zsa Zsa. Did you hear the applause?' Opal jabbered, cradling Zsa Zsa's heavy headdress, which she'd insisted on removing as soon as she got off the stage.

'I didn't see him,' Zsa Zsa panted.

'What? T-Scar?'

'No, that seat you told me about was empty. The only one empty... Third row to the back, eighth seat in, right?'

'Yes, that was the one.'

'Empty.'

A strident, ragtime piano solo blasted out of the speakers in Zsa Zsa's dressing room, signalling the end of the interval. Opal jumped at the sound and hurriedly placed the finale headdress, a cluster of marabou pom-poms, like grapes, on Zsa Zsa's head.

'Was T-Scar's seat empty from the start of your act? Or did he leave sometime halfway through?' Opal asked.

'It was empty from the start. I looked as soon as I came onstage.' Zsa Zsa was patting her bare shoulders with a powder puff.

'Why would he leave after Mei Ling's act?' Opal said, lifting a hairpin, her hand shaking as if the pin had a voltage running through it.

'I don't know... Perhaps he's looking for Mei Ling?' Zsa Zsa said and looked Opal dead in the eye through the mirror.

'Where is she?'

'I don't know. She was supposed to have been getting into her finale costume, but she's not here.'

The girls looked at Mei Ling's costume hanging up behind them through the mirror. The embellished leotard swung very slightly as if a ghostly breeze was touching it.

The girls froze and looked back at each other in the mirror.

Their gaze broke when the intercom fizzed with Claudette's voice. Opal was used to this from dress rehearsals. Claudette would be sitting in the lighting booth at the back of the auditorium, overseeing the show and barking instructions for the tech crew that could be heard in all the dressing room intercoms. The difference this time was that her voice sounded panicked and her frantic breath caused muffled disturbances on the microphone.

'What the hell is going on? Can someone please report back to me... Is Clementina alright? Do I need to close the curtain?' Claudette screeched. Opal stared up at the intercom, her eyelids pulsing in alarm.

'What's going on?' Zsa Zsa said.

In a matter of thirty seconds, Opal and Zsa Zsa had flown down the stairs and were panting in the wings. At first Opal couldn't see anything out of the ordinary onstage. The chorus girls were still kicking and leaping in their elegant jellyfish-like costumes. They were facing the audience so wouldn't have noticed if there was something wrong.

Opal let go of Zsa Zsa's hand and glided to the next wing so she could get a clear view of Clementina. The front of the Salacia's Castle prop had already been lowered, revealing to the audience the front glass pane of the water tank.

Opal swallowed slowly. Now she understood why Claudette had been panicking. Clementina was not in her usual starting pose. She was usually head out of the water, wading and kicking her legs, arms in a 'V' shape, smiling brilliantly.

But now, she was submerged about a metre under the water, limbs flaccid and drooping below her torso. She turned in a very slow barrel-roll, her face rotating towards the front pane of glass. Opal stepped forward to get a better view and very slowly covered her mouth with her hand.

Clementina's face, with that beautiful heart-shape, was a translucent blue-white. A swollen, purple vein cracked her forehead in two. Her eyes ballooned and her lips were parted like a suffocated fish, emitting no air bubbles. It was quite obvious she was dead.

TWENTY-FIVE
ELLE EST MORTE

Opal felt Zsa Zsa grab both of her shoulders from behind and squeeze them. There was a wave of whispering sibilance in the auditorium. They were obviously realising something was wrong and it was not part of the show. The dancers had still not turned around and were continuing to perform, completely oblivious, like a kind of sinister circus. The conductor had not realised either and the musicians continued as normal. *Why is nobody doing anything?* Opal thought.

She and Zsa Zsa jumped as someone spoke in the darkness behind them. 'Close the curtain! Close the curtain!!' David hissed loudly. A technician swished past and disappeared again into the dark, then came the sound of squeaking levers.

The grand velvet curtain began to lower. One of the dancers looked up and nudged another. They inched backwards to get out of the way but continued to dance, bumping into some of the other girls behind them who stopped dancing in confusion. One of them turned to the back of the stage and slapped her mouth with both hands. There was a domino effect of screams and a couple of the girls dashed to the tank, others ran towards the wings.

The band whittled out in a cacophony to silence and the audience's volume increased to a thundering ruckus. There were a few camera flashes that just managed to get a shot under the curtain before it shut off the audience completely.

Zsa Zsa let go of Opal's shoulders and ran to the tank to join some of the other dancers, their faces and hands pressed against the glass. Opal stood as frozen as a piece of taxidermy, her eyes moved back and forth, witnessing the commotion. It just seemed so surreal.

Claudette emerged from the other side of the wings carrying a ladder. Joshua, Clementina's fiancé, ran out behind her and grabbed the ladder off her. He propped it up against the back of the tank and clambered up, his feet slipping several times in his desperation to get to the top.

Claudette tried to peel the girls away from the tank. 'Everyone go to the green room and stay there!' she shouted in desperation.

'Has anyone called an ambulance?' yelled Joshua from the top of the ladder.

'I'll get somebody to call them now!' screeched Claudette, running.

A woman's voice could be heard in the auditorium's speakers. Like a pleasant wireless announcement, she spoke in French then repeated in English: 'We apologise but there has been an emergency, and we must close the theatre. Please make your way to the exits. When you arrive at the exit please queue in an orderly fashion. You will each be checked by Security for a stolen item.'

Opal stepped back into the shadows as she saw Claudette herd a cluster of performers away. She slipped around into the next wing to avoid being told to leave with them. They disappeared through the exit to the outer corridor, the door closing and muting their wails. Opal looked back out at the commotion on the stage.

Joshua by this time had dived a few metres down into the tank to grab his girlfriend under her arm. He heaved her up so that her head was out of the water.

'Somebody help me!' Joshua yelled breathlessly, treading water.

David and a technician appeared from the other side of the tank and lurched at the ladder. David jumped on it first. At the top he reached his arms forward as far as he could and took Clementina's underarms from Joshua.

Joshua dove back underwater and heaved her up from her hips, David pulled her backwards. The technician and a dancer were at the bottom of the ladder reaching upwards in case David fell back with Clementina's weight.

'Make space!' David shouted when he got to the last rung of the ladder. Clementina lay in his arms, drips hammering down onto the stage from her fingers and toes. Her head lolled upside down and it seemed to Opal as if she was looking right at her, with shining glass eyes void of spark or spirit.

David laid her out in the centre of the stage floor, removed her diamond choker, tilted her head back trying to free up her air passage. A clatter of footsteps came from the other side of the stage curtain. The velvet whipped open in the centre and Leon Dumoulin slid through. He was followed by Augusto and four security guards.

'Is the ambulance coming?' a dancer shouted to them.

'Yes, it is on its way, what's happening? Is she alive?' Augusto demanded, hurrying over, kneeling down and putting his hands around Clementina's head.

Leon kept his distance, he watched silently as if in a disso-ciative nightmare. His jaw was clenched hard shut as if he was trying to prevent himself from bursting into hysterics.

David reached two fingers towards Clementina's neck. He drew them back an inch, as if dreading to find out the result. He then breathed in loudly through his nostrils and placed his fingers on her artery.

'She is dead,' he said.

TWENTY-SIX

THE GREEN ROOM

Opal hugged her own stomach. *No! Cousin Clementina!*

David took his fingers away from Clementina's neck and stood up, his head bowed.

'No!' Joshua yelled. He was soaked to the skin, rattling down the ladder. He slid on his knees to his girlfriend's body, pressing his fingers into her neck, then with a last desperate gasp, laid his ear to her heart.

'She's dead? How in God's name could it have happened like this? How could she just drown?' Joshua whimpered. He began to weep in short expulsions of air.

Everyone else was silent. All that could be heard above Joshua was the water in the tank gently lapping the glass sides.

'I will wait with Joshua and some security for the ambulance. Everyone else, congregate backstage in the green room,' Augusto said after a moment. He then turned to the dancer who'd helped Clementina down. 'Will you please tell everyone to stay in their dressing rooms until told to come out. Nobody is to leave until we say they can.'

Everyone dispersed in different directions and Augusto

noticed Opal in the wing's shadow. He walked over to her and gently grabbed her shoulder.

'You should wait in the green room until we know what to do. It'll all be okay, just stay calm. And best not tell anyone that she is dead yet.' His hands were warm and helped her shake off her catatonic stare.

'I think they all know she's dead,' Opal replied. 'They all saw her face.'

'Still, please say nothing.'

A barrel-chested policeman strode into the green room, hands knotted behind his back.

Opal was relieved, her leg had been jiggling with suspense for about an hour and a half and could finally relax. She wriggled her slouched back upright on the leather chesterfield and squeezed Zsa Zsa's hand, damp with tears.

'I assume everyone is here?' The policeman addressed Leon, who stood, ankles crossed in the corner. He nodded with his head propped up by an index finger and thumb.

'Good evening, everyone. I hope you are all okay. Two very awful things have happened this evening. The first was that the Apolline Diamond necklace disappeared, and the second was far, far worse an incident... As you may all already know, Clementina Lalonde is dead.'

Nobody in the room seemed to react to these words as it was what they all knew and had come to terms with in the past hour.

The policeman continued, 'You'll be escorted one by one to fetch only the belongings that are essential to you, like your handbags and money. All your other belongings must be left exactly as they are. You will be able to collect them in a few days' time. On the way out please give your address to my assistant so that you may be contacted if needed to make statements.'

The policeman stepped back and swept his palm to prompt Leon to speak. He rubbed his face with his hands, creating bloodless streaks on his cheeks, and cleared his throat with two raspy grunts.

'As for the show, which was going to run for another two weeks, it cannot go on as we do not have our starlet anymore.' He looked at the carpet. 'You will all still be paid your full wages for the entire run. Those of you not from Paris whose accommodation I have paid for, you may stay in Paris for the remaining weeks.'

Opal sensed Zsa Zsa twitch, as if wanting to go over and comfort him. But he turned and left the room swiftly. A policeman followed him out and shut the door behind him.

Opal waited in silence as people were escorted one by one out of the green room to go and collect their essential belongings. A gaggle of girls moved to reveal Mei Ling, leaning on the credenza in the corner of the room, still in her beautiful white dove costume. She was sharing a cigarette with Christophe. Christophe looked cool and collected. Not a crease on his white tie attire, though he had undone his collar. Opal took the opportunity to speak to them.

'Mei Ling.' Opal outstretched her arms and embraced the dancer, who accepted it warmly. 'Are you alright?'

'No, but I don't think anyone in this room is. Are you?'

'I... I will survive. But where were you? We expected to see you in the dressing room after Zsa Zsa's act. We thought you'd be getting into your finale costume.'

'I couldn't,' Mei Ling snapped and sucked hard on her cigarette. 'Mr Dumoulin had locked me in the atelier. He was berating me, thinking I had something to do with the stolen diamond.'

'Why would he think that?' Opal enquired.

'Something about my background. Who he *thinks* I am. But he's wrong.'

'Who does he think you are?'

'Never you mind, Opal,' chimed in Christophe. 'Who do you think *you* are, a detective?'

'I only came over to see if Mei Ling was alright,' Opal said and folded her arms in outrage.

'Well, I was in the atelier with her when Mr Dumoulin was questioning her. She is absolutely fine. He let us out when he realised he was being a fool.'

'Right. Well, I bid you a good evening.' Opal spun swiftly on her heel and walked away from them. There was no point trying to get anything out of them when they were in this unpleasant mood.

Opal noticed the usherette girls nattering with their elbows up on the bar. She blinked swiftly and listened to them. They were talking about how they would announce the news to all the celebrity attendees in the morning. Opal knew the usherettes had the list of the full attendees of the night. She narrowed her eyes and glided over to them.

'Excuse me, ladies, I know this question may seem a tad odd, but I desperately need to know something, and I would be much obliged if you were to assist,' she asked them in her politest voice.

The girls twisted their pillbox-shaped hats in her direction and looked down their neat noses at her curiously.

'What is it?' one of them asked.

'There was a man sitting on the third row, eight seats in on the right. Do you have his name on your seating plan?'

'Errr. Why?' the other one asked.

'I...' Opal peered over her shoulder and then back at the usherettes, hushing her voice. 'I have a man who's been following me and I saw him sitting there. I've never known his name so I wondered if you have a record of it?'

After a blinking pause, one of the girls got her seating plan out and started to tap her pen on it.

'Okay... that would be row C seat 8... Ah. That one was empty. A cancellation. A man who said he was a fan turned up and wanted a seat so we just let him in. It doesn't look good to have empty seats on press night, you see. There was only one and we must have given it to that person without getting their name.'

'Are you sure you didn't get his name?'

'*Non.* I'm sorry.'

'Do you remember him? He was very tall, a harsh purple scar on his cheek?'

'*Oui, oui*, that scar, I felt sorry for him. The scar was just so ugly and unfortunate.'

'Well, did you see him leave?'

'*Non*, mademoiselle. When all of this erupted, we were called to a meeting backstage and didn't see the guests leave.'

Opal sighed. Would she ever be able to get any information on this man? Perhaps the barrel-chested policeman would take her more seriously than Detective Inspector Prosper Delacroix. She sidestepped around a gaggle of dancers and tapped on the policeman's shoulder.

'Monsieur, monsieur... I need to report some suspicious behaviour...'

TWENTY-SEVEN

BLUE

The curtains in Opal's suite had been closed for two days running so there was no hint of whether it was day or night. She was lying flat in the four-poster next to a slumbering Zsa Zsa. Napoleon was passed out on her feet like a reverse footstool.

Opal's breath was shallow and quick, fuelling a freight train of thoughts about the horrid night her cousin died.

She rolled onto her back and let her arm loll off the side of the bed. She didn't want to leave Paris, but she might have to now. It would take a few days more for her telegram to reach her parents in Papua informing them of Clementina's death. And it would take another three days to get a reply, although the papers in Port Moresby may have covered the story by then.

Opal wedged her hands behind her backside and pulled herself up to a sitting position. She punched a few of the bolster cushions up, leaned back on them and folded her arms. Napoleon scrambled up onto her lap like a furry lap tray.

She knew one thing for sure. She wasn't going to give up on figuring out what happened. *I owe it to Clementina,* she thought. *I'm not sure I can live a fulfilled life without knowing I'd done everything I possibly could to avenge her.*

It would be a small consolation for missing out on having a cousin. Opal had only known her for a few weeks, and Clementina had been torn from her. And Valentine's family deserved the truth too. Meanwhile, the Apolline Diamond had not been found and Estelle was still missing.

No, Opal thought. *I can't leave Paris now. If only I knew where to start...*

She pulled a crunching newspaper from her bedside table onto her lap. Through the curtain of her unkempt hair, her eyes gazed at it. A patch of yellow light from the bedside lamp made it visible. *Diamond Heist and Dancer's Death* was the heading for the *Evening Standard*.

She had swiped a London paper at breakfast because she couldn't take more depressing Clementina Lalonde articles in the French papers. But evidently the incident had become an international story and it was the hot topic of the British news as well.

Zsa Zsa had evidently been stirred by the crunching sound of the newspaper and rolled to face Opal.

'Read it out,' Zsa Zsa said in a tone that you would use if listening to your own jail sentence.

'Hundreds have gathered at the Casino de Paris to pay their respects to the cabaret queen who died onstage on Friday, at the age of thirty-five,' Opal read out faintly.

The first image on the page was the snapshot the blaggard photographers had taken of Clementina in the tank before the curtain fell. It was grotesque but the only dignified blessing was that her hair was floating in front of her face. Underneath was a more respectful photo, showing the hordes of people who had turned up. Many of them were female fans, Clementina-looka-likes, shivering in their Clementina emulation furs, embracing each other.

'The heist and the death must be connected, don't you reckon?' Zsa Zsa said.

'I have an inkling it is, yes. Let me read the coverage about the diamond.' Opal cleared her throat and turned the page.

'*The Apolline Diamond, the renowned Dumoulin necklace, valued at twelve million francs, disappeared as if by sorcery last night from a room in which it was being viewed. Detective Prosper Delacroix, leading the inquiry, remarked, "It seems the work of a magician. But possibly an inside job and publicity stunt."*'

'A publicity stunt? Leon Dumoulin has had to reimburse buyers of thirty-six thousand tickets for the two-week run. Why would he lose all that money for publicity? It doesn't make sense!' Zsa Zsa said outraged.

'That Prosper Delacroix *would* say it was a publicity stunt,' Opal snarked. 'He takes everything at face value. I think he's wrong. I saw Leon's face; he was devastated and dumbfounded. Prosper can't work out how it was done, so it's just like him to make accusations like that.'

Opal's eyelids flapped, not unlike a small sail in a sudden gust, and peered at the photograph of the magnificent necklace printed in the paper. 'What will the thieves do with the necklace now they've got it?' she pondered. 'They could have wanted simply the necklace itself, or revenge on Leon, or the cash. But how would they sell a distinct necklace like that without it being discovered later?'

Zsa Zsa coughed weakly and pointed to the bottom paragraph of the article. 'It's explained here; diamond thieves launder the stones through middlemen until they are clean enough for a legitimate jeweller to set them in new jewellery. Thefts of this scale are becoming easier to liquidate. Another tactic is to sell to foreign princes on the down-low.'

'I see.' Opal nodded, petting Napoleon's ear.

The telephone trilled next to Zsa Zsa's pillow. Matted, black spirals of hair fell over her face as she heaved herself upright to take it.

'Oh... finally. It must be Leon,' she croaked.

'I *told* you he'd be in touch,' Opal said, relieved that Zsa Zsa would stop fretting about not hearing from him.

'He asks if we're okay and if we want to meet him and Clementina's beau, Joshua, at Angelina on the Rue de Rivoli at three. He says that Joshua doesn't know many people in Paris and it would be good for him to have some company between now and Clementina's funeral. Losing his fiancée has got to be very hard.'

'We need to go. We've been festering in here for two days. We need to get out and do something. I wonder if they know any more about Clementina's death?' Opal said.

Zsa Zsa thudded back down on her pillow and moaned. 'Oh... I don't think I want to go. I'm so blue. After we're allowed to collect the rest of our things from the theatre I might just go back to Stepney Green. I mean... what is there left here for us? The show's cancelled. I didn't get any press. No future job offers.'

Opal's toes curled in a fit of dread. A fresh wave of anxiety had crashed upon her. If Zsa Zsa hightailed it back to London, what hope was there for their friendship without the glue of the Casino de Paris? She had to do everything in her power to keep Zsa Zsa in Paris; after all, they had mysteries to unravel, and losing her newfound friend was simply out of the question.

'Leon has paid for our rooms already. We've got another fortnight. We still get paid for the entire run. We don't need to be back in London. I think Leon needs you and we should stay,' Opal said.

'He ignored my calls for two days.'

'That's completely normal, his friend has just died, his diamond's been stolen. Let alone the huge monetary loss of the show. And imagine how busy he'd be with it all. Stop being such an insufferable prima donna.' Opal poked her friend with a fingernail and Napoleon puffed his nostrils in agreement.

'Ouch. Urgh. I guess you're right. Blimey, I don't know if I even have the energy to get dressed.'

'Have a cigarette, Zsa Zsa.' Opal winked.

TWENTY-EIGHT
ANGELINA

At three o'clock in the afternoon, two English women sat opposite two American men. Opal Laplume, Zsa Zsa Desmarais, Leon Dumoulin and Joshua Davenport sat under a pastoral mural of the South of France, while waiting for their orders at Pâtisserie Angelina. The sound of scores of teaspoons stirring in teacups and scraping the inside of ice-cream glasses tinkled above the humming vocal cords of satisfied customers.

Opal rubbed her lips together as the smell of rich confectionary wafted over her shoulder. The waiter clinked a plate down onto the marble table. *Now this is just so Parisian,* Opal thought as she visually consumed the whopping, cameo-pink coloured macaroon. About a dozen raspberries and thick cream was wedged inside with meticulous piping. On top was sprinkled violet petals and a solitary, plump, cerise raspberry. Napoleon's blackcurrant nose twitched as he eyeballed the sweet from under the table.

Opal's eyes scintillated at the sorbet creation that was placed in front of Zsa Zsa. Apricot and peach boules were ice capped with meringue and tufts of whipped cream.

The waiter was pouring Joshua's thick *chocolat chaud* from

a silver pitcher into his teacup. If the consistency was any thicker it would have been a pudding. Joshua seemed to look right through the chocolate into the bottom of the cup, his high-set eyebrows paralysed.

'I thought some sugar and gateaux would cheer us all up a bit,' Leon said, slicing his croissant in half with a knife. His pallor was the colour of cold tea and his smile wavered up and down as if he was fighting to not look miserable.

'It was a great idea,' Zsa Zsa said softly, touching his sleeve. 'Thank you for getting us out of the Hôtel Reinette.'

'I concur,' Opal joined in. 'We've been awfully wretched cooped up in that room.'

There followed a silence in which Opal could feel Joshua's gloom. His fiancée, the beautiful Clementina, was dead and there was nothing anyone could do about it. He sipped a minuscule amount of his *chocolat* and winced as if it was salty rather than sweet.

'It's just impossible,' he muttered.

'I know, I know, it's so hard to believe she's gone,' Leon consoled.

'No, not that...' He shook his elfin head. 'It's impossible what the medical examiner told me.'

'Oh...' Opal looked up at him and gave a quick little blink. 'What did you find out?'

'Well, I knew Clementina used to use this medication to help her sleep. It was a type of nasal vapour called Nictoform. She suffered terribly from insomnia. She had a private doctor that prescribed her this when she was really suffering and nothing else helped. It's actually illegal and not prescribed by normal doctors because it's so potent. It's pretty much a general anaesthetic. After inhaling it, it takes roughly twenty minutes to knock you unconscious.' He paused and picked up his spoon, expelled a pocket of air from his chest, then continued, 'The toxicologist found it in her system the night she died.'

'Oh my God,' Zsa Zsa breathed.

'What do the police think happened?' Opal asked, unable to blink, she was listening so hard.

'They think she took the Nictoform during the interval. While the curtain was down the tank was wheeled onto the stage. She got inside it and the castle prop was erected around it to conceal it. While she waited in the water, the Nictoform in her system would have sent her to sleep and she would have slipped down and drowned while all the chorus girls were dancing at the front of the stage. Of course, none of us in the wings or audience could have seen her slip under because the tank was concealed. It was only when the front panel was lowered to reveal the tank that she could be seen, *twenty* minutes into the act... dead.'

'Oh God, why on earth would she take the drug before her performance?' Zsa Zsa asked.

'That's the impossible thing. She didn't. I was with her and watching her the entire time at the theatre. You know how anxious we all were after the death threat. So since arriving in Paris I'd been at her side constantly. She never inhaled the Nictoform and I never even saw the bottle of it. She'd lost it. She had been looking for it for days. She'd been trying to call a private doctor of hers to get some more, but he was away visiting family in China.'

'That is so, so odd,' Opal said. 'I remember her saying that she was looking for her vapour at the absinthe soirée. So you think someone took it and perhaps administered it to her in the interval?'

'That would be my hunch.'

'Was the Nictoform bottle found anywhere in the theatre by the police?' Opal asked.

'No. I just don't understand any of it.'

'Perhaps the bottle just hasn't been found yet?' Opal hesitated before asking the next thing on her mind. 'She... wasn't suicidal, was she?'

'No way. She had been dreaming of headlining at the Casino de Paris all her life. She would never want to ruin it,' Leon said very assuredly.

'She was always talking about the future and planning every last detail of our wedding, down to the serviette ties,' Joshua added. 'Clem was not suicidal.'

'And what about the death threat?' Opal asked. 'And the connection to Valentine, Estelle vanishing and then the Apolline Diamond going missing? Those incidents could support the probability she was murdered.'

'I'm hoping the police will be able to get to the bottom of it. Detective Inspector Prosper Delacroix seems to think it was suicide or an accident. But there is no way Clementina would have done this to herself. She was at the very apex of her career and engaged!'

'He's an indolent man. He put Valentine's death down to the same things,' Opal said with a sniff.

'Well, he's our only hope,' Joshua said.

'Nonsense. You have Napoleon and me on the case,' Opal said, stirring a little whirlpool in her tea.

The other three at the table exchanged faintly amused smiles.

'Can you go through the events during the interval, step by step?' Opal asked. 'The answer has to be in that.'

'Well, let me see... we were with Christophe in the dressing room. He always insisted on dressing her himself. He gave her a little pep talk and said "*merde*", apparently that's the equivalent of "*break a leg*" in French. Then I held her hand and we walked her down the stairs because it was hard in that costume.

'Then,' continued Joshua, 'David came over and said that he had been out in the foyer during the beginning of the interval and that everyone was raving about how great the show was and an avid fan had given him a gift for Clementina. David said that this fan had wanted Clementina to receive it immediately for good luck. It was a single rose. She took it and read the notelet.'

Joshua stopped and tapped his spoon on the table to try and remember more. 'David was then talking about how he was sure the water was the right temperature for her. He took the ladder out there for her to get up into the tank. I told her how wonderful she was going to be and how much I loved her. David then helped her up into the tank and that was that. Then I went to my seat in the auditorium to watch.'

Opal made a mental note to speak to Christophe and David and hear their version of events during the interval.

'The woman who died from the drug she never took,' Zsa Zsa mused, pouting. 'It certainly sounds impossible.'

'Well, I'm sure the police will find some rational explanation,' Leon said, a flake of croissant falling from his lips. 'I'm glad you girls haven't gone straight back to London. I need you here for moral support.'

'Oh, Leon. You've had some terrible luck. I can't believe Delacroix told the papers that the diamond heist could have been a publicity stunt.'

'He's a moron,' Leon said, his knuckles turning white as he clenched his knife and fork. 'Why would I orchestrate this? I already have enough publicity for my jewellery, and have lost a fortune on this venture. Why would I put myself in this position?'

'I have a hat repair saga going on with him. At this rate his homburg is looking more like an iceberg.' Opal snorted. 'But I have to get it right for Laplume Millinery's reputation.'

'Well, I don't want to see that half-wit chump ever again.' Mr Dumoulin dabbed the corners of his mouth with his serviette.

'I was meaning to ask you, Mr Dumoulin,' Opal said. 'Zsa Zsa and I were a little spooked when Mei Ling told us you locked her in the atelier the night of the show thinking she had something to do with the missing diamond.'

Mr Leon Dumoulin fidgeted in his seat and showed his pearly veneers in a mildly embarrassed way. 'Yes, I saw red when the diamond went missing. I had a suspicion that Mei Ling might have something to do with the heist. Because of the tattoo you girls described to me...'

Opal leaned forward and almost got cream on her blouse. 'What is the significance of it?'

'It's the symbol of a Russian crime family in the under-world. An auction house in Saint Petersburg was stormed by them last year and one of my pieces was taken. They're known to have that tattoo and to use young people and women to do their dirty work. When you first told me she had that tattoo I just kept an eye on her. My security team is very strong so I didn't worry too much beforehand.'

'Blimey... Mei Ling? A member of the criminal under-world?' Zsa Zsa said, and fired up her lighter with a swift thumb gesture.

'She burst into tears and said she had indeed been kidnapped by them two years ago while dancing for a Russian circus. She went on the run across Europe and has tried to put it behind her. She said she had nothing to do with the diamond going missing.'

'Did you believe her?' Opal asked, her eyes as wide as they would open.

'I half did. Christophe was in the atelier with us and calmed me down and told me that we had searched her and there was not much more we could do until the show was over.'

'I guess we would have found the diamond on her if she was planted to steal it,' Opal said, strumming her nails on her teacup. 'But Mei Ling isn't really connected to the string of murders. Valentine was killed before Mei Ling even came on the scene. And we don't know for sure if Valentine's death,

Estelle's disappearance, and Clementina's murder have anything to do with the stolen diamond.'

'All we need is a clue to connect it all,' Joshua said. He'd barely touched his *chocolat* and was staring absently into the mural on the wall.

Napoleon started to yap at a sparrow that had landed on a table outside the window. He put his paws on the brass ledge and pulled himself up to standing. As Opal wrestled with his collar to bring him back down, she noticed across the street a sign, shining in green and gold lettering.

'*Pharmacie*,' it read. Her lids flicked closed and open again as she wondered what she could find out in there about Nictoform.

TWENTY-NINE
THE CLUE OF THE RUSTED PIN

The girls, with dog in tow, exited Angelina's. Opal grabbed Zsa Zsa's arm and pulled her across the street to where she'd noticed the pharmacy. Their feet tottered over the cobbles at twice their normal speed and Napoleon cantered confidently behind.

A bell tinkled as they stepped inside. Rows and rows of blue glass bottles lined the walls behind the counter. The smell of iodine reminded Opal of the sanatorium at school. Napoleon whined as it evidently reminded him of his veterinary clinic. A young pharmacist with horn-rimmed glasses was crushing something with a marble pestle and mortar. *Tap, tap, crunch, swivel, tap, tap, crunch.*

'*Excusez-moi*, monsieur,' said Opal politely, then continued in her best French, 'I was wondering if you could help me... you see... I have terrible insomnia. Someone suggested Nictoform. I have no idea what this is and wonder if you could tell me about it.'

'Nictoform? I know it well as I used to work at the dentist's. It has been taken off the market. I am sorry, mademoiselle, we cannot stock it anymore, I'm afraid.'

'Oh... why was it taken off the market?'

'Its potency is dangerous,' he said, while beating away with the marble pestle. 'Nictoform is a colourless and scentless vapour. It was originally developed as a general anaesthetic delivered via inhalation. It is most commonly used in dentistry, but there has been a demand for it on the black market as a sleeping agent.'

'I see. How long does it take to take effect?'

The tap, tap, crunch of the mortar and pestle stopped.

'Why all the questions? I said we don't sell it.' He looked up and squinted intently.

'It's very important that I know,' Opal said, folding her hands over the top of her handbag and lifting her nose in the air like she'd seen her mother do when trying to get her own way. Her mother would then usually say 'Do you know who I am?', but as this was Paris and not many people would give a blithering fig that Opal was an Honourable, she didn't follow it up with this.

'I'm not going to discuss unauthorised chemicals with you.'

Opal scanned the shelves behind him.

'May I please have some lip pomade by Labello. The one in the stick form. I've never seen it packaged like that before, isn't that interesting,' Opal said and got out the largest franc note she had. 'You may keep the change if you're willing to help me with a little bit of pharmaceutical knowledge.'

The young man tossed the pomade on the counter and plucked the note out of Opal's hand with a disapproving glance over his horn rims.

'My employer is due back any moment and I do not want to be overheard talking black market soporifics with a couple of young ladies, thank you very much.'

He then gave Opal the correct change and went back to pulverising his powder. Zsa Zsa was busy spritzing the perfume samples on her fur. Napoleon was starting to get bored and was pawing at a jar of lavender bath salts on a low shelf. Opal put her foot between him and the bath products, but this did give her a bright idea.

'Monsieur, I will be honest with you. I am anxious to know about how long it takes Nictoform to take effect because I have a friend who is currently in the bath in our hotel and she took Nictoform shortly before getting in. I told her I didn't think it was a good idea and a drowning hazard, but she ignored me.'

'Mademoiselle!' The man pushed his glasses up onto the bridge of his nose. 'This is indeed very dangerous, you must go at once to check on her. Is she alone?'

'She is indeed alone. How long does she have before she falls unconscious?'

'Roughly fifteen to twenty minutes. Go, go, mademoiselle.'

'Oh, she only took it right before we came in. So we have a few minutes. What does it feel like when you take it?' Opal asked, blinking in interest.

'At the dentists, before falling unconscious the patient would experience dizziness, breathlessness and sometimes muscle weakness. Did she start to feel these?'

'She didn't say. How long were dentistry patients out for?'

'Between four and six hours. Now please, mademoiselle, go and check on your friend in case it has kicked in sooner. And suggest to her that she should be using something like veronal. Much less potent. And not to use it in the bath.'

'Thank you kindly, monsieur, I will go back and get her out of the bath.'

With that, Opal scurried to the exit, pretending she was in a hurry. She took Zsa Zsa's furry and pungently perfumed arm and pulled her out of the shop. The bell tinkled frantically as Opal shut it with pretend haste.

'What's the hurry?' Zsa Zsa asked in surprise, checking with her hands to see if her hair had fallen out of place.

'I had to spin some yarn to get information about Nicto-form,' Opal said. They were still in front of the pharmacy but shielded behind a window display so that the pharmacist couldn't see them. She then got her sketchbook out and scribbled everything the pharmacist had said about Nictoform.

'Clementina must have had pretty bad insomnia to be taking black market drugs for it,' Zsa Zsa acceded, getting out her lipstick and swooping it over her bottom lip in a compact mirror. Her elbow brushed over her chest as she did so and a clatter noise sounded on the cobblestones.

It was the half-moon costume brooch that Clementina had given Zsa Zsa.

'Oh dear, I thought I'd fixed it! I managed to straighten the pin but it's still coming unclasped,' Zsa Zsa screeched.

'Let me see if *I* can fix it,' Opal said, putting her sketchbook away, plucking the brooch off the ground and turning it over in the palm of her hand.

Opal blinked once, then twice, steadying her gaze on the pin. She focused on the rusted tip. The brown rusty substance on it was cracked and flaky. Her brain jigged and she gasped. She looked into Napoleon's deep-brown eyes and thought hard. The dog tilted its curly head back at her.

'What?' Zsa Zsa said.

'Zsa Zsa...' Opal said. 'This brooch pin *isn't* rusted.'

'What? Yes, it is, it's all brown. What are you on about, you ninny?'

'Not a *rust* brown though. And look! It peels off the pin to reveal silver underneath. Rust doesn't do that.'

'And?' Zsa Zsa said, puckering her lips in bemusement.

'It's *wood varnish!*' Opal exclaimed; she could feel her eyes pulse.

'And?' Zsa Zsa repeated herself with identical bemusement.

Opal ignored her and riffled in her handbag. She pulled out a tissue from a zipped pocket. Inside was the flake of wood varnish she'd taken off Clementina's headboard that night after the death threat. She held the varnish chips flat in her palm and placed the brooch, pin upwards, next to it.

'See... the varnish on the pin is identical to the varnish I peeled off Clementina's headboard. The note was scrawled with *this* brooch pin.'

Zsa Zsa clapped closed her compact mirror and blinked at Opal's palm. 'How does that help us find out who scrawled the note?'

'It's very odd...' Opal lowered her voice to a whisper, remembering they were on a public street. 'You remember when we met Clementina outside her apartment at eight o'clock? She'd just come back from the shops with cocktail ingredients. She was wearing this brooch. So, if this brooch pin was used to scrawl the note, the note must have been written *before* she left for the shops.'

Zsa Zsa pouted vacuously. Napoleon whined and pulled on his lead in the direction of the Tuileries Garden.

Opal continued, 'Clementina must have scrawled the note *herself!*'

Zsa Zsa and the dog blinked at her. Opal sighed.

'She didn't go into her bedroom all night while we were there. Neither did anyone else. The brooch fell off her at the end of the party. Then she went into her bedroom. After discovering the death threat, she swore the note definitely wasn't there when she left for the shops. She said it must have been done while she was *at* the shops.'

'So? I'm confused.'

'*So...*' Opal whispered, exasperated, 'she *lied* to us. It was scratched with her own brooch *before* she left.'

'Why would she lie?'

'I don't know.' Opal paused. 'But she wanted us to believe it was a *genuine* death threat. Perhaps the whole reason she'd thrown a soirée was to have us witness her discovering it.'

'Goodness gracious, Opal, you're positively giving me brain

ache. Why on earth would she write a *fake* death threat to *herself*?'

'I mean, it would get her out of the suspect line for Valentine's murder... but she wasn't really a suspect in the first place, so I don't think it is that.'

'But how do you explain Clementina's death then? If she wrote the note herself, would that imply that she committed suicide by taking the Nictoform and wanted everyone to think it was murder?'

'I don't think it was that either. She wasn't suicidal, and the Nictoform bottle hasn't been found at the theatre.'

'What then? Why would she write her *own death threat*?'

The horn-rimmed spectacles of the pharmacist slowly rose above the shop window display. He eyed Opal with a mixture of concern and perplexity at why she hadn't run off to save her friend from drowning in the bath.

Opal bared her teeth and tweaked her fedora at him, before pulling her entourage out of sight down the street. She stopped again in front of the next shop and turned to continue her brooch discussion.

'Remember the words used in the death threat, "*Don't sleep alone... You'll be next to die.*" I think there's a clue in the words. There must be, otherwise why would she have chosen those specific words?'

THIRTY
IMPROMPTU MILONGA

'Ah, here are the London girls, monsieur,' said the plump receptionist from behind the desk, waving her wine glass in their direction.

Augusto turned his head and nodded at them each in turn. 'Opal! Zsa Zsa. Napoleon.'

'Augusto!' Opal smiled at him with warmth, rather pleased that he'd said her name before Zsa Zsa's. Napoleon trotted over to Augusto, his theatre babysitter, and sat to attention, tail sliding back and forth on the varnished tiles.

'Good afternoon, girls. I came to see if you're alright.' He ruffled the dog's head, stood up and held his trilby to his chest, his chin more stubbled than usual.

'That is kind. We've just come back from a tea with Mr Dumoulin and Clementina's fiancé, Joshua. It was quite miserable,' Opal said.

'I was wondering if you'd like to go and watch the milonga under the Eiffel Tower with me, mademoiselles? And the little curly gentleman on the leash, of course.'

'What's a milonga?' asked Opal intrigued.

'Oh, it's a tango dance event. There is an impromptu one

happening now with a handful of musicians and dancers. It's rather quite a sight. I might sketch it.'

'No, no,' Zsa Zsa said. 'I'm going up to write home to my old man, but you go, Opal.'

Opal knew her friend had sensed the frisson and had ducked out to let her get some alone time with the handsome Spaniard.

'I'd be delighted. I've never heard anything like it!' Opal said and blinked acceptingly. 'Napoleon would too, of course... he has missed his Marshal Augusto. In fact, I may go up and fetch a beret to wear. For an activity as French as this I must go dressed accordingly. Will you wait one moment with his lead?'

As Opal ascended the stairs she wondered whether this afternoon she'd get an inkling as to whether Augusto had taken a liking to her. Not that she would be able to entertain any kind of real dalliance with such a man. Her mother would positively skin her alive. But he was the first male of the species she'd ever truly felt any connection to. He was just so hard to read...

Half an hour later, Opal found herself on a bench next to Augusto. Their sketchbooks open on their laps, charcoal in Augusto's confident hand and lipstick crayon in Opal's tentative one. Napoleon's leash was anchored by the bench but it didn't stop him from rising onto all fours and twirling in emulation of the dancers under the Eiffel Tower.

The vast, wrought-iron latticework of the monument created the drapery of an imaginary royal court for tango. The band, a ragtag assembly of virtuosos that looked as if they'd been procured from a jumble sale, played hypnotic Argentine tango, something utterly alien to Opal's ears. The dancing couples were a circular current of Parisian bohemians, the petite bourgeoisie and the odd tourist with a questionable grasp of rhythm.

Opal was utterly transfixed on sketching the charming accordion player in his silk top hat. His notes sailed through the late spring air, mingling with the strumming of the guitarist, whose fingers danced across the strings like a tipsy spider. The violinist, a woman with a plum beret and peasant blouse, provided a soulful undercurrent, occasionally breaking into a spirited jig.

It was easier to draw the musicians than the dancers who were rotating and undulating. Augusto was far better at capturing the milonga as he sketched fast and impressionistic. He had focused on drawing a woman in a beautiful flowing cape dress with butterfly sleeves. She was a blur of red but her legs made strong angular lines as they stepped forth and kicked back unpredictably. Opal felt a tad sorry for her partner, a monocled, diminutive chap in a morning suit who would be whipped in the face on occasion by her long beads.

'She's going to smash his monocle with her necklace if she's not careful,' Opal said, and tittered.

'I think she needs you to design her a hat,' Augusto said and handed her his sketchbook.

'Oh, I simply couldn't deface it,' said Opal in politeness, though she really did enjoy the co-working exercise that they had invented.

'You can only improve it with your talent.' He smiled with his dark eyes, and Opal could almost see how happy she looked inside them they were so reflective.

Opal looked back down at the sketchbook. He was so dashing it was hard to look away. She didn't let her mind interfere with her hand and just started drawing, in the red waxy pastel, a kind of pillbox with flowing plumage emerging from its centre.

'Had you worked with Clementina for a long time?' Opal took the opportunity to probe him.

'I've been her bodyguard for about three years.' His voice

became hollow and sad. 'I feel like I've failed. I was supposed to protect her.'

'It's not your fault, there's nothing you could have done.'

'I know.' He sighed and looked over at the musicians as if for some inspiration to change the subject, but he seemed to be struggling.

'So, who are you going to work for next?' Opal asked in a brighter tone.

'Well, Mr Dumoulin might make me part of his security team... We'll see.'

'What do you think of Mr Leon Dumoulin? What's he like to work for?' Opal asked.

'I like Leon very much. Apart from thinking his veneers look a little silly, I respect him. He has a lot of power and seems to handle it well and doesn't abuse it.'

'I concur,' Opal said. 'He doesn't seem to take himself too seriously either.'

'I'm surprised you're still in Paris, Opal. Didn't you want to go home after everything that's happened?'

Surprised or pleasantly surprised? Opal thought but didn't have the gumption to ask this.

'Well, I am awaiting a telegram from my parents, who are on the other side of the world. It will take several days. Leon's already paid for the hotel room for the length of the show's run, so I'm staying for the time being. We still need to collect our belongings from the theatre when the police have finished investigating. So, there's quite a few reasons to stay.'

'What on earth has been happening this past month?' Augusto shook his head and his dimpled chin brushed his cravat back and forth.

'I don't know. But I'm dying to find out,' Opal said.

She was also dying to impress Augusto with her new discovery about the brooch pin and the death threat, but she could not be one hundred per cent certain she could trust him just yet, though his gentle disposition made her want to think she could.

She looked back down at the sketchbook and, with her lipstick, she daubed the dancing gentleman's monocle over his eye in one finishing stamp.

'Bravo, Mademoiselle Laplume.' Augusto clapped. 'We must do a series of these. All over Paris.'

'That would be top-notch,' Opal said, scrunching her toes in excitement. Perhaps it was his way of saying he liked her, or perhaps he just wanted an illustration buddy. But she was thrilled either way.

'I think it's time we joined the milonga, Mademoiselle Laplume. Have you danced the tango before?' Augusto stood up above her and looked down over his protruding silk cravat at her.

'I most certainly have not.' Opal gulped, but reached her hand out to take his before she could stop herself.

'Not a problem at all. I shall lead.'

Before Opal could take a preparatory breath, Augusto had swirled her into the tango traffic. His hand on the small of her back, pulled her closer than she had ever been before to him. She smelt the faint mixture of cigars and Brilliantine in his cravat. She held onto his warm shoulder and hand as tight as she could as her feet barely touched the ground.

'Gosh, Augusto,' Opal shrieked. 'You seem to be very well seasoned.'

'Oh, I learnt in Spain. Don't resist me with your hand. Feel the direction.'

'This is nothing like the foxtrot,' Opal said.

'Of course it isn't. It is Latin.'

A delicious warmth spread over her, like she was touched by the Iberian sun. With it, the nagging sensation of being dreadfully alone, which had hitherto clung to her for years like an ill-fitting garment, seemed to dissolve, leaving her feeling seen and safe in the arms of this man.

The vibrant song ended, and another more sombre and strict tango strummed up. Augusto slowed his pace and Opal thought she'd take the opportunity to probe Augusto further on his thoughts on the murders.

'So, what do you think about Clementina's death?' she asked, treading on Augusto's toe by accident. 'Oh, I do apologise. Clementina's fiancé swears blind she didn't take the Nictoform, though it was found in her blood. The police seem to think she took it to calm her nerves or to commit suicide even. But the problem is, they didn't find the bottle. If she took it herself, they would have found it somewhere.'

Augusto's hand grip stiffened. 'As I said before, Opal, I was Clementina's bodyguard and the fact that this happened to her, whether it was self-induced or not, is hard going and I'm still coming to terms with the fact she's dead. I'm not thinking about how it happened.'

'Do forgive me, I just wanted to know whether you thought it was suspicious. Whether someone could have administered the drug somehow?'

'Well, she received a death threat and now she's dead. What are we supposed to think?'

Opal thought again of telling him about the brooch, and the likelihood that Clementina had written the death threat herself. But she still didn't know who she could trust. Besides, it would probably sound like balderdash, as she still hadn't discovered the reason *why* Clementina would have written it to herself.

'I guess after such a long time you must have got to know her exceedingly well,' she said instead.

'I did know her well. She was very close to the people she worked with. David, Christophe. But I can't imagine why anyone would want to kill her.'

'Hmmm,' Opal mused. 'The only people Clementina interacted with during the interval were Joshua, Christophe and David. What was her relationship like with each of them?'

'I believe there was something funny going on between her and David.'

'Oh?' Opal blinked speedily and listened intently over the music.

'Well, David and Clementina would meet at Lapérouse every now and again. I thought that was odd. David is just the set designer and they'd never gone out together in the past, not until summer this year.'

'What is Lapérouse?'

'It's a historic Parisian restaurant. Perhaps they were talking business or having an affair even.'

'Oh?'

'Who knows what people get up to. But it's not like her fiancé Joshua would have ever found out about it, being in New York.'

Opal thought back to when she saw Clementina and David chatting at the absinthe soirée. Their body language was pretty ambiguous. Then again, perhaps they wouldn't want to show affection in public, if they were having an affair. Opal made a mental note to pop into Lapérouse to ask if any of the staff noticed anything.

Suddenly there was a ruckus at the opposite end of the milonga circle. Opal peeked over Augusto's shoulder. Napoleon, keen to join in, was jumping on his hind legs and pulling the wooden bench along with him. The sketchbooks they'd left on the seat jittered as it dragged along.

'Napoleon!' Opal shrieked in delight and humour. 'I'm not sure the bench wants to dance with you.'

She dashed through the dancers to where a bunch of people had stopped to laugh at the silly pooch. The band clashed and tinkered to silence and Augusto helped unloop Napoleon and drag the bench back into place.

The lady in red that Augusto had drawn, saw her picture and picked it up.

'I adore this. I'd do anything for a hat like that!'

'Oh, I can make one for you. Take my business card. Laplume Millinery in London. But we can ship anywhere.' Opal wasn't going to miss an opportunity to get her name out.

'Thank you, my dear,' she said and took it with scarlet nails. She then turned her gaze on Augusto. 'You dance with the soul of a *porteño! Eres Argentino?*'

'*Non. Soy de España,*' he replied, shaking his head.

'You are about as Spanish as a gauchos' poncho!' the woman retorted with her hands on her hips and narrowed eyes. She was determined to prove he was Argentinian but only in jest.

'I'm sorry to disappoint you, madame. But I am not Argentinian,' Augusto said firmly and sternly.

Opal was a little taken aback at how the woman's comment seemed to irk Augusto so much. *Was he hiding something?*

'Opal, we've worked up an appetite. Why don't we go to a crêperie?'

'Indeed, I could eat a horse after all that. But... you mentioned Lapérouse... where Clementina and David would rendezvous. It sounded ever so historic and interesting. Could we perhaps go there?'

'We are not dressed for such an establishment, mademoiselle.'

'Well perhaps we can book a table, get changed and then meet there? I mean, it's only five thirty now.'

'Alright, *señorita.*'

He called me señorita. Opal scrunched her toes in excitement. *Now what on earth should I choose to wear?*

THIRTY-ONE
LAPÉROUSE

Opal had chosen to wear the purple ruffled taffeta gown she'd worn to the opening night of the Casino de Paris. There might not be another nice enough opportunity to wear it. She'd paired it with a midnight-blue cloche, the heavy beading of it creating a waterfall down the left side of her face. She thought she could make sultry looks up at Augusto in it with heavily shadowed lids.

They had booked dinner for eight o'clock but took the opportunity for a sundowner in the bar first. The Lapérouse bar was tucked away in a secluded alcove of the restaurant. The walls were lined with rich mahogany panels which exuded the scent of polished wood. Behind the bar, rows of gleaming bottles stood like sentinels, their contents jewel colours of amber, ruby, green and gold.

Augusto, his shoulders looking broad in his dinner suit, pulled back a stool and Opal perched upon it. Napoleon, freshly brushed, settled at her feet and placed one paw over the other like he did in snazzy establishments. Opal slid a menu along the marble worktop.

'Shall we go with a champagne, Augusto?' Opal asked.

'I am going to order Fernet and water to start with,' Augusto said.

A waiter nodded at Opal with rushed acknowledgement. She assumed from the speed in which he was chopping up mint with samurai-like precision, he had a backlog of drinks to make.

'What is Fernet, Augusto?' Opal frowned.

'Oh, just a drink from back home... in Spain,' Augusto replied rather hurriedly. He always seemed a little embarrassed or dismissive when talking about his Spanish home life, Opal noted. She turned her attention to the bartender.

'Monsieur, can I ask you something?' Opal fluttered her eyelids and the bartender extended his neck and ear towards her. 'I heard Clementina Lalonde used to come in here. Is that correct?'

'Err... I am new here, so I don't really know...'

'Did you say Clementina Lalonde?' The head of another waiter bobbed up from where he'd been riffling in a cupboard. He placed his hands on the bar, fingers splayed out. The other waiter rolled his eyes at him and turned his back to fetch some glassware.

'Yes,' Opal chirped, as friendly as she could.

'Are you a journalist?' he asked, visibly excited. Opal thought for a split second whether to lie so she could get more information. But then again, staff might conceal certain things from the press, and she didn't want Augusto to think she was loopy.

'No.'

'Oh, I see.' He frowned, confused. 'Then why do you ask if she used to come here?'

'I am just a big fan of hers and was wondering.'

'I am too.' He beamed, then the sides of his mouth curled downwards. 'Well. *Was.* I saw her perform many times all over France. I am so devastated at what happened to her. I even had tickets to see her at the Casino de Paris.'

'Is that so?' Opal asked but didn't elaborate on the fact that she worked at the show. She didn't want to excite him too much and have to tell the whole story.

'I cannot believe she died onstage!' he continued.

'Yes, it's awful, isn't it? But I heard she used to come here? Did she?'

'Yes. Quite a bit. Earlier this year. I served her once, it was my favourite day ever working here.'

'I say!' Opal sat up straight and craned forward. 'That must have been exciting.'

His colleague tapped him on the shoulder and muttered something. He quickly put his hands down and picked up a lemon.

'*Un moment*, mademoiselle, I just have to prepare a cocktail.'

He began chopping a lemon and started talking about what Clementina wore on the occasions that she had come in. Opal humoured him, nodding and humming, but began to get impatient, crossing and uncrossing her legs.

'Who did she come here with?' she interrupted him mid passionate gush about a pair of shoes she wore.

'Oh... with this unattractive man.' He winced distastefully.

'Did you catch his name?'

'*Non.*'

'What did he look like?'

'He was all skinny and tall. Sort of lopsided and had a long mouth and brown hair, he was talking about stage set design at one point.' He pulled the side of his mouth outwards with a finger. *Definitely David*, Opal thought, amused at his impression.

'It wasn't a date, was it?' she pressed.

'I don't know. Because I know she was in a relationship at the time, with that director in New York... Joshua something.

But they would always book the private salon upstairs and that is usually booked for romantic couples.'

'Did you see them kiss or were they affectionate in anyway?'

'*Non, non.*'

'Did you hear any of their conversation?'

'Not really, I only heard him mention the set design for a water tank or something when walking up the stairs behind them. They didn't converse when I was in the room. I do remember them laughing from outside the door in a very loud kind of mischievous way and I remember Clementina saying, "*Let's do it.*" But that's all I can remember.'

'Did you hear them say anything else?'

'Oh, it was a while ago! I can't remember... But I got a little souvenir from her visit. That I will always treasure.'

He put his finger up in an indication for Opal to wait. He ducked below the bar. There was the sound of a drawer opening and shutting. He stood up again and produced a crumpled piece of tissue with a red lipstick smack on it. Opal's eyes fluttered with a gentle tremor, recalibrating to the new discovery. It wasn't the lipstick she was intrigued by; it was the pen markings scrawled next to it in blue ink.

~~10/2~~ ~~9/3~~ ~~8/4~~ 7/5

This was followed by an upside-down sunrise with rays and an arrow pointing down into the sun.

The numbers were dates, Opal concluded, and she wondered why the first three had a line through them. And what was the curious diagram drawn underneath them?

'What is this?' Opal asked.

'Oh, I don't know. She left it on the table screwed up when they left and I kept it. I'm so glad I did. I have her blotted kiss.'

He then started to ramble on about how many of her shows he had seen and which ones were his favourites. While he did so, Opal reached into her handbag and opened the sketchbook. She copied the dates and diagram with her lipstick, but did so inside her handbag so the waiter wouldn't think it was odd.

'Your champagne, mademoiselle, your Fernet, monsieur,' the first waiter said curtly, nudging his rambling colleague discreetly with an elbow and clinking the glasses down. The other shut his mouth and gave Opal an apologetic look. Opal thanked both the waiters and smiled, before turning to Augusto.

'What was the wicked plan that David and Clementina were discussing upstairs? Perhaps the answer is in those dates and the diagram on the serviette.' Opal realised that the champagne had loosened her tongue. She hadn't wanted Augusto to know she was investigating Clementina's death but the more time she spent with him the more she relaxed.

'They said, "Let's do it?" and laughed wickedly? They could have been talking about necking the last of the absinthe. Or to go and watch something obscene at a cinema in Pigalle. It could have been anything, *señorita*.'

'Well, when you put it like that.' Opal sighed as she realised how silly it was to speculate. 'I'm going to have to do a lot of questioning at the wake tomorrow and see what those dates on that diagram mean.'

Once seated at dinner, Opal used her powers of observation to read the dashing Latino. Any body language that might signal what this meal could mean to him. Was it a pally chinwag? Or did he find Opal more charming than a mere theatre-crew chum?

He spent a large portion of time looking down into his crab cocktail rather than into Opal's eyes. Opal couldn't blame him, it did look exceedingly good. The crab meat, pale and tender, was nestled elegantly in a crystal coupe, its snowy whiteness contrasted by the blush-pink Marie Rose sauce. A whisper of lemon zest crowned the whole affair, releasing a citrusy perfume.

Perhaps he was shy. But why would such a hulk of a gentleman be shy?

The conversation emitting from his dancing moustache was all about an exhibition he dreamed of putting on and about how he would love a collaboration with Opal and her red overmarking. Opal chewed her delicate escargot and nodded. She decided to follow his lead and treat the meal as a business meeting, whether it truly was or not.

'I've never thought of myself as creating artworks. Only fashion illustrations and sculptures upon people's heads. But I would be delighted to work on something more serious with you, Augusto. I take it as an immense compliment.'

'If you go back to London, we can send each other work to collaborate on,' Augusto said, lifting his fork in the air as the idea hit him.

What a wonderful excuse to keep in touch, Opal thought. *He was either very clever or he really was very earnest about making work together.*

'Or I could hop back over on the Golden Arrow every so often.' Opal blinked at him, head balanced in her cupped palms.

'I just loved your audacity when you leant across and drew over my work. The lipstick is ingenious. You know, Édouard Vuillard used wallpaper in his works, Francis Picabia used iodine... so why not lipstick? You see, to me, Paris is a woman, and lipstick is the paint of a woman. If it is good enough for a woman's lips, then it's only going to add intrigue to my work.'

'You are *mad* as a march hare, Augusto!' Opal giggled. 'But I like it.'

'You think I sound mad? Wait till you hear the bohemians speak at a literary salon, that will make me sound dull.' He put his fork in the air again. 'There is also something in the way that only the hats are red. A hat is something subconsciously drenched in meaning in society. Especially female society.'

'I always say that a hat gives women authority.'

'That one certainly is dominating.' Augusto drew his eyes over Opal's cloche. 'In the most sparkly and animated way.'

'Why thank you for saying so. I beaded this myself. It was a bit too racy to go in Mother's shop though,' Opal replied, shimmying her head back and forth so that the beads could swish.

'Take a look at some of these sketches,' Augusto said. 'We can make them larger and add your touches to them.'

'We would have to add powder to dry out the lipstick and stop it from smudging,' Opal commented, flipping the pages. On reaching the most recent page, her hand froze as she recognised one of his subjects. 'Oh gosh.'

Augusto's pencil had almost indented the page with the way he had scrawled the T-shaped scar on the man's face. He'd caught the man smoking through his Citroën window.

'Where did you draw this man?' Opal said, the paper shaking slightly in her hand.

'Oh, this questionable chap. He was waiting outside here in his car earlier; he drove around the corner when you arrived. I was here early.'

'Wait, how on earth did he know I'd be coming here?' Opal gasped.

'What do you mean, Opal?'

'This man... he's been following me the entire time I've been in Paris. He carries a pistol. I told Detective Inspector Prosper Delacroix about him. He said he has a licence for the gun and works and lives by the theatre and hotel so it's just a coincidence and that he can't convict him without harassment. The fact he came here tonight means he is in fact following me.'

'If I see him again I will vanquish it for you, I promise. He won't bother you further,' Augusto said in a calm and assuring voice.

He put his hand on top of hers, and it stopped shaking

under the warm hood of his palm. He took his hand away again when the waiter walked past.

'The bill, please,' Augusto called to the waiter.

Opal reached for her purse. She did not expect Augusto to be footing the entire bill. It was far too expensive an establishment for someone of Augusto's occupation. Everyone in the restaurant seemed to be an aristocrat or haute bourgeoisie. She had been prepared to pay. He shook his head and smiled as he noticed her gesture. He seemed to be able to afford it. Who *was* this man?

THIRTY-TWO

CLEMENTINA'S FUNERAL WAKE

Clementina's funeral wake was held at three o'clock in the afternoon at a club called Gaîté. Opal's black shoe froze in the doorway. Why had she not considered before now that she may be meeting Clementina's mother, her long-lost aunt, the Honourable Florence Laplume today? She had not come to Clementina's show and Opal was not sure why. Her heart fluttered nervously. She arranged her black cloche lower onto her face and pulled Napoleon inside with her.

Gaîté was a traditional Parisian cabaret, situated among all the other cabarets in the Quartier Pigalle. Clementina, when she had been seventeen years old, landed a job there and danced there as a chorus girl for years, before she got chosen to go solo and became a star.

The now elderly owner of the venue, Edgard, had been very fond of Clementina and had seen her career blossom. It seemed to him his venue was the most appropriate place to celebrate her life as a showgirl, so he offered to host the wake.

It was a miniature theatre, its capacity around two hundred and fifty people. It was nothing like the magnitude of Casino de Paris but it had an intimate charm of its own. The ceiling was a deep midnight blue emblazoned with white stars. The stage curtains were the same colour in gathered velvet at the pelmet. The auditorium was arranged with lamplit cabaret tables with white tablecloths.

The scene inside looked to Opal like one of Picasso's Blue Period paintings, not only because of the forlorn expressions on attendees' faces, but because the venue had been lit entirely by blue light.

Opal took Clementina's favourite cocktail off a tray that was floating round. Even the absinthe drink, which should have been green, appeared a melancholic, bluish concoction.

'Apparently it was the owner Edgard's idea to light the room blue this way to reflect his sadness,' Opal said to Augusto.

'I am feeling it.' Augusto nodded and swallowed half his entire glass.

She stood next to him, away from everyone else, under a shadow made by the balconette. She fiddled with the black funerial feather she'd stabbed into her hat and listened to sniffs and suppressed sobs as people, one by one, made speeches on the stage.

Opal listened to the tributes being given and even though she couldn't catch every word they were saying, felt a lump swell in her throat. She didn't want to break down. Her mother always said it was unseemly for a lady to cry in public. It would be self-indulgent. This was not the time to draw attention to herself. She looked at Augusto. He stood like he was still Clementina's bodyguard, a silent, uninvolved hulk of muscle, but there were teardrops lightly balanced on his lower lids.

'I enjoyed last night,' Opal said quietly, looking at him sideways under her black brim.

'Me too. I'd like to do some more illustrations with you this evening, in fact, a good opportunity has arisen.'

'Oh...Yes?' Opal said, pleasantly surprised.

'I'm going to take you somewhere I think you'll like. It's a surprise. If you don't like it, then we may leave.'

'Oh, how very mysterious... But why wouldn't I like it?'

'Well, it's not an ordinary kind of place with run-of-the-mill types. You may feel uncomfortable. But you'll be charmed by it... I hope.'

'I could certainly do with cheering up. Get me on the blower later and we shall make the arrangements,' Opal said over her shoulder and walked away in search of Zsa Zsa.

She couldn't find her friend in the thick wedge of guests and didn't want to push through and disrupt people when Clementina's childhood friend was speaking on the stage. She then tried again to search for her aunt. She did not know what she would look like. She glanced at older ladies' faces, trying to see if she could recognise a Laplume chin or resemblance to her father.

She gave up for a moment and exited through the double doors to the foyer where she came across David standing with Mei Ling, who was patting tears from her cheeks with a handkerchief. This handkerchief was striped with the colours of the French flag.

Mei Ling noticed Opal staring and gave her a weary nod hello. Opal smiled back and carried on out of the exit.

A tricolour handkerchief. Blue, white and red, she pondered. She had seen that before. It was the colours of the thread she'd seen on the plinth at the scene of the diamond heist. *Could it have come from Mei Ling's handkerchief? Had she wiped the plinth for some reason when nobody was looking?*

A posse of bottle-orange-haired girls were drinking wine on the pavement. Opal assumed them to be Clementina's fans, having their own little wake as they weren't invited to the official one.

When a couple of them parted, Opal could see Christophe on the other side of the street, a cigarette in a limp wrist. He was looking his best in a magnificent Victorian-style black waist-length jacket and silk cravat. But his body language had none of his usual zesty confidence.

'Christophe, how are you doing?' Opal asked.

'Opal. Oh, the wake was irritating me, so I had to come out for a bit.'

'Why?'

'It's too morbid. I thought it would be a party. A celebration of her life.' He said it like he'd been looking forward to an outrageous knees-up and had been robbed of a good time.

'You don't think she would have wanted this?'

'*Non*. Clementina Lalonde, the world's greatest cabaret star? She loved to dance and enjoy herself. She would have hated this.'

'Well, maybe you can hold a party of your own?' Opal suggested.

'*Non, non*, I've had enough of these people. Now she's gone I won't have anything to do with her entourage.'

'Oh... What will you do now?'

'I don't know, Opal, it's a nightmare. She was my muse. Who am I going to dress now? Nobody could do my costumes the justice she could. I knew her measurements so well I could whip up a pattern for her without even checking. It's the end of an era for me. I have to rethink all my goals. I will miss her as a friend, obviously, but it's all too much to compute.'

'I'm so sorry,' Opal said and took a few seconds to think of a consolation. 'You can make anyone look amazing, no matter who they are. You're Christophe Tasse.'

'Mei Ling and Zsa Zsa did look fabulous, I must admit. But I need a celebrity. A star. I worked with the best for eighteen years and I'm not going back to work for anything less.'

'Eighteen years? Gosh, that's a long time.'

'Yes, we met around the year 1912. I was an apprentice corsetière and she was working as a dancer here at Gaîté.

Clementina stood out and she shouldn't have been part of the chorus. We helped each other and it turns out we both became very successful together.'

Opal realised that this could be the last time she would see Christophe and would have to sensitively ask him his thoughts on the circumstances of Clementina's death and about the dates on the napkin she found.

'I wonder if you could help me put my mind at rest about my cousin's death. I'm not sure what the police are coming up with is satisfactory.'

'Oh, the police will never care too much about a *danseuse de cabaret*. Even a world-famous one. They seem to be caring more about the diamond.'

'I think you are right. But the night she died... the police seem to think she inhaled the Nictoform during the interval. Her fiancé didn't see her take it, even though he was watching her the entire time. The Nictoform bottle wasn't found at the theatre and he thinks that something is not right about it all. What do you think?'

He snorted a kind of bitter laugh. 'Clementina was the biggest nervous wreck I'd ever met. I think she took it to calm her nerves. I didn't see her take it either, but I reckon she did.'

'But what do you think about the death threat?' Opal asked.

'I can't say who that was, and it may have simply been to scare her, not a real threat.'

Opal did not reveal to him that she thought Clementina wrote the threat herself. She certainly did not trust Christophe yet.

'Can you go through exactly what happened in the dressing room the night she died and any possible time she could have inhaled the Nictoform?'

'I was so frantic getting her ready I can't remember much.' He snorted bitterly again. 'My last word to her was *"merde"*. That is what the French say for good luck.'

'Well, in the context, it was a nice thing to say,' Opal said brightly.

'I wish people would stop thinking she was murdered. It was an accident, she took the drug for her nerves. After the diamond was stolen she got extremely nervous.' He tapped the end of his cigarette briskly into the road.

'Do you know anyone who might have wanted her dead?'

'If she was administered the drug somehow by someone with ill intent, then it would have been Zsa Zsa. That girl is cut-throat. Has a questionable background. God knows where she is really from. She tried to throw me under the guillotine for Valentine's suicide. All because I was not complimentary of her performance style. She wants to be famous like Clementina, so she has the perfect motive to want her killed,' Christophe said, looking at Opal with cold eyes.

'I came across something odd.' Opal pulled her sketchbook out of her bag, she was about to tell Christophe she had found these dates on a napkin at Lapérouse but didn't want to reveal too much information. 'A little note she'd written with these dates on them, 10/2, 9/3, 8/4, 7/5. Can you tell me what they might mean or what she may have been doing on these days?'

'I don't know. Could have been anything. In February and March she was in Saint Tropez with her greyhound to escape the cold. What's the significance?'

'That's what I'm trying to find out. Shall we go back inside?' Opal asked, suddenly chill.

'*Non, non*, I think I might go home. I'm not enjoying it,' he replied bitterly.

'I have to leave now too.' The words came from David, who was crossing the street towards them.

'Oh... why are you leaving, David?' Opal asked him. She'd been wanting to speak to David about his last interaction with Clementina in the interval and, as with Christophe, didn't know when she'd ever see him again.

'I've got to go and oversee my apprentices in my workshop. We're making props for a film set at the moment and I have to get back.'

'Oh... can I come with you?' Opal thought fast. 'I... I have a business request for you. From my mother's shop in London, Laplume Millinery. We'd like to commission some props for the shop window. Increase the footfall of the shop, you know. I'd love to see your studio and get some ideas.'

'Well, I don't see why not. We can have a quick coffee there, then I'll have to get back to work. Come on, I'll drive you.'

THIRTY-THREE
DAVID MILLER'S WORKSHOP

David's car swung into the industrial neighbourhood of Boulogne-Billancourt. As the sun was descending, it cast a peach hue over a sprawling Renault factory. Tall chimneys pierced the sky, expelling smoke that, in the dusk, resembled cotton candy that had been dipped in ash.

David gently stopped the car outside the warehouse next door to the car manufacturers. The walls were streaked with soot, windows grimy from years of industry. Opal opened her door to the sound of clattering machinery and hum of motors. David helped her out with a warm hand and took Napoleon's lead for her. He then unlocked a hefty padlock at the entrance with delicate long fingers.

Opal tasted sawdust in the air as they entered a small reception room. It had a dilapidated, paint-splodged chaise longue up against one wall. Opposite was a wooden desk, also paint splattered, a mess of pens, paper and teacups on it. Photographs of sets and props that Opal assumed David had made were in glass frames lining the brick walls. A chaotic worker but he was evidently very proud of what he'd been achieving in the theatre world.

'Wait here, I'll get us some coffee,' David said and disappeared through some swing doors.

Opal sat on the squeaking springs of the chaise longue and waited, listening to the faint sound of a saw scraping back and forth, interrupted by hammerings and short remarks made by male voices.

After ten minutes Napoleon started to get impatient, straining on the lead, whining to go exploring where the action was taking place. *Couldn't do any harm to have a nosy*, Opal thought, and let her dog pull her through the swing door. It groaned open to a long corridor with many more doors. The concrete floor was dribbled with paint and lumps of resin.

She couldn't tell which room the noise was coming from so she decided to poke her nose in each as she passed. After wedging open the first door, she was hit with the smell of turpentine. Rows and rows of paint tins lined metal shelves. The next room had boards and planks of wood stacked against the walls.

The third was a much larger room, obviously storage for pieces of set and props. Among the chaotically crammed items were a half-dismantled merry-go-round with swans on it. Their bulbous eyelids were gathering dust. By this were a couple of fake lamp posts twisted with silk ivy, leaning diagonally against a bonfire-sized heap of pieces of prop furniture.

She was about to try the next room when something caught her eye and made her stop. Beyond the merry-go-round was a metal table with something gold on it. It was a metal bowl with an acorn nut shape underneath. In a flash of memory, Opal realised this was identical to the bowl underneath the chandelier in the room where the diamond was stolen.

Opal glided over, lifted the bowl and turned it over. It was about as wide as an average cereal bowl but quite shallow, a couple of inches deep and very heavy. Her lashes danced as she inspected the empty vessel. Why had it been unscrewed from the chandelier, and what was it doing here?

Opal looked back down at the table and noticed a rusty paint-tin opener. She picked it up in her other hand and brought it close to her right eye. One corner of the blade was covered in a dried drip of a dark-red liquid. It had dribbled down the side of the handle and small blobs had dried on the table. More had dribbled onto the floor below. There was also a faint circle of the liquid, about the diameter of a paint tin on the surface of the table.

Opal shivered. *It looked like blood.*

The scuffing sound of two sets of footsteps sounded somewhere back at the entrance to the room. Napoleon whipped his head around. Opal's shoulders jolted and she hastily placed the objects back on the table. She turned around so fast her cloche hat slid back.

At the door was David. His linear mouth was shortened in a pinch. In his right hand were the handles of two cafés noisettes cups. An axe was brandished in his left, dangling down by the leg of his corduroys.

'What are you doing in here?' he said in a belligerent manner, his hairline rising in reprimand. His knuckles were white around the axe and Opal gulped as she wasn't sure what he was planning to do with it.

'Oh... David, I'm sorry. I was waiting for quite a while out there and just came to find you. I thought I heard someone in here,' she stammered, backing up against the table. Napoleon stayed put, his chest puffed out, a faint growl vibrating in the back of his throat.

David's knuckles became pink as he loosened his grip on the axe and his face fell back into a less livid, more exasperated expression. 'Well, please, if we can go back to the office that would be good. There are too many breakable things in here.'

'Oh, I'm ever so sorry,' she panted in relief. 'The props are beautiful, I couldn't help but have a look round. It's alright, Napoleon, come here.'

Opal thought his 'breakable' remark was rather strange, as the things in here had not been placed inside with any care. It seemed more of a dumping ground.

'It's quite alright,' David said, gesturing with the axe to follow him out of the room.

As Opal glided forward sheepishly, she noticed that the dribbles of dried red liquid continued along the floor all the way to the door. They continued up the corridor also. They were standing out in brown-magenta against the other coloured paint dribbles. She felt her heart rate rise and the headband in her hat moisten with sweat. As Opal passed the door where the paint tins were stored, she saw that the trail of drips led inside. Napoleon's nose seemed to be analysing them too. But she couldn't go in to investigate, she had to follow David into the reception room.

'Come along,' he said, turning back.

Opal smiled over-brightly and caught up.

He opened the swing doors with his shoulder and gestured for Opal to sit herself down on the chaise longue. He leant his axe against the leg of the desk and handed her her coffee.

'I almost did my back in using the axe a minute ago. I had to show one of those fools in there how to do it properly.' He groaned, arching his back and then slumping down next to her.

'Oh dear,' Opal said.

'Now, young lady, how can I help you with these props for your shop window? I made a helter-skelter for handbags once for Galeries Lafayette. But that's the only venture into the retail sector I've ever made. And London... that would be a new stomping ground for me.'

Oh gosh, please don't get too keen, thought Opal. *I only wanted an excuse to snoop around the workshop.*

'Well, Mother wasn't absolutely certain what she may want

or what kind of budget we would have either, but I thought perhaps you could come up with some ideas to start with.' Opal gulped. 'A helter-skelter for handbags? That sounds simply ripping!'

'It was. Red and white striped. As tall as a bus standing on its nose. We put thirty handbags sliding down as if they were little people enjoying themselves.'

'I bet they had a jolly good time. What prop could work with hats? The shop window is only about ten by ten feet, mind.'

'I wouldn't be able to get anything done for the Christmas season now. But Easter perhaps... a sort of pastoral backdrop with the hats hanging from an Easter tree covered in ribbon and birds?'

'That would be the bee's knees,' Opal said, quite taken aback at his colourful imagination. She suppressed a tiny giggle. She knew Lady Phyllis Laplume would have a heart attack if she came back to the shop and the window looked like a farmyard fete. 'Let us correspond by post when I'm back in London. By then I won't be as shaken up as I am at the moment and able to get my business head back on.'

'It has been unsettling,' David said, leaning back in his swivel chair. 'A twelve-million-franc diamond heist, two deaths and a missing person all in the space of a month.'

'And all of the crimes seeming to be committed by a revenant,' Opal said. She took a sip of coffee, trying to prevent her voice from shaking. 'What do you think could have happened to the necklace?'

'Between you and me,' David said, downing his café noisette in one and placing his cup onto the saucer very delicately, 'I agree with Detective Inspector Prosper Delacroix. The American fat-cat clown pulled a publicity stunt and faked the heist of his own jewel. He's probably going to claim it on insurance. As for Clementina, perhaps it was her own twisted publicity stunt too. Perhaps she wanted to go out with a bang? Fame was always her motivating force, and people who seek fame in the way that she did are the most unhappy people, living through the eyes of others. Fame was almost like a religion to her, and to die unknown by the masses would have been her worst nightmare. And I know she wasn't happy with her fiancé being so far away all the time. She had dark things to say about her life. I would not put suicide past her.'

'What kind of dark things did she say?'

'She was unhappy about never having known her father. Her mother is a bit of a lunatic by all accounts. A bohemian émigrée. She wasn't interested in Clementina's stardom, even though Clementina had tried so hard to impress her. Oh, that's your aunt, isn't it? Apologies.'

'That's quite alright, I've actually never met her. But if Clementina really did commit suicide, then what was the death threat about?'

'I don't know, perhaps someone wanted to scare her into quitting the show. It seems to me there were various villains at play here.'

'You were one of the last people to see Clementina before she climbed into the water tank. Did you see her take the Nictoform?'

'No, I didn't see her take it either.' David sighed and stood up as if wanting to wind the conversation down.

'What did she say to you? What happened in those last minutes?' Opal continued, ignoring his body language.

'I came and met her in the wings. I told her that the temperature was right in the water tank. I carried the ladder out for her and helped her climb up. I told her she'd be smashing. She didn't reply, she just slipped into the water while I walked back into the wings with the ladder. I mean, she did seem dazed, but I put that down to nerves.' David began tweaking the levels of the frames on the wall and Opal could not see his face.

'You two seemed to have become good friends.'

'Yes... I owe her my entire career, a bit like Christophe does. When she got more successful, then so did we.' He shrugged his shoulders. 'I will call you a cab now, Opal. I have to go and kick my set builders into action. The blighters are really lagging.'

'Just one last thing, David, if you'd be so kind. I need to know what Clementina was doing on certain dates earlier this year.' Opal didn't want to reveal she'd found the napkin in Lapérouse, so instead she said, 'I saw she'd crossed some dates off on her calendar and I just have a feeling they might be significant.'

'I wouldn't know everything that woman got up to. You'd have to ask her greyhound.'

'Oh, darling Yvette. How is she getting on?'

'She's with me for the moment, but we're going to send her back to Clementina's beloved château where her housekeeper will let her in the gardens to bound about. I guess the château will be taken up by her mother now as she had no husband.'

'Goodness, yes. It is a shame that she didn't maintain a close relationship with her mother. I think that may be why she suffered from insomnia. A troubled mind.'

'Well, that could be what was on her calendar. Her trips to Doctor Ding Shanyuan were monthly, I believe.'

It was a possibility. She hastily scribbled the doctor's name in her sketchbook to see if she could follow it up later.

David riffled in his desk drawers and produced his own business card. It contained his postal address for her to be in touch about the window display. Opal thanked him and waited for her car. She had a lot to absorb. Had it really been blood on the paint tin opener? And if so, whose was it? And what on earth was the significance of the chandelier part?

THIRTY-FOUR
THE NUMBER 12

'Thank you kindly for your time, Doctor Shanyuan. Good day to you,' Opal said and put the receiver down. She then sighed. She'd followed up on whether Clementina had visited her doctor on the dates on the napkin, but he'd informed her that she had not. She had thought as much. It wouldn't exactly have been the kind of thing she would have discussed or needed to write down with David at their Lapérouse rendezvous.

'It's getting late, shouldn't you be getting ready to meet Augusto?'

Zsa Zsa peeked up over the bathtub in Opal's suite. Steam swirled around her arms and evanesced off her elbows.

'Oh, I'll be fine. I'll get ready in a minute,' Opal replied. She was on her bed peering at her sketchbook. She had open the page with the copy of Clementina's cryptic dates and diagram from Lapérouse.

'Where's Augusto taking you again?' Zsa Zsa asked, lathering her calf with shaving soap.

'Oh... it's a surprise. He said I might not like it but, if I don't, we can leave. Sounds rather peculiar, doesn't it?'

'How queer? I'm dying to know where it is.'

'I jolly well am too.'

'I mean, you do have *the pash* for him, don't you?'

'I'm a tad impassioned, I must confess. But it's hopeless. If they don't have a title, they would at least have to have an ancestral pile – a decent property – to pass with my folks.'

'My parents would be happy with anything as long as he wasn't a crim. They might accept a petty crim, but nobody that could get me in the soup.'

'How lovely and free that must be.' Opal sighed, not exactly sure what she meant but it sounded as if her folks were liberal.

'You've got to stop trying to figure out that stupid napkin and get ready. Those numbers on it could mean anything. They could be the dates she's had the nit nurse round, for all we know.'

Opal inwardly agreed with a sigh. She stuffed the sketchbook back in her handbag and started recurling a feather that she was going to stab in her hat. She didn't even need to look at that page of the sketchbook anymore. She knew it by heart, she'd been looking at it so much. It was like she'd scrawled it in lipstick across her own brain. It frustrated her that she just couldn't see the significance or symbolism in it.

On the bed, wedged under Napoleon's curly hindquarters, was the front page of the newspaper that had published the story of the Dumoulin diamond heist. *Twelve Million Apolline Diamond*

Twelve. Opal's eyes gave a swift, instinctive blink, the revelation landing firmly in her mind as she gazed at the number. Something had clicked. *Twelve, twelve, twelve.* Opal took out the sketchbook from her handbag again. She looked at the numbers she had previously assumed to be dates: 10/2, 9/3, 8/4, 7/5.

All the groups of numbers added up to twelve!

Perhaps they weren't dates after all. Could it possibly be... An idea started to brew in Opal's mind.

She then squinted at the diagram Clementina had drawn below the numbers. An upside-down sunset with lines like rays pointing outwards. *A sun? Rays? Light? Beams? Chandelier? Chandelier!*

Opal visualised the chandelier dangling above where the diamond necklace sat. She pictured the bowl-shaped fixing on the table in David's workshop.

The drawing wasn't a sun, it was the removable bowl of a chandelier! She looked at the scribbled arrow pointing down into the drawing of the bowl, her eyes electrified. *Was Clementina's idea to hide the necklace in the bowl of the chandelier?*

Opal's mind flashed back to the conversation with the waiter at Lapérouse. He'd said Clementina and David were laughing mischievously and Clementina had said, *'Let's do it.'*

Opal continued to curl her feathers with her scissors in faster and faster motions. She thought back to the night of the heist. She pictured the door of the dressing room opening inwards. David entering the room after her. She pictured the tricolour thread on the plinth after the necklace disappeared. The tricolour handkerchief that Mei Ling had next to David at the wake. The dismantled chandelier bowl in David's studio.

She shuffled the images round and round in her mind, illustrating the scenario. One that made perfect sense. She stopped curling the feather and dropped her scissors onto the bed. Napoleon scarpered out of the way and looked up at her, his pom-pom tail wagging with anticipation. Opal had come to the conclusion that her suppositions were *right*.

'Zsa Zsa...' Opal blurted. 'I've just realised how the heist was done! And who did it!'

'What?' Zsa Zsa splashed some water over the sides of the tub. 'You're off your onion! How could you possibly work that out? How was it done? Who did it?'

'I...' Opal considered going through it with her but knew

that Zsa Zsa would be sceptical or laugh at her. She also couldn't trust that Zsa Zsa wouldn't go blurting to Mr Dumoulin or someone else. Someone that perhaps shouldn't be trusted. 'I can't tell you yet. I want to wait until I've unravelled the mysteries of the murders. I want to get to the bottom of everything, get proof, then let everyone know what's been going on.'

Zsa Zsa pouted her lips and swung her legs to the side. 'You are funny. Oh, just go out with Augusto and stop winding me up.' She flicked a lump of foam off her razor at Opal and then slipped back down into the water.

Opal slid off the bed sheets, feeling light and content. She was finally getting somewhere. She knew she'd be able to help. She glided over to her wardrobe; her neck elongated, proud of her cleverness. *Now, what to wear to meet the dashing Spaniard?*

THIRTY-FIVE
SALON DES ARTISTES

Opal sighed and her eyelashes danced while looking up at Augusto's face. He was standing in front of the door he had just rapped his knuckles on. She could have a good stare without him knowing she was gawking. His brow protruded, a dark canopy hiding his mysterious eyes, protected further by spiked lashes. His dimpled chin twitched impatiently.

Augusto's thick knuckles rapped again louder on the cream lacquered door. *Where on earth had he taken her?* Opal could hear a soup of sounds coming from behind it; a piano tinkling an arabesque tune, a lady counting to eight in French, clusters of voices exchanging kisses and casting out morsels of gossip.

Opal fizzed with excitement from the extremities of her toes to the tip of the peacock tufts on her head. She inspected her Chanel coat for any curlicues of Napoleon's fur. The dog barked when someone rattled the door handle from the other side.

A mature woman's head poked out. She had a tortoise-like face with walnut-like skin around the eyes. A green conical hat was wrapped around her head in pleats and splayed out like a palm at the side of her head.

'Augusto,' the lady said in an interesting European accent. She slid her eyes up and down his body approvingly and then gazed at Opal. 'And who might this be?'

'Opal Laplume. How do you do,' Opal replied, offering her hand.

'Ah, *magnifique*,' she said, taking the hand. 'We actually have another person with the name Laplume here. I'll have to introduce you later.'

Opal was surprised. She had never in her whole life met another Laplume apart from Clementina. Who could it *be*? Though it was a French surname so it would be bound to be more popular in this country than in England.

'And *my* name is Misia Sert.' The lady beamed welcomingly.

Her eyes flickered when she caught sight of Napoleon as he stood up on his hind legs, paws lifted high for attention.

'*Oh là là, qu'il est mignon!*' Misia extended her neck like a delighted tortoise and clasped her hands together. 'Perhaps we should draw you!'

'Napoleon is quite the poser,' Augusto said.

'Napoleon! Come with me.' Misia scooped Napoleon up under her armpit and carried him inside like a limp doll.

'Drawing?' Opal looked up at Augusto.

'We're at Misia Sert's Salon Des Artistes.' He nodded and gestured into the room. 'A private gathering of Paris's finest artistes and aesthetes. Do you want to come inside? I thought you might find it daunting.'

'Not at all. And Misia was ever so welcoming, I couldn't turn away now.'

The grandeur of the room caused Opal to gasp. Tall, slender windows overlooked the twinkling night lamps of the Tuileries Garden and the curtains fell like large swathes of cream falling from a wedding cake. On the parquet flooring were a scattering of chairs that spilled with people clutching books and charcoal. Smoke rose from their fingers like mini chimneys in a colourful city.

Opal had never seen such an array of à la mode headpieces. She pulled at the tips of her gloves nervously, almost feeling intimidated. If she came again she would have to dress far more boldly.

There was a grand piano by the bookshelves where a man was tonking an Egyptian tune and humming under his thick moustache. Misia Sert carried Napoleon to the piano lifted high like a prize lamb and guests swirled around him.

'His tiny bicorn hat!' one voice piped up above the hubbub.

'The little pom-pom tail!'

'What is she going to do with my darling pet?' Opal asked Augusto, half enchanted and half terrified as if it might be some kind of artist sacrificial ritual.

'He will be a drawing subject, I expect,' Augusto said.

'So it's an *art* club?' Opal asked, following Augusto into the room. Using his shoulders as a shield. She felt awfully shy.

'Of sorts. It's a mixture of drawing, lively discussions, fashion presentations, performances, music, poetry. I come here every month. It is my favourite thing to do. But very hard to get an invite.'

'Oh goodness. And you wanted to bring *me*? I feel so honoured,' Opal said, not knowing whether she was more over-joyed at being at a prestigious event or the fact Augusto was sharing his favourite activity with her.

'Well, I know how much you want to get Laplume Millinery known here. I thought this would be the best place to mingle. Give out business cards.'

'Oh yes. That is ever so thoughtful, Augusto.' Opal smiled.

'*Mesdames et messieurs*, welcome to my May Salon,' Misia addressed the room with a double clap. 'The theme of the evening is "Napoleonic". Take inspiration from that word as you will. The theme initially was something quite different but this *petit chien* has set the tone. We must draw the Poodle on the Piano!'

Napoleon stood proudly with his chest puffed out and chin high like a prize thoroughbred at Ascot.

Misia continued, 'Later we will have a poetry recital from Alphonse Martell trying out some new work. A discussion by Vionnet and Chanel on bias-cut fabric and the contour of the body, and then a debate about the current obsession with red squirrel fur and whether it has gone far enough.'

Chanel! Opal scurried her eyes over the landscape of cloche hats, for she expected this may be what the famous couturier would be wearing. She could not pinpoint her yet.

'Then, our Josephine Baker will model new silk printed crepes by Fantasia A.G.B. Now let us get our creative juices flowing and spend fifteen minutes on our canine muse. He will probably move a little, but that will just add something... I will turn the hourglass.'

Misia turned the hourglass propped on the bookshelf and heads bowed. The sound of charcoal scratching came from all directions like an exodus of insects scurrying out of the wood-work. Opal bit her lip and watched Napoleon. He was already whipping his head back and forth to look at the scribbling instruments in people's hands.

'Let's sit here...' Augusto gestured to a love seat.

Opal's cheeks pinked as she sat in the chair, ensconced next to the dashing Latino, closer than ever before. She took out her sketchbook and placed it on her pinched knees. She plucked out her notebook crayon and bit her lip.

'Use the lipstick... they will appreciate the innovation,' Augusto suggested, reading her mind.

Ten minutes later, the drawing session was over. It had ended abruptly when Napoleon had leapt into someone's lap. The sketches, or watercolours, were laid out on top of a long banquet table for people to discuss. Opal's submission stood out very much in red.

As Opal walked along the table gazing at all the works, her eyes faltered on something. Someone had used ink to draw the ladies surrounding the piano with small catlike feet, tiny high insteps. Napoleon too. They had shaded everything with tiny criss-cross strokes. *Where had she seen this style before?*

Opal picked it up. It was on thick textured paper. She lifted her thumb to reveal the signature in the corner... *R.S 1934*. The same initials in the corner of the costume design book that she'd found in Valentine's dresser drawer. The one which Christophe snatched off her.

'I wish to buy this,' she said.

'It is a good depiction.' Augusto nodded. 'I like the feet.'

'Who is it by?'

'I don't know... perhaps we will need to go around asking?'

Opal clutched the drawing to her chest. She felt a tad shy again. Everyone was so stylish and so... bohemian. How could she ever hold a conversation on their level? Augusto sensed her coyness and offered his arm to be linked.

'Let's try the people by the jardinière,' he said. 'They also have champagne.'

As they headed over, Opal couldn't help but overhear a conversation to her left. It echoed around the marble alcove the people were sitting in.

'I am dreadfully sorry to hear about your daughter Clementina, Madame Laplume.'

Opal scuffed to a halt, blinked rapidly, then pulled Augusto in the voice's direction, where she saw an elderly lady sitting in a wheelchair in a low mushroom hat and tasselled shawl slung around her shoulders. Bending over her was a gentleman with red hair and an overly filled coupe of champagne. It dribbled on the parquet flooring as he noticed Opal and Augusto approaching.

'I'm terribly sorry to interrupt. But I think you might quite possibly be my aunt. I'm the Honourable Opal Laplume from London. Lord Edmund Laplume's daughter.'

The mushroom hat slowly lifted. The Laplume heart-shaped jawline became visible, and then two wrinkled but piercing blue eyes popped up. Opal held her breath.

'Opal?' the lady said in a quavering voice. 'My goodness, you look like your father.'

It was the plummiest English accent Opal had heard since she'd been here.

'Aunt Florence, it truly is a delight to make your acquaintance,' Opal said, taking her aunt's hand in hers. Despite her cotton gloves, Opal could feel how cold Aunt Florence's hand was.

'And you, my dear. I must apologise; I had every intention of making an effort to visit you since your arrival in Paris.'

'Oh, please don't apologise, Aunty. I should have made a greater effort to visit you.'

'Well, you know I simply could not abide the circles Clementina moved in... the superficial celebrity lifestyle – the paparazzi trying to shoot you down like snipers. It's precisely why I didn't attend the event the night she... she passed. I suppose it was fortuitous that I wasn't present to witness it.'

'That was indeed a small mercy,' Opal conceded, and squeezed her aunt's hand once more.

'But I never attended her performances. That sort of thing never appealed to me. If it had, I would have remained in English society, attending the London Season and State Banquets, the glitz and glamour. I have no interest in such affairs. I fled to Paris as soon as I could. How do you find it all?'

'I do quite enjoy it, but I'm not sure how good at it I am. Keeping up appearances, I mean. I made a complete mess of my court presentation. There was a bee that got in the palace because of all the roses and blooms everywhere. The queen batted one away and made her tiara wonky. I just couldn't let her be ignorant of this. I felt the politest thing was to tell her highness that her tiara was askew. Queen Mary thanked me but Mother was so terribly embarrassed and refused to speak to me for a month afterwards.'

'That sounds like your mother, indeed. I expect she's keen on marrying you into the old boy network, a duke or something,' Aunt Florence scoffed.

'She has set her sights on Viscount Cecil Turks-Leyton for me.'

'The Turkeys?' Aunt Florence laughed. 'I remember them. A terribly old-fashioned lot. A rather cumbersome estate. I cannot fathom where these people find the energy to sustain such responsibilities.'

'Well, it seems that Turkey and I are not quite a natural match.'

Opal glanced at Augusto, almost involuntarily. He was standing in his bodyguard stance, shoulders square, politely smiling in the way you do around old ladies.

'I must apologise; I neglected to introduce Augusto. He was Clementina's bodyguard... I don't believe you've had the pleasure?'

'We have not. *Bonsoir*, Madame Laplume,' Augusto said, taking her hand and bowing his head. 'Please accept my deepest sympathies for your loss, madame.'

'Thank you, my dear. Is this Turkey's replacement? He appears far more suitable from where I'm sitting.' Aunt Florence smirked.

Opal blushed furiously. 'No, no. Augusto and I have struck up a friendship as we both enjoy fashion drawing. I enjoy sketching hats, and he enjoys sketching people, so we combine our talents.'

'You've become friends, have you? I see.' She winked. 'Now what is this you have in your arms?'

'Oh, it's a drawing I want to purchase. It's not my drawing. It is of my dog though.'

'That cherub is your pet?' she gushed. 'You simply must introduce me... though I can't imagine your mother liking having him around the house.'

'Well, she didn't at first... but then we got lots of attention in Regent's Park because of him and it attracted new clients for Laplume Millinery.'

'I thought of coming to visit, you know. The shop. But your father said it was best he simply visit me alone in Paris.'

'Oh, I didn't know Father would visit you.'

'He does from time to time. It's your mother, you see. There are reasons why she's tried to keep you away from me, Opal. I know things that... I'm sure she would not want you to know. Do not blame *me* for our estranged situation. It's all her, I can assure you.'

'What things?'

'I'm not at liberty to say.'

'But she suggested I come to Paris. She wanted me to work with Clementina. That wouldn't be her trying to keep me away.'

'Well, that is a queer turn of events, I can agree. I was terribly surprised when Clementina mentioned you were coming.'

'I also haven't quite clarified why I've been sent here.'

'That, I cannot answer, my dear. But I must say... I am glad we have met.'

'You know, I'm going to try to uncover what's happened to Clementina. I will make sure they face justice, whoever the blighters are. I've made a few discoveries.'

'My niece, I never worry about justice. The cosmos has a way of dishing out justice to those who deserve it. And I don't mean that in the kind of Church of England way your mother would. I mean, it's science. It's what they call *karma* in India. I've lost my daughter and that is what I need to overcome.'

Opal opened her mouth to express further sympathy, but Aunt Florence tipped her head sideways and changed the subject.

'So you want to buy this drawing?' She pointed at the sketch.

'Yes, do you know who it's by?'

'Yes, Renaud Sauvé. I don't even need to look at the signature, you can see from the style. Lovely gentleman. Costume designer and teacup collector. He's over there talking to Chanel.'

Opal turned in the direction of her aunt's knobbly finger and frantically rearranged her hat. *Chanel!*

THIRTY-SIX
ROSES

Chanel and Renaud Sauvé, the costume designer, conversed with limp-wristed hand gestures, patting the air with their cigarettes, causing smoke to build up around them like a silver bush. They stood in front of a ten-foot painting, an impressionist depiction of a Moroccan village in a palette of pinks and oranges.

'Come on, Opal,' Augusto said, offering his arm. 'I've met her once before. Madame Coco Chanel is very pleasant, she doesn't bite.'

'I need Napoleon for moral support,' Opal said, handing Augusto her handbag and the sketch and scurrying over to the windows where a couple of ladies in tuxedos and monocles were ruffling Napoleon's tummy. She grinned, gingerly attached his lead and dashed back to Augusto.

'Are you ready now?' Augusto asked, brows raised.

'Yes. I am. I couldn't meet her without letting Napoleon meet her also. He could prove a good conversation piece if I get tongue-tied.'

The pair approached and found themselves enshrouded in the bush of smoke.

'*Bonsoir*, Madame Chanel. And you are Monsieur Renaud, I believe,' Augusto said charmingly.

'Augusto... What a pleasant surprise. I haven't seen you since the summer at La Coupole,' said Chanel. Her voice was calm and deep and her eyes shone like black pearls, a stark contrast to the white ones layered around her neck and dabbled on her hat. She looked *simply ripping*, Opal thought, mouth agape.

'I'd like to introduce my friend, Opal Laplume, from London. And her trusty mascot, Napoleon.'

'*Enchanté!* Delighted to meet you both. I've been wanting to inspect this petite bicorn,' Chanel said, peering closely at Napoleon's cap. 'The pattern is interesting, like an upside-down boat.'

'Oh, thank you. I hand-stitched it myself.'

'You sew?'

'Indeed, I do. My mother, Lady Phyllis Laplume, owns the Laplume Millinery Shop in Marylebone, London. And I help her make and sell the hats. She hasn't completely let me take over with the design side yet, though.'

'Oh, I have not heard of that shop. I am very fond of hat boutiques – it is where I started out in the fashion world.'

'Yes, well, I suppose you're used to shopping in Kensington or the King's Road. We are based in Marylebone, which is slightly off the beaten track for hats, so perhaps that's why. Here, please take a card.'

'Thank you, mademoiselle. And I am assuming you also made your charming fedora. Exquisite bouquet of peacock feathers you've attached.'

Opal tried to move her tongue in thanks but it seemed to have melted. She couldn't believe Chanel had told her that her fedora was charming and exquisite. She felt as if a bright red, first-prize rosette had been pinned to her breast.

'Goodness gracious. I very much appreciate the compliments, Madame Chanel. My mother will be so pleased to hear this.'

'Come and see me at my boutique anytime. Thirty-one Rue Cambon. I'll be upstairs scrutinising toiles, so I rely on the presence of chic company to keep my spirits lifted.'

'Oh, I shall, Madame Chanel. Thank you very much.'

Renaud, a pencil-moustached tiny man in a red beret, leaned forward and blew some smoke on to the sketch in Augusto's hand.

'Is that my sketch you have in your hands, monsieur?' Renaud asked Augusto.

'It is. Opal wanted to purchase it,' he replied.

'Oh that. It's just a rough scribble of a dog. But I am flattered, mademoiselle,' he said in a bored and expressionless manner.

'It's a very darling depiction of my Napoleon on the piano. Very sweet, tiny feet.' She pointed her red fingernail at the inked tootsies. 'They remind me of some illustrations I've seen before.'

'Oh yes? Where?' Renaud asked, still sounding a little uninterested.

'Well, I've been working in the atelier at the Casino de Paris for Christophe Tasse and I came across a book of designs. I was a tad taken aback because, well, I saw your signature at the bottom, monsieur, and they were drawn in the same style.'

Renaud blinked rapidly at her, as if trying to hurry his brain along and think of a reply. Chanel, obviously sensing the awkward air, started a conversation with Augusto about her Leo astrology reading.

'Christophe Tasse has a very similar style to me, mademoiselle.'

'But the signature read R.S 1934 at the bottom. Not C.T.'

'Perhaps the C.T looked like an R.S.'

'Honestly, Renaud, I don't know why you're covering for

him,' Chanel interrupted curtly. 'Christophe Tasse does not design his own costumes. He's an exquisite pattern cutter, tailor and needleworker. Clementina's best friend. But he is *not* a designer. He pays you to keep quiet, I know, but I think you need the recognition. Now the job is finished, you can move forward putting the name to your work.'

'I don't have the contacts to get the kind of work he gets,' Renaud said bitterly out of the side of his mouth.

'We will talk,' Chanel said.

Renaud rolled his eyes as if she always said that to him.

'May I purchase the pretty picture?' Opal asked, trying not to look too satisfied with her discovery.

Renaud eyed Opal up, as if weighing up that she was sitting pretty. He named an amount. He was probably adding tax due to the insight she had gleaned about him. Opal rummaged for her money and handed him a note.

'Oh, keep the change, monsieur.' Opal smiled and rolled the artwork up neatly.

'Please do not repeat this conversation,' he replied. And slipped the rolled-up note into the side of his shoe.

Opal nodded and Augusto gave her a sneaky side eye. *So,* she thought, *had Valentine been blackmailing Christophe with the sketchbook she'd found of Renaud's original costume designs? To reveal that he was merely a maker and not a designer would have been a blow to his reputation.*

A gong was beaten in the corner of the room. Napoleon's ears fluttered. The crowd pressed backwards, distorting Opal's view in a forest of berets and wisps of smoke.

She raised on her tiptoes to see Misia and a man at the grand piano. Misia introduced the evening's poet, Alphonse Martell, a pink-faced, gargoyleish man in a paisley cravat. He lifted his notebook and began his recital.

'Death, a silent gardener,

Tends to his blooming shadows,
Each rose a sigh from the beyond,
A delicate requiem for the lost.
And in the quiet of the eternal night,
Where time folds into itself,
We become the blooms, the scent, the silence.'

Opal listened to the maudlin lines with slow blinks of intense concentration. She'd never really been the best at following poetry at school. But the last line. Why did these words ring in her head? *The blooms, the scent, the silence.* She thought about the time in Pâtisserie Angelina's when Joshua said Clementina had been given a rose from a fan during the interval.

Opal gasped and held her breath. *That was it! She knew what the murder weapon was!* But who had used it, and why?

THIRTY-SEVEN
NICTOFORM

Opal burst back into her hotel room and slammed the door closed, causing the chandelier to rattle. Napoleon whined with anxiety and his eyes became round marbles of concern. Leaning back on the door, she pressed her adrenaline-pulsing hands to her chest in a futile attempt to steady her racing heart.

Her eyelids flickered briefly, almost as if shielding her from the sudden spark of interest as she eyed what she'd propped up against the trifold mirror on her dresser. It was the single white rose in the transparent gift case that she'd found in Valentine's room.

Slowly, she approached the dresser, the floorboards creaking beneath her as if emitting tiny, sharp cries of alarm. She picked up the cellophane rectangle off the dressing table, cracked it open and took out the rose. She twirled the stem in her fingers and looked at the edges of its petals, browning with age.

Could a rose have been dosed with Nictoform and presented to Clementina for her to inhale? She wouldn't have known, and just smelled the rose, as one does. Nictoform is a scentless substance so she wouldn't have smelt or detected it on there.

Opal pondered. She would have to consult Joshua to see if

he remembered her sniffing it. Lost in thought, she brought the velvet petals to her nose and inhaled deeply.

Napoleon looked up at her with his head tilted, quizzical at whether she was going to play fetch with the rose.

She placed the flower back on the dresser and decided to give Napoleon a good brush on the bed while she ran through the clues in her mind. After a while, her shoulders started to sink into the shroud of pillows at the head of her bed. She felt like her bones had become a soft marshmallow and her hands weren't able to make the swift and precise brushing motions.

Why do I feel like this? It wasn't mere fatigue; it was something far more insidious.

The brush in her hand started to skip in and out of focus. She became aware of how deeply she was breathing due to her corselette compressing her lower ribs. Napoleon turned his head to her, puzzled by the sudden cessation of his pampering. She slid with gelatine limbs off the bed and decided it was time to put her nightdress on.

She floated, a serene smile painted across her face, past her dressing table towards the wardrobe. She suddenly stopped and took a few steps backwards. She twisted her eyes towards the dresser and affixed it on Valentine's rose. It reminded her of a miniature glass coffin, encasing a deathly bloom, the notelet inside a little epitaph.

She had a terrible thought. The symptoms of Nictoform she'd heard about were the ones she was experiencing; lightheadedness, shortness of breath, dizziness. *God oh God! Was this rose, the one she'd found in Valentine's room, also doused in Nictoform?*

She snatched up the notelet that was nestled in the pink tissue paper in the cellophane box. She'd forgotten that this rose had been addressed to Clementina. Not Valentine. Clementina had simply re-gifted it on to Valentine to cheer her up one night after rehearsals.

What if this particular rose had been spiked with the Nicto-form too, intending to test how long it took for Clementina to fall unconscious or to kill her during one of the rehearsals in the tank? It could have been a test or a failed attempt.

Opal looked at the message on the notelet and translated it.

Dear Clementina,

Inhale deeply the sweetest smelling rose in Paris. An eternal fan.

Whoever sent it had put it in a cellophane gift case on purpose so the vapour wouldn't escape.

The notelet slipped out of Opal's hand. Her knees dipped. *Am I going to pass out? I can hardly breathe! I need to get this corselette off.* She tried to pluck at the laces but she was feeling too weak to pull. She needed oxygen, so, with a great effort, she managed to open the balcony door.

Urgh! Get off me, get off me! Opal shouted in her head, tugging at the strings on her back. Her eyelashes quivered in a hazy reflection. *Isn't that what Valentine had shouted the night she died? 'Get off me.' She had also been wearing a corset, was that what she'd been shouting about? And Christophe made it for her...*

Opal held onto the brass balcony door handle for balance and panted, the epiphany clear as day in her mind.

There wasn't anyone in Valentine's room after all! She'd taken home the rose Clementina had given her. She was prac-tising in her corset, smelled the rose and became breathless. She tried to undo her corset, using Christophe's technique with the pencil, which then broke, she cursed Christophe, came out onto the balcony for air, and...

Opal glanced at the low balustrade and the twilit cityscape beyond. Napoleon barked and clasped her skirts in his jaws. He pulled at her skirts to get her away from the balcony edge. She stumbled backwards and collapsed at the foot of her bed. *Valentine must have fallen unconscious at the balcony and then fallen over the balustrade. That was why there was no scream when she fell. She was unconscious.*

Opal's head slung backwards with a thud on the wooden bedpost and the last thing she saw was the chandelier in the canopy. Discs of light swirled and danced in a dizzying freak show. Her consciousness flew away, leaving her in a black, impenetrable sleep.

THIRTY-EIGHT
ISOBEL-MARIE, FLEURISTE

Opal glided up the Rue Jules Lefebvre, overtaking the other morning pedestrians, the plumes on her fedora billowing. Napoleon trotted at her heel, his bicorn fashionably askew. The Nictoform had given Opal the deepest and most enriching sleep of her life; no wonder Clementina was addicted. Aside from a bit of a stiff neck due to the French windows being open all night, she felt rejuvenated.

She stopped when she'd reached a red-fronted shop and held the notelet that came with Valentine's rose up to her nose. Her nose then pointed up at the shop sign. 'Isobel-Marie Fleuriste' was written in bronze unfurling italics. *This is where the rose was bought. Whoever put the Nictoform on the roses must have come here to purchase them.*

A bell tinkled as she opened the door. Her nostrils were hit by a concoction of aromas and she felt like she was out on one of her papa's explorations. She squeezed through a forest of spring blooms; sweet peas, lilac, iris and peonies hugged together in the present seasonal hues of pinks, purples, yellows and whites. She heard snipping noises and a female voice humming to tunes on the wireless. Opal careered around a towering spray of gold-dipped china berries and found her.

The goldfish-bowl bespectacled florist was in a green apron chopping heartily at the stems of lilies. Opal hoped she would remember who bought the 'death' roses.

'*Bonjour*, madame,' she cooed.

'*Bonjour*, mademoiselle,' the florist said brightly, then sneezed and cursed at the lily stamens.

'I'd like to buy a single white rose in one of those cellophane boxes, please.' Opal thought it rude not to buy anything if she was going to bombard the woman with questions. She could also use it as a way in to ask about the roses the killer had bought.

'*Oui*, mademoiselle, choose one, please. They are at the back, over there in the bucket.'

Opal fetched one of the snowy buds and put it to her nose to sniff. It was completely scentless, like smelling damp paper. Must be rather a cheap variety.

'This is strange.' Opal blinked hard and eyed the florist. 'This rose doesn't really have any scent at all, but I know someone who got someone white roses from your shop and the notelet read, "The sweetest smelling rose in Paris."'

The woman's eyebrows frowned below her spectacle rims and she stopped chopping the leaves.

'That's peculiar,' she said. 'I do remember the man that made me write it on the notelet.'

Opal made a mental tick as the florist continued…

'But I'm sorry, mademoiselle, no. They don't smell of anything because they haven't been bred well. If you try the red ones, they have a wonderful, sweet perfume. Your whole apartment will be heavenly.'

'Oh, no, it's quite alright. I'll take this white one, if I may. But I don't know if by any chance you remember the man's name? The one who made you write that notelet?'

'No, I don't think I took his name.' She picked up another lily and continued snipping. 'Why do you ask?'

Opal looked down at her flower and thought fast. 'Oh, err... He's an admirer of mine who sent me one. I don't know who he is and just came to find out.'

The woman smiled, but in a pitying sort of fashion. 'I'm sorry, mademoiselle, but I don't think he'd be your type. Even with my eyesight, he was nothing a pretty girl like you would go for.'

'What did he look like?'

'Well, I only really remember him because he got me to write that strange note. I never would have otherwise...' the florist said, then reeled out a description of the mystery man.

Opal let out the breath she'd been holding. She fumbled in her handbag for a brochure from the Casino de Paris show. She flipped through to the page which had a photo of the man inside.

'Ah ha!' Opal said, then turned the page to show the florist. 'Was *this* the man?'

'*Oui*,' the florist confirmed.

Opal clasped the rose to her chest and shut her eyes in relief. She was going to avenge her dear cousin, and Valentine...

'But that brochure... the Casino de Paris. That's where my darling daughter was a chorus girl before she went missing,' the florist continued in a quivering voice.

Her secateurs moved a branch of pussy willow out of the way and pointed at a poster. Opal sucked in a breath when she saw what it read.

MISSING: Estelle Dufour, twenty-three years old with a photo of the smiling dancer who so closely resembled Opal.

THIRTY-NINE
THE BAKELITE STAIRCASE

Opal and Zsa Zsa had been informed that the police had finished their investigations in the theatre. All performers were requested to congregate at the Casino de Paris at one o'clock in the auditorium. Opal made sure she brought Detective Inspector Prosper Delacroix's homburg hat with her to return to him.

'Where are you going? The meeting's in here,' hissed Zsa Zsa as she held the auditorium door open with her red nails fanned out.

'I'll join you in a minute, take Napoleon for me, please,' Opal whispered back over her shoulder and continued up into the wings.

Enveloped in the darkness of the wings, she got out her miniature torch. She could see the police had left everything exactly as it was on the night Clementina died.

The quick-change chorus girls' costumes were flung on the floor and dangled from rails like shed skin. Feather fans, canes, headdresses and half-drunk glasses of water were scattered on the props table. Looming above her was the giant block that was Clementina's water tank. It had a huge tarpaulin thrown over it.

Then, sitting solitary on a wooden chair, she saw exactly what she was looking for: a single white rose in a cellophane box, a little notelet nestled inside the tissue paper. Opal checked the notelet. *Yes.* It said the exact same thing as the one found in Valentine's room. She stuffed the box into her deep coat pocket.

She joined the cast meeting, entering the auditorium through the side door so nobody would know she'd been poking about up there. Detective Inspector Prosper Delacroix stood on the edge of the stage.

'I think everyone's here now.' Claudette nodded at Prosper to start speaking.

His blond head tipped up and he addressed the auditorium first in French, then in English. 'Good afternoon. I'd first like to say thank you for your patience. We are now finished with the inquest and you are free to go up to the dressing rooms and remove your belongings.'

'Aren't you going to tell us how Clementina died?' someone asked.

'She inhaled her medication, Nictoform, to help her nerves and unfortunately it knocked her unconscious in the tank and she drowned. The information has not been released to the press yet, so I'd appreciate it if this was kept quiet.'

'Do forgive me for interrupting. But I regret to inform you that that's not what happened,' Opal piped up, in as loud and confident a voice as she could muster.

She felt everyone's stares as she glided up the stage steps and sat midway up the Bakelite staircase. She wanted to loom above Prosper, not stand next to him. He turned as if blown by a gust of wind and looked up at her, his arms folded, his chin twisted to the side in surprise.

'Opal, please, we haven't got all day, can you please just cooperate,' Prosper said in a patronising tone.

'I have an announcement to make.' Opal looked beyond

Prosper into the red glare of the seats, she knitted her hands around her knees and stuck her chin up. 'I have figured out exactly what happened to Clementina. *And* Valentine. *And* the twelve-million-franc Dumoulin necklace. There's only one thing I have not yet been able to find out and that is where our dear Estelle has disappeared to.'

'Opal, this is very interesting, but I think people want to go and get their belongings,' Prosper said, inviting her to leave the stage with a sweeping arm.

'No. You haven't told us anything, so I'd like to hear what she has to say!' shouted one of the chorus girls.

'Yes, let her speak,' Zsa Zsa joined in, squeezing Leon's hand nervously.

Mr Dumoulin was leaning forward, his ear inclining to the stage.

Opal rose and floated up a few more steps, turned to face them all and lifted the tip of her nose. 'There is someone sitting among you who is responsible for it all.'

Bottoms fidgeted in the velvet seats. Opal could feel a bead of sweat develop on her forehead. Prosper folded his arms and tapped his foot.

'I'll start at the beginning,' Opal continued. 'The twelve-million-franc diamond was the cause for all of the atrocities. Everything revolves around the beautiful yellow jewel. Clementina was as astute as she was comely. However, her ingenious scheme to purloin the Apolline Diamond necklace proved to be her undoing.'

The lower row of Mr Leon Dumoulin's teeth became visible as his jaw slackened.

'Leon Dumoulin and Clementina decided to put on a dazzling Grande Revue and to show off the diamond necklace. Clementina, as we all know, had a very lavish lifestyle. She was very materialistic indeed. Even her greyhound had a Cartier collar! I believe she wanted the necklace, and she devised an ingenious heist in order to acquire it.'

Opal swallowed and hovered her eye over David. He was lounging in a seat on the far left, stroking the head of Yvette, eyes meeting Opal's like swords in a duel.

Opal continued, 'Clementina knew she'd need David's help to orchestrate the theft. She hired him as set designer for the show and to make a special prop to assist with the heist.'

Mr Dumoulin laughed in an incredulous fashion and shot David a glance. David's lips stretched into an amused grimace.

'Clementina met David to discuss the details of this theft. But she left a clue behind – a tissue with a little scribble showing the strategy. She would split the twelve million francs profit with David,' Opal said, recounting the crossed-out numbers on the napkin.

David sniggered through his nose and Opal ascended the steps higher.

'So, David designed a special object for their plan. He made a false bottom for the chandelier in the room in which the necklace was to be displayed with a small cavity in which the necklace could be hidden. This could be removed later and nobody would notice.'

Claudette interrupted Opal. 'You mean the diamond necklace was hidden in a removable dish as part of the chandelier design? But how did he get the necklace inside it without anyone noticing?'

'Well you see, on the opening night, Clementina insisted we all view the diamond necklace before the show started. I entered the dressing room with nine other people, including David. The door to the dressing room was opened inwards by Clementina. When we all left the dressing room, David hid behind the door. To everyone outside, it would look as though there was no one in the dressing room. Clementina gave David thirty seconds to do the job while she counted the next group of people to be let in. Inside, David took the necklace from the velvet display and hid it in the chandelier. He must have noticed he'd left a footprint on the plinth, which he cleaned with his tricolour handkerchief, unknowingly leaving a thread. He stood back behind the door again so that when it was opened it would look like nobody was in there. When the guests gasped and rushed inside, seeing the necklace had vanished, David came out from behind the door and pretended to be shocked with them.'

'You are ridiculous.' David Miller brought his hands together in mock applause and Yvette's chain rattled.

Prosper rubbed his forehead, disguising his face from Opal.

She continued, 'When the police and security team had searched everything to no avail, Mr David Miller was asked to come into the theatre to advise them on how the tank worked in conjunction with Clementina's drowning. While nobody was in the diamond viewing room, he took the Apollina Diamond and the false chandelier bottom back with him to his studio. He probably intended to launder the diamonds through middlemen and get the cash or sell to a foreign prince – I'm sure he would have met a few on opening night.'

'And he killed Clementina so that he could keep her share?' one of the tap dancers asked, outraged.

'Yes. Originally the idea was that they would split the cash. They negotiated the ratio on a napkin found at Lapérouse. But David wanted to cut her out because she wasn't needed in the actual heist. All he needed from her was the *idea*. So, he decided to get rid of her in the most undetectable way possible.'

David clapped his hands together and stood up. 'Very imaginative, my darling. I think you'll find you have no proof of any of this. It is utter rot.'

'Oh, I have proof, alright. Wait till I get to that part!'

'I'm looking forward to hearing it. Go on, tell everyone how I managed to *drown* Clementina!'

'You chose the most undetectable way of killing her you could think of – Nictoform, a sleeping agent. It takes twenty minutes to knock someone unconscious, and you knew she would drown in the water tank as a result. But how could you administer the drug to her and make her inhale it without her knowledge?'

Bottoms on velvet fidgeted again.

'Roses!' Opal smiled.

'This is getting more absurd by the minute,' David sniggered, shifting his weight from foot to foot.

'But first you wanted to test the potency of the doctored flower. So you gave Clementina a trial rose, probably saying it was from a fan you'd bumped into outside. But she didn't smell it like you'd planned. She re-gifted it to Valentine to try and cheer her up after an argument with Christophe. I found the rose in Valentine's room and kept it. I inhaled it in my room the other night and in twenty minutes I was unconscious.'

'That's ridiculous.' David gulped, perspiration starting to sparkle on his brow. 'How can you hope to prove any of this?'

'Joshua saw you give her the last rose before the interval. And I went to the florist, who described you as the customer who bought them.'

'I am very amused. You said that I killed Valentine also? How did I miraculously get into Valentine's room unseen, push her off the balcony and keep the door locked from the inside?' David flung his arms out, dropping Yvette's chain.

'Well, you did kill her, but unintentionally. That night, Valentine smelled the rose, and soon after she found it hard to breathe. She opened the French windows to get some air. She was becoming faint, perhaps because her corset was too tight. She tried to get it off with a pencil, but couldn't. She screamed so loudly that Zsa Zsa in the room below could hear her. She was screaming at her corset and cursing Christophe, who made it. That's why we thought he was in the room, but he never was. She then fell over the balustrade to her death.'

Christophe sat up straight and proud. He raised one eyebrow and darted a sly look at Zsa Zsa, who had suspected him. Prosper stopped rubbing his forehead and looked at Opal, impressed.

The auditorium was as silent as if it was empty. Opal clasped her hands in front of her and tried to catch her breath.

David killed the silence. 'Well, why then was there a death threat scrawled on Clementina's headboard? There would have been no point in me doing that!'

'You're right. You didn't scrawl the threat. Clementina scrawled it there herself, with her brooch pin.'

'But why would she write it to herself?' David laughed, arms flung out like a scarecrow.

'She wrote it so Joshua, her long-distance fiancé, would come back from New York. She tried everything to get him to come, and when Valentine died, she had the idea to *scare* him into coming. She wanted him to think there was a murderer after her – and it worked.'

'Mademoiselle Laplume. You've really stunned me with all this. And it's certainly all possible. But with *real* police work you will need to have proof,' Prosper said.

'Oh... I have proof alright.' She pulled the cellophane case out of her pocket. 'I have the Nictoform-doused rose in its box. Just before this meeting, I grabbed the rose that was used to drug Clementina on the night she died from where it was left in the wings. In my other pocket I have the rose that I found in Valentine's room. The one that knocked me unconscious. If you test them both, I'm pretty sure they will be doused with Nictoform.'

David turned as if to leave but Leon marched over and put a hand in his way. Yvette crawled backwards away from David and cowered behind Mr Leon Dumoulin, seeming to prefer Mr

Dumoulin's scent. It was clear the dog had not warmed to her new owner.

Mr Dumoulin pulled the handkerchief out of David's pocket. They both looked down at it and then back into each other's eyes. It was hard to tell whose facial contortions were the angriest.

'This is all rubbish, I've been set up,' David exclaimed, throwing up his hands and glancing desperately at Prosper. Prosper walked slowly down the steps.

Opal ascended further up the Bakelite staircase and went on, 'No, no. No setting up, because the last piece of evidence I have is the most valuable of them all! On a visit to David Miller's workshop I found the false chandelier bowl. On a table next to the chandelier was a paint tin opener. I noticed there was a drop of blood on the corner of it. Probably from opening a tin. The blood dripped all the way to the room where the paint tins were kept.'

Mr Dumoulin shot his chin up at Opal. 'You think the necklace may be in a paint tin at his studio?'

'It's just a guess, but evidence leads to it.' Opal shrugged. 'The diamond necklace may be sitting in an old paint tin now, waiting for David to figure out how to liquidate it or sell it to a foreign prince on the sly.' She put her finger in the air with a last thought. 'Oh... and why do I guess it's your blood on the paint tin opener, David? Well, to my joy, you have a plaster covering your left thumb.'

Prosper took David's left hand and lifted it into the air, revealing to everyone he had been caught red-thumbed.

Opal giggled with satisfaction. 'Prosper, I suggest you go and check David Miller's studio now. Have these roses tested for Nictoform, and call on Isobel-Marie, Fleuriste, and Joshua Davenport for witness statements.' She held up a cellophane-coffin-encased rose in each hand.

Mr Dumoulin let out a gusty breath and his face turned purple. 'How could you kill Clementina? Just for a *diamond?*'

David's horizontal mouth twisted from its usual, humble slant into a grimace that seemed to come from the very core of his bitterness. 'Because I have no respect for you!' he spat explosively. 'This grotesque, elitist lifestyle you lead. You're so disgustingly rich, stealing a diamond from you is like stealing a macaroon from a morbidly obese elephant.'

Leon lunged towards him and David stepped backwards, a warning fist in the air. 'It isn't even immoral! I gave Clementina the dramatic death she'd always dreamed of! She was on the cover of every paper, magazine and gazette! All she cared about was fame. She even said to me once that to die without being famous was to die like an animal – unknown and without status. What would she do when she got too old to dance? She died gracefully. No blood. No violence. She just fell asleep from the sniff of a rose!'

'Get him out of here or I'll kill him,' Leon said, low and cautioning.

The greyhound could sense the upset in the air and snarled with her head low to the ground, ready to pounce at anything that may hurt her or Mr Dumoulin.

David threw his arms out in a crucifixion as if welcoming the arrest, grinning remorselessly. Prosper put his hands on David's forearms gently and pushed his arms down. He proceeded to restrain the criminal in handcuffs.

'Give me Yvette.' Christophe marched up to them and picked up the dog's chain. 'She's coming with me now.'

David turned his head to Prosper, who was shackling his wrists, and said, 'Whatever you do with the Apolline Diamond, don't give it back to Mr Dumoulin. There is a dispute as to who legally owns it and found it in the first place.'

'*What?*' Mr Leon Dumoulin yelled so loud the acoustics of the auditorium bounced the word around.

'Clementina said it was found by her uncle, Lord Edmund Laplume, in Papua on a field trip. It was robbed from him at gunpoint and sold illegally to Mr Leon Dumoulin. Mr Laplume knew Clementina had ties with Leon and asked her to devise a plan for it's return. She persuaded Mr Dumoulin that she should be a brand ambassador and plotted with me to get it back.'

Opal felt her weight falter on the steps. Napoleon broke from Zsa Zsa's grip and bounded up onto the stage. He seemed to Opal to be running in slow motion.

Why was her father being mentioned? What on earth had been going on in Papua? Who had held him at gunpoint?

'This is outrageous... The Apolline Diamond is mine. I bought it from a private collector. It was found on their own land and the tax had already been paid.'

'I think we will need to involve the Papuan authorities and consult the Bureau of Foreign Affairs to sort this out,' Detective Inspector Prosper Delacroix said curtly. 'But in the meantime, Monsieur David Miller, you will come with me.'

'You may need your homburg hat when you exit...' Opal Laplume called down to the detective. 'It's here in my hatbox. Good as new.'

FORTY

ABDUCTION

About half an hour later, Opal and Zsa Zsa exited the stage door of the Casino de Paris for the last time. They stopped underneath the stained-glass window and Opal gazed into its mosaic of Grecian dancers, twirling and celebrating something triumphant.

Zsa Zsa lit up a final, reflective cigarette. The gold-foiled Sobranie tip swung in and out of her magenta lips and silver smoke veiled her face as she watched the police cars in the road.

David's shoulders jutted back due to his cuffed wrists and his head stooped in the posture of a vulture that had had its winnings stolen. His head was pushed down inside the back of the police car by Detective Inspector Prosper Delacroix.

Prosper turned and gave Opal a rather embarrassed tip of his pristine homburg with his chin pulled into his collar.

'You look simply ripping in your homburg!' she called out to him and pulled her fedora further over her left eye. *How deliciously satisfying it was to beat him in solving the case.*

Through the car window, David gave Opal an almost cross-eyed look of hate, his linear lips curling down at the very edges. Zsa Zsa blew a kiss at him mockingly and Opal chortled.

Napoleon strained on his lead, yapping at the vehicle removing the culprit from society as it sped away. Another police car zoomed off in the other direction, probably to break into David's atelier and inspect the blood-spattered paint tin. Would they find the Apolline Diamond within?

'Oh... I don't know what was more satisfying. Seeing David's face or Prosper's,' Opal said.

'Yes, they can't get over the fact you solved it... all by yourself,' Zsa Zsa said. 'They were both outsmarted by a ditzy milliner.'

'I am *not* ditzy!' Opal nudged her friend.

'But... how exactly did you do it? I mean, I know you notice things. Even a missing rhinestone on the inside heel of a dancer's shoe. You found Clementina's ring at the audition. But this was a multimillion diamond heist and two reason-defying deaths.'

'I don't know... but details mean everything. Once you notice one detail, it sheds a spotlight onto others,' Opal replied, batting her lashes like a free butterfly and sighing with satisfaction. She hadn't really until this moment taken in the scale of what she'd achieved.

'Yeah. Well, I guess we can say *au revwarr* to Casino de Paris. It was a complete disaster. But at least I've got Mr Dumoulin.'

'What are you going to do now? Stay in Paris with him?' Opal asked with a tinge of anxious shrillness. The idea that it was all over meant that she may be separated from her big-sister figure. She cherished Zsa Zsa Desmarais.

'I don't know. I mean, I've got no work in London. I'm not going back to being Mrs Mop 'n' Bucket in Stepney Green, I can tell you that,' Zsa Zsa scoffed.

'As long as we stay as thick as thieves and don't drift apart, that's all I care about.' Opal looked Zsa Zsa dead in her brown eyes.

'You've got to be kiddin'! How could we let the glitterati of the glove-and-garter brigade split up?'

'Never,' Opal chortled. She was jolly pleased with Zsa Zsa's answer.

'What's your next move?'

'I'm going to have to try to get hold of Mother. And Father. I can't believe he was the one who found the Apolline Diamond. I'm so proud of Clementina for planning to get it back for him. It wasn't greed on her part after all.'

'But does that mean... if David was right and Mr Dumoulin acquired it illegally, then the diamond will go back to your father?' Zsa Zsa's eyes sparkled. 'You could buy back the mustard factory!'

'Oh, dash that. We could have the world's monopoly of mustard.' Opal giggled.

'The Mustard Magnates!' Zsa Zsa guffawed, almost choking on her smoke.

'Silliness aside, I haven't the foggiest about whether Papa will own the diamond or not. The Papuan government may want to seize it.'

'Devil!' Zsa Zsa said emphatically. 'Well. Speaking of gems, are you going to keep in touch with that gem of a Latino if you go London town?'

'Perhaps... if he wants to, that is.' Opal felt her cheeks warm and she looked down at her Mary Janes.

'Oh, he wants to alright.'

'How can you tell?'

'You solved all these mysteries and you can't see when a bloke's sweet on you? Come on, Opal Laplume.'

'Well, he never said anything. And it's no use. We're far too different for it to go anywhere. Mother wouldn't have it.'

'Why don't you take after your aunty and just stay here with the wayward artistes?' Zsa Zsa flashed her eyes and pouted her lips mischievously. Opal debated this for a moment.

'There's so much more I want to know. I wonder whether I'll ever get to the bottom of what happened to Estelle and who the man with the scar was.'

A breeze stroked Opal's cheek. It carried the unique scent of Paris in late spring – sweet narcissi, newspaper ink, the briny Seine and fruit beers.

'I'm going to head off with Leon, he's taking me to dinner. Though I don't suppose he'll be in the best mood, seeing as his diamond's going to be seized. Do you want to be dropped at the hotel?' said Zsa Zsa.

'No, thank you. It's almost dusk and I love Paris in the twilight, so I'd prefer to walk.'

'Alright, see you later.'

Opal walked backwards so that she could take in the façade of the mythic theatre. Farewell Casino de Paris. The stonework glowed an orangish hue as dusk bleached out the city. Time to go.

Napoleon was starting to drag so Opal spun on her heel. She gasped as she was confronted by an old man right in front of her. He had a sad expression on his face. He was very unusual looking, his face a leathery tan, with piercing, sun-bleached yellowish eyes. A bristle brush of a moustache sprouted orange and black hairs. The hair on his head was an unkempt volume of tight auburn curls.

On top of his head was an ivy cap in Harris Tweed. One did not see many ivy caps in Paris, they were more a hat of the British. He also wore a huge overcoat in some animal skin... could it be horseskin?

Who on earth could this character be? Opal was quite possessed.

'Do you speak English, young lady?' His accent was of a well-to-do Englishman.

'Yes,' Opal replied.

'What is your name?' he asked, rather keenly, his moustache animated.

'Opal,' she replied, and the man's eyes flashed as she said it. Perhaps it was twitty to be so unreserved with her particulars.

'How do you do. My name is Sterling. There is a magpie that is injured and I want to catch it and take it to the vet. It's just down this *ruelle* by the side of the theatre and I need someone to help me trap her.'

Opal was surprised. This burly man having a soft spot for birds wasn't what she'd expected. But helping wildlife was a very important thing and he seemed quite determined to help it. It was a strange request, but she couldn't bear the thought of the poor magpie in pain. She wasn't going to say no to this.

'Oh dear. Yes, I'll try my best.'

He smiled in relief. Opal followed the bulk of his coat down the left of the theatre. It was a dead-end alley where the restaurant rubbish was kept. The staircase which led to the costume atelier spiralled above them. A black Bugatti was parked further up. She followed him to the far wall.

'It isn't where it was before.' He huffed. 'I'll check this rubbish heap. Perhaps you could check under the car? Let's loop the dog's lead here for a moment as it might scare the thing.'

'Just a moment, Napoleon. Please don't moan, good boy,' Opal said and tied him to a bollard. Napoleon emitted a low growl. He did not want to be restrained in front of this stranger.

Opal then put her hatbox on the gravel and bent down by the Bugatti. Napoleon looked up and barked three fast and ferocious barks.

A swishing noise ended in a loud thwack on the back of Opal's skull. She fell forward onto her cheekbone, gasped at the filthy dust on the ground and gave in to darkness.

Opal was slumped sideways, her knees curled up to her chin. Her head lay on grey concrete. Her hair was flung over her face in dark rivers. Her shoulders were unnaturally strained backwards, her hands bound behind her.

A thick metal chain curled around her wrists causing white indents in her skin. It snaked up around a steel pipe against the brick wall behind her and was secured by a hefty, square padlock.

A muscle in her calf spasmed, causing the heel of her left shoe to jolt upwards. Her right eye opened and peered through a slit in her hair. The pupil was constricted and smudgy, like a drop of ink. Her eyelid fell again lethargically. Then opened a second time, dilated and electrified. It darted around like a blue marble shaken in a jar.

It was very dark, but a faint wash of moonlight seeped in from a circular window above. She couldn't make out much, only the silhouettes of crates on the floor ahead of her. She made a barely audible, creaking moan from the back of her throat.

Her head rushed and thumped as she lifted it an inch off

the cold stone. The pain was so overwhelming she wished she could fall unconscious again. Her shoulder sockets ached and her wrists burned. All she could focus on was pain.

But wait, she had to concentrate. *Where am I?* She sat up as fast as she could manage. Her head lolling, a great weight, as if it was filled with her entire body mass of blood.

She twisted and strained her chafed wrists. She couldn't see her hands over her shoulder. She gasped as she saw the thickness of the chain looped around the metal pipe. The padlock, a mass of metal, swung every time she tugged.

Why in God's name am I tied up here? God, oh God... Where is Napoleon?

The sound of liquid sloshing in a bottle came from somewhere ahead in the darkness.

'Who's there?' Opal gasped and pulled her knees into her chest. Her heart beat like horses' hooves in her ribcage.

There was the sound of a switch being flicked and a fluorescent bar on the ceiling flashed and fizzed. Opal blinked and flipped hair away from her eye with a jerk of her head.

Now she could see she was in a wine cellar. The walls to the left and right were lined with wooden wine compartments; the corked ends of the bottles pointing inwards like rows of cannons.

Her sightline moved up a wooden staircase ahead of her, step by step, until she reached two bulbous, leather boots. They stood wide apart; the brown leather finished at the knee like thick trunks.

Bunched into the boots were plus fours, lichen green and a little grubby at the knees. The horseskin coat shrouded the rest of the body and was done up tight to a bristly Adam's apple.

Smoke, encircling a fat cigar, clouded the face and slowly thinned to reveal the visage of the man named Sterling. His eyebrows, identical in shape and texture to the moustache, were roofs over the eyes, casting shadows over them so they appeared as black holes. He had a bottle of champagne in one hand, swirling with liquid.

Opal sucked in a huge mouthful of damp air. *What does this man want with me?*

'Opal.' Sterling's voice lacked any kindness whatsoever, like he was talking to a bird he'd trapped on a hunt. 'So here we finally are. This is going to be a very cathartic evening for me.'

'Who... who are you?'

'I'm Lord Sterling Peregrine.'

Opal frowned, and it hurt to do so, so she stopped. *Where had she heard that name before?*

'And... Where *am* I?' Opal's voice was just air.

'The cellar of the Champagne Pavilion. It was built for the Exposition of Jewellery and Goldsmithing, I believe. So that the gold aficionados can drown themselves in the liquid gold. It's after-hours now, so nobody knows you're here.'

'Why are we here?'

'Well, it wasn't exactly part of my plan. I was going to drive you out of Paris into the countryside. But you see, when I abducted you in the alley and bundled you into my Bugatti, someone attempted to stop me.'

'Who?'

'Never you mind!'

Lord Peregrine went on puffing at his cigar as he spoke. 'They chased my car all over Paris. I was only able to throw them off down here by the Seine. I managed to break into this cellar and tie you up. Everyone seems to have gone home so nobody knows you're down here. It's a stroke of good luck that we're surrounded by all this champagne. It's top-notch stuff.'

'Why did you abduct me?' Opal asked, her eyes pulsing in distress.

Lord Peregrine rubbed his moustache with an aubergine-like finger.

'It's what you could call... a vendetta, my dear,' he replied.

'What?'

'It's all your father's fault.'

'My *father*?'

'Yes. You see, we were good friends, your father and I. We studied at the University of Edinburgh together in the 1890s. I'm also an ornithologist. Don't you remember me? I recall you came on one of our field trips to Papua when you were, perhaps, ten?'

'I... I think I remember, yes. I went on many trips with Papa, they've sort of moulded into one in my memory.'

'Your father and I were together on the most recent exploration in Papua. Well, not actually working together – we had different agendas.'

'You were recently in Papua with him?' Opal was finding it hard to focus with the pain in her head.

'Yes, you see I hunt the birds of paradise out there in Papua. They fetch quite a pretty penny now that there's an embargo on the trade. My son overheard your father talking about a diamond he'd found in the river. We approached your father on his way to the bank to get it weighed and documented. Long story short, he shot my son dead and I took the diamond in retaliation.'

Opal's mind patched the scenes together. She couldn't make it seem real that her papa would kill his friend's son over a diamond. Someone as gentle and clement as Papa. Someone who did not value riches over human life.

'But even if this was true and Papa did kill your son, what's any of that got to do with me?' she blurted. 'Are you trying to get the diamond back?'

'Diamond? No. I sold that to the American *diamantaire*, Mr Leon Dumoulin. Got a jolly decent amount of cash for it. No, what I want with you is something different. I want you dead, my dear.'

'Me? Dead? Why?' Opal twisted her wrists in the chains to

no avail. 'Please don't kill me!'

'Because your papa killed my only son. *That* is why, my dear Opal Marion Laplume. I considered killing him, but that wouldn't be enough of a punishment, now, would it?'

'Please, stop this madness. Why didn't you go to the police if my father really did kill your son?'

'It would flag up too many things, my dear. I have my poaching business to think of. And there's more than one way to get justice.'

'Please stop this. Untie me!'

'Oh, I'm not going to stop now. It's taken so much effort to track you down. And another girl had to suffer in consequence. A brunette girl with bright eyes like you. I mistook her for you a few weeks ago.'

'Estelle?' Opal gasped.

'Yes, I think that's what her name was. You see, I popped over to your London address to track you down, but the neighbours said you'd dashed off to Paris. Showed me a newspaper, too. There you were, clear as day, a dancer at the Casino de Paris. So off I went, and outside the place, I spotted someone in your coat. Naturally, I thought it was you, so I nabbed her and gave her a dose of the old chloroform to keep things simple. I'd driven a jolly long way out into the countryside before she awoke. I found a beautiful vineyard with coiling, snakelike vines. Tied her up in an empty monastery there. It was rather bothersome to find out she wasn't you. Most inconvenient. I let her go, of course, but not without a firm word about staying out of Paris. Sorted the whole thing neatly.' Lord Peregrine sucked a large glob of smoke from the cigar.

Opal breathed a massive sigh of relief to know Estelle wasn't killed.

'Where is she now?'

'Well, I felt a little sorry for the rotten luck I'd bestowed upon her and got her a job at a local vineyard. You see, I'm not all evil.' Lord Peregrine sipped from the champagne and continued, 'This is delicious, don't you want some?'

'No. I want you to untie me. I have done nothing. Can't you see the injustice? You will surely hang for this. If not, then the guillotine. They still send murderers to the guillotine in France!'

'You're boring me.' Lord Peregrine looked at his pocket watch. 'I'm going upstairs to wait for the fireworks to start.'

A rush of panic came over Opal, she rattled her chains and yanked at her wrists.

'Help!' she screamed at the top of her lungs like a wounded lark.

'Oh, there's no point in screaming – nobody will hear you in this concrete cellar. They could probably hear my Remington rifle, though, when I shoot you. That's why we're waiting for the fireworks.'

'The fireworks?'

'The Exposition fireworks. They've been letting them off every night at nine o'clock. Nobody will notice my shots then. You see, I have to be as discreet with your murder as possible and be long gone before they find you in the morning.'

He stomped up the steps of the cellar and left through the door at the top. The door slammed closed with a resounding rattle.

FORTY-TWO
BALLISTIC CHAMPAGNE CORK

I can't let him kill me! Opal's heart beat in her head so hard she thought she might have a nosebleed. She wriggled as hard as she could. She wrenched and twisted her wrists, riddled in chains. She scrambled to a crouch on her feet, kicking off her high heels and tried to stand up. She was restrained too tightly to stand. *I have to think fast.*

She eyed the cellar for some inspiration. Brick walls, wine storage and a circular window above. *How can I possibly get out?* Her eyes pricked with tears and she kicked her legs in terror and desperation.

Mid-fit, her eyes caught something that made her freeze. It was a group of champagne bottles standing on the floor a few metres away. Looking down at her stockings and back at the champagne bottles, she sniffed, and her tears ceased with a sparkle of inspiration. Her slim chance of escape was inspired by Zsa Zsa. How she'd seen her once remove her stockings with only her toes.

She rubbed her knees together and managed to peel a stocking down to her calf. Then used the toe of her other foot to grab the stocking and peel it off completely. It fell to the floor in a crumple. She used that bare toe to peel down both the garter and stocking of the other leg. She panted from the effort. *She had to be quick!*

Using her toes to drag the stockings and garter backwards along the stone floor she managed to pass them to her hands, bound together at the base of her spine. With fiddling fingers, she tied the stockings in a tight knot to create a two-metre long rope. She then knotted her garter onto one end to create a kind of lasso.

She pinched the garter in her right big toe and aimed it out in front of her. She stretched it back with her left foot's big toe and held her breath. *I only have one shot at this.*

She squinted at the champagne bottle with her right eye, two and a half metres away. She pinged it hard and it landed over the bottle. *Yes!* The satin garter spun down to the base, the stocking, knotted to it, trailing behind.

She sighed with relief and grabbed the end of the stocking with her outstretched toes. She tugged and the bottle fell on its side. She reeled it in with her feet.

She repeated this trick with another champagne bottle and now she had two, rocking by her side. She kicked one of them back towards her hands and managed to undo the foil with her sharp nails and twist open the cork wire.

She took the other bottle between her feet, then slammed it down onto the stone floor in an effort to smash it. It didn't work, so she lifted it higher and swung it down again. *Hurrah!* It smashed. Champagne splashed and frothed all over the floor. She then foraged in it with her toes, cutting one of them in an effort to find a small, sharp shard.

She found one. It was a two-inch long, lightning-bolt-shaped jag of green glass. She wanted it to be longer but she had no more time. She didn't know how long she had until the fireworks would start and he would come downstairs. She could hear obnoxious whistles and booted footsteps somewhere in the building above.

She scraped the shard back towards her hands with sore feet. She managed to pierce the shard through the top of the cork of the champagne bottle that she'd taken the foil off. She'd created the perfect champagne bayonet!

A sudden sound from outside made her freeze. It was a firework going off. *Oh gosh, it must be nine o'clock.* Piercing whistles and explosions came one after the other, ending in crackles and pops.

He'll be coming back now the fireworks have started. Dear Lord, help me. With a desperate flick of her restrained hands, she rolled the pierced bottle forward towards her feet. She wriggled her shoes back onto her shaking feet and lifted the bottle between her shoes.

She balanced the cork end to face the door at a forty-five-degree angle. Her other heel rested on the lip of the cork ready to push forward. Her heart stopped as she heard Lord Peregrine take the door handle.

His muffled voice was a cheerful howl. 'At last, I get to shoot the pretty bird I've been hunting.'

Then the 'click-slide-click' of a pump-action rifle sounded, making Opal almost drop the bottle. His boot kicked the door open with a squeal of hinges.

Lord Peregrine stood with his rifle aimed right at Opal's face. His bonfire eyebrows interwove as he saw her in her unexpected position: legs raised with a bottle balanced on her feet, a shard of glass sticking out of the cork. He lowered his gun a fraction and pulled his head back, his moustache twisted in perplexity.

'Well, congratulations on almost catching this bird,' Opal said.

She raised her legs up a fraction and swung them to the left to get a good aim at his eye. Her own eye pulsed with concentration. She dug her heel into the lip of the cork and simultaneously kicked outwards with all the force she could muster.

The cork, stuffed with a blade of glass, flashed under the light as it flew and impaled itself straight in Lord Peregrine's left eye. Champagne exploded over Opal's legs in a triumphant wash and the bottle clattered to the floor.

Lord Peregrine's hoarse scream lasted a good ten seconds, then it broke into a high-pitched, self-pitying cry, 'You bitch!'

Opal's heart sank. She hadn't killed him or floored him. But it had at least bought her a fraction more time. She wriggled at the chain binding her hands, trying to squeeze them out once more.

Lord Peregrine held his hand to his eye, blackish blood oozing through his fingers. His gun thudded to the ground and he doubled forward. He plucked the offending, glass-speared cork out and rocked himself with agonising groans. Opal's wrists burned unbearably as she tried to free herself.

Lord Peregrine then seemed to balloon with rage. He gasped, pulled his gun off the floor and rolled upright, blood dripping down his coat. He tried to aim with his wounded eye, seeming to forget it was blinded. He roared with more rage. 'You blinded my aiming eye!'

He tried to use his other eye and shot wildly at Opal. She crumpled her body into a tight ball, screaming inaudibly through the deafening, bursting bullets. It took her a split second to realise she wasn't hit and that he'd shot the brick wall above her head. He was clearly too injured and manic to aim properly.

He blasted again and again at the wall, inches from Opal's head, choking her with brick dust. The brick dust cleared enough for her to see the double-barrel holes of death pointing directly at her face, three yards away. She watched his bloody knuckle curl around the trigger and swung her head to the left.

BANG.

A loud chink of metal sounded with the shot. *I think he's broken my chain! Yes, yes, he has!* She clambered forward, her hands still twisted tight in the chain that was dragging along the floor behind her. *Oh my God he's reloading.*

She peered up at the cellar door, gaping wide at the top of the steps. She managed to break apart her wrists as she ran, though the chain was still looped around one of them. Lord Peregrine's hand grasped her ankle and tugged her backwards. She fell, hitting her shins hard on the wooden steps. She flung her wrist backwards, the chain swinging out and whipping him in the bloody face. Flecks of scarlet flew sideways. He roared, pulled the chain from around his neck and flung it back down the steps below him.

He grasped his whipped cheek and groaned, stumbling backwards. His boot seemed to get wedged under one of the steps, causing him to fall back. He crashed down the steps and rolled head over heels to a broken heap on the concrete below. His neck would surely have been damaged. No time to check if he was alive. She carried on upstairs.

But Opal froze when she saw a hefty shadow looming above, the purplish lesion on his face striking her comprehension like lightning. It was the man with the scar. She tried to pull away but he held her by both shoulders and pressed her against the wall.

FORTY-THREE
T-SCAR

'It's alright, Opal, it's alright, dammit. Stop struggling!' His voice was a hoarse cockney.

'Who are you? Why have you been following me?'

'My name is Benjamin. Your mother hired me to watch you while you've been in Paris. To protect you... from that man. Lord Peregrine.'

'What?'

'Is he down there?'

'Yes, yes, he is... but...'

'Let's get you to safety in case he comes after us.'

Benjamin led her out of the venue's staff quarters and into a pristine bar. The vast semicircular windows seemed to shatter with golden fireworks spreading across them. They emerged onto the marble slabs outside. They crept along the wall of the Pavilion in a thick wedge of shadow. Opal didn't know whether she'd been deafened by the gunshots or whether the fireworks still bombarding the skies were the cause of her numbed and ringing lobes.

There were masses of spectators right up by the edges of the Seine some distance away, their hats moving from left to right as the fireworks jumped out in every direction from the Eiffel Tower.

It really was a magnificent view. She let herself appreciate the spectacle for a few moments so that her heart rate could ease. The Eiffel Tower appeared a blossoming bouquet of colour as the display played out. The buildings in front of it were floodlit and absorbed all the sparklers' hues.

Opal took a deep breath in of the sulphuric atmosphere. It was a blessing the fireworks were so loud. Nobody would have noticed them and connected them with Lord Peregrine's attempt to murder her. She looked up into Benjamin's eyes. The lids were half open and reflections of blue fireworks were dancing in them. She knew from their sincerity he was telling the truth – he was here to look after her. And it did make sense. Though she had many questions indeed.

'Are you alright?' he asked, loosening his grip on her shoulders. 'Let's go somewhere you feel safer to speak.'

They found a quiet spot away from the Seine on a small park bench, fenced by some tall shrubbery. He put his camel coat around her shoulders.

'I may have really hurt Lord Peregrine. Or worse,' Opal whispered when she felt calmer. 'He's at the bottom of the cellar stairs in the Champagne Pavilion.'

She went on to explain how she'd bested him.

'You *are a* clever one,' Benjamin said. 'I'm sorry I wasn't able to get him myself. He was just manic with his driving, and I almost crashed twice.'

'Do we have to go to the police?'

'Considering the state you may have left him in, I think the best thing to do is leave him to be discovered by the police in the morning. Nobody saw you, did they?'

'No... no, I don't think so.'

'We should arrange a call to Port Moresby with the operator in the morning, try to get hold of your parents.'

'Yes. I sent a telegram when Clementina died, but I've had no correspondence yet. We shall have to update them now. But... why didn't Mother just tell me that Lord Peregrine was after me and that I needed to flee London?'

'They didn't want you to worry and to know that a rogue, poaching maniac was after you with his rifle.'

'Well, a lot of good that did! Instead, I just thought I had a man with a daunting scar creeping after me!'

'I'm really sorry. It was hard for me to conceal myself from someone who notices everything!'

'I know you did your best. I'm sorry, I'm still in shock. My toes feel numb and my head's still pounding. And do you know where my poodle is?'

'I'm afraid he may still be tied to that bollard around the back of the Casino de Paris. Or at the police station, if someone found him. I'm sorry I didn't have time to grab him when I chased Lord Peregrine.'

'I'll let you off, Benjamin. Unless he's being served as *le plat principal* on the menu at Maxim's.'

'That's not a bad idea, you know... Maxim's, I mean. Let's go for something to eat after we've fetched Napoleon, eh?'

'Grub, sir? Capital thought!' Opal said and they began to walk, keeping inside a segment of shadow. 'What's still baffling me, though, is why your seat was empty while Zsa Zsa was dancing onstage. I thought you'd gotten up to orchestrate the murder.'

'Oh no, I was summoned from my seat by a security guard and taken out into the corridor. He said he didn't like how I looked, that I didn't fit in with the millionaires and glamorous celebrities in there. They then strip-searched me for the diamond and booted me out.' He looked a bit sad at this.

'It's funny how you can be picked on just for how you look.'

'It's hardwired into our psychology, my dear.'

'Talking of psychology, Lord Peregrine should have been lobotomised. What an utter madman!'

'He was no ordinary specimen. Not many of the gentry are. If you'll excuse me for saying so, Opal Laplume.'

'Oh, not at all. Batty, the lot of us, in varying degrees. But... what are we going to do about him?'

'As we say back home... Sweet Fanny Adams. Nothing. Let *les flics* discover that dog's dinner.'

FORTY-FOUR
A TELEGRAM FROM LORD LAPLUME

A week later, Opal had heard and seen nothing in the papers about Lord Peregrine's body being found and her anxiety was high. She'd moved hotels to a humble establishment in the 16th arrondissement of Paris, good for anonymity, and had Benjamin at close quarters to keep watch.

She was coming down the hotel staircase with Napoleon cradled in her arms. He was getting plump. After rescuing him from the bollard down the *ruelle* she'd been giving him extra sausages at breakfast to make up for it.

The hotelier was passing her on the steps, keys jangling in his pocket. 'Madame, there is a telegram for you at reception, it has been forwarded on from your last hotel, Le Reinette.'

Opal's shoes made hard clacking sounds on the marble floor as she dashed to retrieve it. The envelope was a travel-worn thing, dotted with stamps of brightly coloured birds, bold cancellation marks from Port Moresby sprawled across the stamps, while a faint blue airmail label clung to one corner. It was from Papua! *The address in father's handwriting!*

Western Union / Télégramme

Date: 7 May 1934

From: Lord Edmond Laplume, Port Moresby, Papua

To: Honourable Opal Marion Laplume, The Reinette Hotel,
Rue de Rivoli, Paris, France

DARLING BINS (STOP) DREADFULLY CUT UP
ABOUT CLEM (STOP) I'M SORRY (STOP) I WILL
DIVULGE EVERYTHING IN PERSON (STOP)
VOYAGE BACK TO BRITAIN SOON (STOP) YOUR
MOTHER FREED ME FROM CUSTODY (STOP)
FRENCH AUTHORITIES RETURNED DIAMOND
TO PAPUA AND I WAS AWARDED A FINDERS FEE
(STOP) I WILL SET UP A BIRD SANCTUARY HERE
IN CLEMS NAME (STOP) LOVE PAPA

Opal pressed the letter to her beating chest. How wonder-
fully clever of Daddy to turn the deadly diamond into a positive
pursuit, saving those precious birds from evil hunters. But why
did Lord Peregrine think that her father was the one who had
shot his son? Papa wouldn't even shoot a bird out of a tree.
*There must be a way to prove it wasn't him and stop Lord Pere-
grine's vengeful pursuit of me!*

'The good news, Napoleon,' Opal said, looking down at her
pup whose head was tilted to one side, eager for answers. 'Is
that Papa will be flying back to London soon and we can finally
spend Christmas with him.'

FORTY-FIVE

LE FLEURISTE & LE PLUMMASSERIE

Opal had one day left in Paris to tie up loose ends before her Golden Arrow back to London. Her priority was to inform Isobel-Marie Dufour, *Le Fleuriste*, that her daughter was still alive out in the countryside. And to say farewell to Augusto...

Napoleon emerged from the fleuriste's with a bunch of purple dahlias in his jaws. Opal, Benjamin by her side, had informed Isobel-Marie Dufour that her daughter was likely working in a vineyard in the Loire Valley.

'All Lord Peregrine told me about the winery in question was that there was a deserted monastery and coiling, snakelike vines. I remember *"Le Clos du Serpent"* was on the label of a wine bottle I'd seen at my hotel that my dog had knocked over onto a detective's hat. It had an illustration of a monastery too. I checked again and it is situated in the Loire Valley. Could she perhaps be at this vineyard?'

'I shall make enquires immediately.' Isobel-Marie Dufour grasped Opal's hands.

'And she is not to worry about her abductee. He has been—'

'Neutralised,' Benjamin interrupted in stark cockney.

'*Neutralisé,*' Opal translated.

Next stop was the *plummasserie* where she was to meet Augusto and Christophe to help return the mounds of feathers and plumes used in the Casino de Paris revue. They were to be recycled and re-dyed for another production.

In the feather workshop at La Maison Février, the walls were lined with wooden shelves brimming with an astonishing array of feathers. They were sorted by type and colour, creating a spectacular display. Ostrich plumes sat beside bundles of marabou, which were as fluffy as snow. The iridescent eyes of peacock feathers gleamed like tiny gems. There were also wooden racks that held drying feathers, their colours deepening as they absorbed the rich pigments from the copper vats that bubbled away in a corner of the room.

A technician in a crisp, white overcoat went through the returned feathers with pernickety fingers and separated the ones he would not accept.

'Too bedraggled... too limp... this colour we cannot bleach away. What on earth have you done to these?' he said, pinching one of the pheasant tails with his nostrils flared.

'We curled them. You have a pair of eyes,' Christophe said, without curbing his sarcasm.

'I'm sorry these cannot be reprocessed.'

'Oh alright.' Christophe snatched the rejected bundles off the counter and passed them to Augusto, who held them like bales of corn.

He tapped his foot impatiently as the technician filled out the *lettres de change* with a fountain pen.

As they made their way towards the exit, Opal asked, 'What will we do with these rejected plumes?'

'Make very expensive feather pillows. Or dump them in the Seine,' Christophe scoffed.

'What an exorbitant waste... I could take them back to the

shop in London to be incorporated in some new designs,' she suggested brightly.

'Regard it as a gift from me.' Christophe sighed. 'In fact, I have another gift for you, Mademoiselle Laplume.'

Opal's lashes flickered at him with curiosity.

'A friend of mine has asked me to recommend a millinery assistant for a Hollywood production at MGM Studios,' Christophe said with a wave of his wrist like it was nothing.

Opal halted, her shoes squeaking, and looked at Augusto. The dimple in his chin became a comma as he smiled proudly at her. She looked back at Christophe, who was also flashing a rare smile.

'Monsieur Tasse! I am speechless. You have recommended *me?*'

'Your skills are highly commendable. Who else would I recommend?'

'I... I thought you'd be vexed that I revealed your costume-designing arrangement with Renaud Sauvé to everyone at the theatre?'

'Oh, that was somewhat of a relief in the end. Nobody has any interest to gossip about it, seeing as there have been so many bigger things to talk about. I can finally just market myself as a maker. I'm moving on from showbiz now that Clementina is no longer gracing the stage. I'm moving over to haute couture.'

'I wish you all the best with that, Monsieur Tasse, sincerely I do.'

Christophe put his hand on the revolving glass door to leave. Then turned back. 'Rumour has it Coco Chanel will also be frequenting Tinseltown in July, working on a production.'

'Oh, that's simply ripping!' Opal beamed and hugged her shoulders.

The swing door consumed the costume designer, leaving Augusto and Opal alone, with his bundles of feathers between them.

'This may be goodbye for us too,' he said, and the corners of his eyes drooped.

'Quite,' Opal said, hanging her head and looking down at her shoes.

This would certainly be the hardest part about leaving Paris. It meant saying farewell to Augusto, the dashing man who'd embraced every quirk and peculiarity she possessed, twirling her into a tango of unadulterated bliss and making her feel utterly seen.

'What will you do with yourself?' she asked him, looking up.

'Mr Leon Dumoulin has an opening on his security team. He wasn't impressed with how many of them missed the diamond being in the chandelier fixing.'

'Oh, well, so did we all.' Opal laughed.

'*You* didn't. You really are a very astonishingly clever woman.'

Opal looked down at her Mary Janes again and clasped her handbag in front of herself, abashed. She riffled inside the bag and produced a Laplume Millinery business card.

'That's my Marylebone address. When I'm back from Hollywood, if you'd like to send me some drawings as you proposed... you may...' She smiled. 'Or write. I'd love to know how you get on.'

'I will.' Augusto slowly eased the card out of her fingers and dropped it into his breast pocket above the bundles of pheasant feathers in his arms. He stepped closer. Opal felt that if the feathers weren't in the way, he may have leaned in for a kiss. Instead, he transferred the bundles into her arms in a kind of an embrace. 'Here are your feathers. Are you sure your chaperone, Benjamin, can carry them for you?'

'Yes, Benjamin is waiting outside for me with Napoleon.'

'Goodbye, *señorita*,' Augusto said and pushed a segment of the swing door open for her.

'Goodbye, *señor*.'

She glided under his arm like a silk thread through the eye of a needle, her smile to him a picture of unspoken determination as the doors swept her away. That thread, you see, she intended to keep firmly in hand.

A LETTER FROM MILLICENT

Dear reader,

I want to personally thank you from the bottom of my heart for picking up my debut novel, *A Most Parisian Murder*. If you enjoyed the Honourable Opal Laplume's adventure and want to stay updated on my latest releases, please do sign up using the link below. Your email address will never be shared and you can unsubscribe anytime.

www.bookouture.com/millicent-binks

A Most Parisian Murder had simmered away in my head for over ten years and drew from one of my wildest adventures aged twenty-one when I performed at The Gentry de Paris Revue, a burlesque show at the Casino de Paris with my favourite celebutante, Dita Von Teese, back in 2009. Having always been a keen reader and scribbler, I was bursting to set a murder mystery there with its rich history and the colourful 'Icônes de cabaret' that graced the stage. The main starlets being Mistinguett and Josephine Baker.

My favourite animals are the birds of paradise. They're so bizarrely decorated, pretty and comical and are the showgirls of the natural world. Though it's fascinating that it's the male of the species that put on the displays and in our species it is often the females who take on this dazzling role. This curious parallel inspired the settings for my novel, bridging two captivating realms: the bustling stages of Paris and the lush rainforests of Papua, the natural habitat of both the birds and the showgirls. This was my starting point and to connect them was a really fun experiment.

Paris in the early 1930s was alive with performance, exuberance, artistic innovation and crime! In the year 1930 it was teetering on the very edge of the Great Depression and was the last hurrah, marking the twilight of the *Années Folles*. The 1930s is also my favourite era on the fashion front – a dash of experimentation tempered with the lingering elegance of the previous decade. It really was 'anything goes', there was so much to shock and opportunity to be original. Which nowadays, seems to be a recycling centre.

The scope for adventure in writing about the 1930s is also huge. You have to go on a major escapade to acquire tools in order to navigate your way to a clue. Whereas today we simply have Google to discover any kind of information we want. Conversely the 1930s had more opportunity to conceal things that simply can be ferreted out quickly on the internet now. There was true secrecy and the only way to pass secrets on was first-hand and in the physical realm.

I am fascinated with how humans have such a different mix of values and resources that cause them to behave in surprising and conflicting ways. Despite upbringing, class, culture and intelligence. Historical cosy crime is a wonderful melting pot to explore this chemistry and researching it all was a delight – like being a sleuth in a world of sequins and subterfuge. I do hope the resulting pages bring you as much joy as I had in creating their universe.

I would LOVE to hear from my readers – for any reason, ideas on new book themes or adventures that Opal could go on or even just to chat – you can find me if you search Millicent Binks on Facebook, Instagram, Tiktok and X. You can also contact me on my website.

Best wishes,

Millicent Binks x

www.millicentbinks.co.uk

PUBLISHING TEAM

Turning a manuscript into a book requires the efforts of many people. The publishing team at Bookouture would like to acknowledge everyone who contributed to this publication.

Audio
Alba Proko
Melissa Tran
Sinead O'Connor

Commercial
Lauren Morrissette
Hannah Richmond
Imogen Allport

Contracts
Peta Nightingale

Cover design
Tash Webber

Data and analysis
Mark Alder
Mohamed Bussuri

Editorial
Nina Winters
Imogen Allport

Copyeditor
Jane Eastgate

Proofreader
Anne O'Brien

Marketing
Alex Crow
Melanie Price
Occy Carr
Cíara Rosney
Martyna Młynarska

Operations and distribution
Marina Valles
Stephanie Straub
Joe Morris

Production
Hannah Snetsinger
Mandy Kullar
Jen Shannon
Ria Clare

Publicity
Kim Nash
Noelle Holten
Jess Readett
Sarah Hardy